EMPIRE

THE NEW PROTECTORATE STORIES: VOLUME TWO

ABIGAIL KELLY

AUTHOR'S NOTE

For those who wish to see them, content warnings for this book can be found in the backmatter and on my website. You can also find a small glossary and name pronunciation guide, should you need them.

~Abigail

For all my fellow silly girls:
you are never too much
you are always enough

CHAPTER ONE

OCTOBER 2045 - EMPIRE ESTATE, THE ELVISH
PROTECTORATE

THE YOUNGEST OF SIX SIBLINGS, ALL BROTHERS, AND A
consummate cry-baby, Zia preferred to keep things on the straight
and narrow. Rules made her feel grounded. Rules helped her navigate tricky social situations. Rules meant that no one would get
mad at her, or laugh at her, because rules were a clear set of guide-
lines she could follow unerringly.

She had never willingly broken a rule in her life. She never
drank a sip of alcohol before she was legally allowed to, didn't
cheat on a test, or break curfew. Her brothers might have prided
themselves on mischief and mayhem, but she just couldn't
imagine ever *wanting* to cause trouble for herself.

When Zia got the job as Empire Estate's resident rosarian, she
never would have called herself a rule-breaker.

After nearly a year on the job, she wasn't quite so sure that
was true.

She stared out the windshield of her little blue car and into
the waning sunlight with growing dismay. Her deeply ingrained
need for approval warred with her professional pride.

Her brothers wouldn't have hesitated. They would have charged in through the gates, consequences be damned, and done what they pleased, while she idled in the middle of the narrow road that led to the great stone and iron gateway of the estate, wracked with indecision.

If she went through the gate, she'd lose her job.

If she *didn't* go through the gate, a year's worth of work would be destroyed overnight.

Zia's fingers danced nervously over the worn synthetic material of her steering wheel. Outside, the first terrible chill of autumn came on a stiff wind. It buffeted the sides of her car, taunting her.

Maybe they'll be all right, she thought, painfully aware of every second that passed, damning her further. *Maybe the temperature won't drop as far as the weather service says it will. Maybe—*

She watched as the wind snatched at the branches of the sturdy evergreens that guarded the road to the estate. They shook violently, almost as if to say, *"Don't you care about your roses?"*

She *did* care. The estate's long neglected rose garden was her baby, and she had been looking forward to the downtime in the autumn to work on her paper for the Rose Society about the rare variations she coaxed back to life over the past year.

In one night, nature threatened to steal all that hard work from her — as well as her job.

Zia glanced at the clock.

It was just past six in the evening. Since it was early October, it wasn't quite dark yet. The sunset still held on with streaks of baby pink and buttery orange. Overhead, long, wispy clouds looked like unspooled cotton candy. It was sundown, but it wasn't quite *night*.

If she gunned it, she might be able to make it before she broke the *big* rule.

Certainly, no one would get mad at her if she simply cut it close, right? The gates were still open, after all. There was no rule that said she *couldn't* come back to the estate after she left for the day.

If she moved really, *really* fast, she wouldn't break any rules at all.

You can do this.

Holding her breath, Zia let her foot off of the break and hit the gas. The estate's road was spindly but as meticulously maintained as everything else. There were no potholes or ruts to slow her down as she careened down the road, around the gatehouse, and through the massive iron gates. A tiny parking lot for staff lay just on the other side, tucked against a tall stone fence topped with wicked iron spikes.

Zia didn't bother trying to park like a responsible person. All the other staff had gone, and it wasn't like she was going to get a ticket, so she simply left her car in the middle of the lot. Throwing open her door, she hit the ground running.

There was less than a half hour until the sun would go down completely and the gates would shut. She had only that much time to make the long trek to the rose garden, gather everything she needed from the greenhouse, cover all the newly planted roses, and then haul ass back to her car.

The actual procedure of covering the roses for the cold snap to come would only take about five minutes. The *walk*, on the other hand...

Well, there was a reason she normally hitched a ride on Mr. Eisele's golf cart. He managed the whole estate, and even though he was a sour-faced old bastard, he usually waited for her arrival before he puttered off to do whatever it was he did during the day.

On a golf cart, the trip through the trees and around the massive estate to the lush, stonewalled rose garden was beautiful and brief. On foot it was much, much longer.

Wishing she hadn't thrown on her cute, oversized sweater after she got off from work that day, Zia jogged around the sprawling lawn and the glittering fountains barely discernible in the distance. The manor house, old and beautifully built with local granite and gorgeous leaded windows, rose up from behind a wall of stout trees separating it from the rest of the courtyard.

Like every other time she saw it, Zia hastily averted her eyes and moved faster.

Goosebumps broke out across her skin as she picked up her pace. The air was cold in her lungs, scraping at the tender flesh of her throat with each breath. The scents of pine and damp earth clung to the back of her tongue.

Faster, Zia!

The large granite patio that led down to the elaborate gardens was just ahead, but so too was the manor. The back of the home overlooked the sunken, walled area where she typically spent her days — casting a shadow that she could feel clinging to her long after she returned home in the evening.

Zia rounded a bend in the narrow path. The trees thinned out the closer she got to the manor grounds. No matter how hard she tried to keep her eyes on the steps leading to the patio, she couldn't quite stop herself from stealing quick, furtive glances at the home.

Who knew if Mr. Bounds was even inside? He could have been away at some fancy resort, or gone for the weekend to San Francisco. She could imagine him at a sophisticated bar in the city, one with low lighting and shiny, dark wood accents, just as she could picture him at an opera, a black tie party—

Zia banished the train of thought. She did not have time for her usual daydreams about her terrifying, elusive boss. If she didn't hustle her ass, she wouldn't even *have* a boss anymore.

Huffing, a stitch in her side, Zia broke through the last of the trees and onto the patio. Rectangular, with rounded corners and a balustrade on one side, it connected the gardens to the lush land-scaping that filled the immediate area around the manor. On the opposite side from the home, a brick staircase led to her destination.

Turning her back on the manor was always an exercise in will. Something fundamental in her — perhaps the small, nascent part of her brain that remained stubbornly *animal* — recognized the threat which dwelled in that home. It didn't matter that she was never on the premises when that threat could emerge. She *knew* he was in there.

Or at least, her imagination did.

That was the trouble with developing a rich fantasy about the life of her mysterious employer: at a certain point, she couldn't be sure what was entirely made up and what was real instinct.

At least *this* time she had a basis for her acute awareness of her boss. Seeing as she was only twenty-ish minutes away from breaking the *one* rule that governed the entirety of the Empire Estate, she thought her paranoia was justified.

The paranoia, sure, she thought, bracing a hand against her aching side, *but not the goosebumps, or the way you always look at the windows, hoping to catch a glimpse of him.*

She made a disgruntled face. This was not the time to dive back into the psychological reasons for her obsession with a vampire she'd never even properly *seen.*

Desperate to get out of the manor's shadow and away from its watchful windows, Zia beat a hasty path down the staircase. It was split in two, with a fountain built into the top so that water could cascade down the center in a serene waterfall and pool in the large koi pond at its base. Normally, she took a second to admire the water, but seeing as she was taking the steps two at a time, she didn't risk it.

Hitting the brick path at the bottom with an ankle-rattling jolt, she threw herself to the right. Verdant hedges lined the rectangular garden, which was itself broken up into a series of smaller areas. To the right, the stonewalled rose garden and its nearly two hundred year old green house. In the middle, the koi pond and mediterranean garden. To the left, an elaborate gazebo nearly swallowed by climbing jasmine and lush wisteria, where Zia normally ate lunch.

The entrance to the rose garden was marked by a bronze plaque set into the mortar of the low stone wall that bordered it.

In shiny copperplate letters, it read: *The Rose Garden est. 1812 -*
Officially recognized Protectorate Heritage Site & Registered with
The Rose Society 1953

Two quick steps down landed her on the neatly swept gravel
path that bisected the garden. On either side, two huge flower beds
bursting with rose bushes stood. Each bush had its own tiny plaque,
stating the name, the origin of the variety, and the date it was
planted. This late in the season, only a few of her beloved roses still
bloomed. Their colors were bright splashes against dark green leaves.

Zia hustled down the path, her flats crunching in the gravel, to
make her way toward the far end of the garden. That was where
she had planted her newest residents only a handful of weeks
prior.

Pulling her old ring of keys out of her pocket, she came to a
halt in front of the greenhouse at the end of the path. It was as
ancient as the garden was. Rectangular, with a peaked roof and
old, oxidized copper joints between thick glass panels, it had been
nearly overgrown with creeping vines when she first took her post.

It was still old, but now it was also well-loved. Her key slid
into the oiled lock easily, and the door swung open with only the
faintest groan. Inside, the air was warm and wet and thick with
the scent of greenery.

Through the thick, bubbled glass roof, she saw the sky begin
to darken.

Zia shoved her keys back into her pocket and lunged for her
workbench.

Snatching her low-heat thermal sealer, she threw caution to
the wind and thrust it into her front pocket. Hopefully it
wouldn't accidentally turn on and burn a hole through her thigh.

There was no time for a second trip. She wasn't even sure
she'd have time to lock the door on her way out. Frantic now, she
swept her arm across one of the shelves attached to the bench.
Thick sheets of plastic fell onto the grimy brick floor, but most of
them made it into her arms.

She was out of the greenhouse in a flash.

Throw the sheets on, seal them up, run like there's a vampire on your heels. She tried to swallow around the lump in her throat. *Gods, I am not cut out for rule-breaking.*

Her hands shook as she threw the first sheet over the barely established rose bush, then dropped to her knees to use the heat gun to seal the edges around the thick stem. *Maybe he's not here,* she thought again, scrambling to move on to the next one. Rich soil smeared her hands and legs, but she didn't notice. *Maybe he's away, and they won't close the gates tonight because...because maybe they're waiting for him to come home?*

Six more rose bushes stretched ahead of her. The light had begun to fade in earnest, making the LED display on the heat gun glow with a sickly green light.

Maybe no one will notice even if he is *home. Maybe he likes to sleep in a little, like I do. Why would he get up right away on a— a Friday, anyway?*

Zia sank her teeth into her lower lip. Her hands were getting cold, her cheeks beginning to chap under the onslaught of the increasingly icy wind. Her long, thick curls got in her face as she moved from bush to bush.

Four more. All she had to do was four more, and then she could escape.

Escape? she thought, inwardly cringing. *Zia, you dramatic bitch, he's not going to eat you. He's going to* fire *you.*

And still, she felt a shivery little thrill at the idea of being eaten by her vampire.

Was it bad that she felt a deep, dark thrill at the idea of her nearly faceless boss eating her? Certainly. Absolutely. She had officially gone way, way too deep down the rabbit hole of her crush and at some point taken a left turn into weirdo town.

For godssakes, she'd never even properly seen him. He was just a shadow in the window of the manor on the mornings she arrived just before sunrise. Sometimes, when she worked up the nerve to really look, she thought she spied that signature vampiric eye-glow through the leaded window panes.

And that was it.

He was nothing but a shade — a suggestion of a shoulder, a fleeting glimpse of a strong profile, and *menace.*

Everything about him and the rules of his estate screamed that he was dangerous and wanted nothing to do with anyone, least of all the weird woman hired to look after the rose garden in his backyard.

So why on Earth did she think about him *constantly?*

Even that moment, when she nearly slid through the dirt of the bed to reach the final bush, her hands aching fiercely with cold and her heart going a mile a minute, she thought of him.

A large part of her wanted absolutely nothing to do with him. Vampires were *scary.* The dark terrified her. The idea of fangs sinking into her throat should have made her want to run home to her brothers, her parents, and the safety they promised.

The man made every one of her instincts bristle with warning, and getting caught at this moment would mean losing the job she loved.

But a small, dark part of her thrilled at the possibility of finally, finally catching a real glimpse of him. An even darker part found the idea of him catching her, pinning her down, and taking a long, sensual sip from her veins so blazingly erotic it burned.

Not worth your job, you horny idiot, she chastised herself.

Zia held her breath as she dropped onto her hands and knees to seal the bottom of the last plastic sheet. She stared at the display on the heat gun and counted down the seconds. A bead of sweat slid down her temple.

The gun beeped.

Thank the gods. Zia scrambled onto her feet, heedless of the dirt and plant detritus that streaked her cute but apparently unseasonal capris, and turned to jog back to the greenhouse.

She froze, staring at the vague shape of the greenhouse. Her stomach dropped.

"Shit."

Sometime between getting down on her knees and getting back up again, night had fallen. The garden was nothing more than blue and violet shapes. The sky, when she lifted her wide eyes to see it, was a deep, velvety blue. Only a razor thin line of orange gilded the treetops in the distance. When she blinked, it vanished.

She stood amongst the roses, now safe from the coming freeze, in complete darkness. The estate had no outside lights, seeing as vampires didn't need them. There wasn't even a moon to light her way.

Zia stood frozen for several terrible seconds as she grasped the enormity of her mistake.

The number one rule you need to remember, Mr. Eisele had lectured on her very first day of work, *is to never, under any circumstances, stay on the grounds after sundown. Doing so will result in immediate termination, understood?*

When she asked why, he simply answered, *Because Mr. Bounds should never even have to know you exist, Miss North.*

His stern voice echoed in her head as she frantically considered her options. Getting to her car required she walk past the manor house and back down to the lot in complete darkness — something she wasn't even sure she could work up the courage to do.

Even if she could manage to push through her fear of the dark, when she got to the parking lot, she was certain that the gates would, in fact, be closed.

Mr. Bounds did not play around with his security, no matter how much she hoped there would be a glitch in the system, or a dropped shift in the rotation of guards he employed. The gates locked at sundown, just as they did every single night before.

If she could get all the way there — in the *dark,* that was also the *woods* — she would then have to request permission to leave. The guards would contact Mr. Eisele, and she would be summarily fired.

Knocking politely on Mr. Bounds's door would result in

much the same. Not that she could ever work up the nerve to do it even if he wouldn't immediately fire her. As much as he tantalized her, he also scared the shit out of her.

It was half the fantasy, really, but not at all useful in her current situation.

Sneaking through the woods and back to the main road to hitchhike was out of the running, too. Her initial briefing when she took the job went over many details of the estate on the whole, including the state of the art sigil-lined electrical fence that ringed the entirety of the grounds. It not only kept people out, but it worked beautifully to keep foolish rosarians *in*.

Seeing as she desperately wanted to keep her job, had no desire to be electrocuted to death by the fence, and was more than a little skeeved out by the dark, there was only one option, really.

I have to hide.

Holding her hands out to her sides, she crept slowly between the rows of rose bushes until her shoe hit the edge of the bed. The heat gun fell out of her hand, lost to the inky darkness. Deciding that she would just have to pick it up in the morning, Zia wrapped her arms around her middle and tried to breathe. *It's okay. Just get to the greenhouse. Don't focus on the dark, or the woods.*

She could just make out the lip of the bed as she stepped over it and back onto the gravel path. Breath short, she tried to make as little noise as possible as she inched her way back toward the relative safety of the greenhouse.

Certainly Mr. Bounds wouldn't go in there, right? He wouldn't have any reason to. As far as she knew, he had never stepped foot in the greenhouse. Likely, with the weather as bad as it was, he wouldn't even think to take a stroll through the garden. Everything would be fine.

And if anyone questioned why her car was left overnight, she could just say that she'd come back to cover the roses and then had car trouble. A friend had come to pick her up, perhaps, and that was why she'd left it. None of the staff would be able to call her bluff, since none of them knew she didn't have any friends.

Her numb fingers found the old brass handle of the greenhouse door. Quickly pulling it open, she slipped inside and swung it shut behind her. The latch clicked. Somewhere outside, an owl threw out a haunting call.

Zia stood in the rapidly cooling greenhouse, surrounded by the ghoulish shapes of her familiar workspace, and thought, *Oh, this isn't going to be a very nice night at all.*

Chapter Two

Harlan Bounds didn't want for anything. Not anymore.

Born in the darkest point of the Great War, left in the gutter for the sun to ravage, and raised as a soldier in the Amauri Family, he clawed his way to power and wealth. He broke nearly every law in the United Territories and Allies. He killed. He sold secrets. He lied and he took what wasn't his. He became one of the most feared assassins to walk the filthy streets of the New Zone — the stretch of neutral territory between the Draakonriik and the Shifter Alliance — and he was good enough to retire from it all when it pleased him to do so.

He wanted for nothing, because he'd taken everything he desired with his own claws.

Except her.

Harlan looked for her every sunset and every sunrise.

He looked for her even when he knew she would not be there, simply because he could not bear the thought of accidentally missing her. It didn't matter that he had surveillance sensors installed around her home so he always knew when she came and went. It didn't matter that he knew her schedule, her routines. He *looked.*

He wanted Zia North with every fiber of his being, and at some point in the year since she stepped foot on his estate for the first time, his entire life had become shaped by her presence. He rose early enough to catch the last fading streaks of sunset and stayed up until as far past dawn as he was able. He moved his bedroom furniture so that his view out into the rose garden would be entirely unobstructed.

He *looked*, he hungered, and he thought of her relentlessly.

As he always did, Harlan checked the notifications from his security team as soon as he woke. The driving, instinctive need to see to her safety made it a damn compulsion.

It had been nearly two years since anyone tried to make their name by attempting to kill him, but he still worried about her, about what some young, bloodthirsty pricks would do if they knew how much he valued her.

Two hundred years of working for the Amauri Family as their personal assassin meant he accrued more than his fair share of enemies. Most of them were smart enough to leave him alone, but those green fools who thought they could build a reputation by taking out *the* Harlan Bounds were a nuisance.

They were gnats. Killing them was easy, almost routine. It took more effort to ship their body parts back to their pitiful little factions than it did to execute them. But when he thought of his witch being targeted, Harlan was gutted by cold, merciless fear.

It was irrational, of course. They didn't have a relationship and he'd never had the privilege of sinking his fangs into the hot, silken flesh of her throat or breast or thigh. She hadn't taken his venom. She didn't smell like him, or wear his bite. Unless one of his enemies got through the steel vault of his mind to pry out his innermost thoughts without him noticing, no one could know how much that lush creature meant to him.

Still, he assigned his guards to watch the surveillance equipment, just in case.

That was how he knew she had gone home before sunset that day, her trowel and clippers and advanced soil testing equipment neatly shelved in her greenhouse. The sensors registered that she returned to her little home and then left again just before nightfall.

He had to read the notification twice before he processed the words. *Zia never leaves her home after dark,* he thought, stomach sinking.

There was only one reason he could think of that might explain her sudden departure from routine: she was with someone.

Harlan tried to rein in his agitation as he tossed off his charcoal gray sheets and padded, naked, into his ensuite bathroom. He did not gnash his fangs as he took a quick, cold shower. He didn't think about how she might be on a date at that very moment, out to dinner with someone else, while he tugged on a pair of running pants over a cock that hadn't gone completely soft since the day he caught her scent through the open kitchen window.

He didn't curse the short winter days, which meant she left for home earlier and earlier each day, as he cracked open a bottle of synthetic blood and watched balefully as the proprietary tech in the bottle heated it to the perfect body temperature.

And he tried very, very hard not to think about how sweet her blood would taste in comparison to the synthetic crap he'd lived on for so long.

"Fuck," he groused, lowering the bottle to wipe at his mouth. It tasted like fucking *nothing*.

He needed to get out of the house and burn some energy off, or else he'd do something stupid, like track her down.

It was a tempting thought, too. The predator in him lunged toward the challenge of hunting his sweet prey in the dark. It would take so very little.

He'd never touched her, never spoken to her, but he knew her scent like he knew his own. Even without all the advanced technology available to him — and her home address, of course — he could find her with terrifying ease.

Because she was *his* prey, and had been from the moment he saw her in the rose garden a year ago.

Slamming the half empty bottle down onto the marble countertop in his mostly unused kitchen, Harlan swore again.

He was a civilized vampire now. He was Harlan *fucking* Bounds, owner of the Empire Estate and respectable businessman. He did not hunt down sweet, sensual bits who walked his grounds in flirty little shorts and smiled brighter than the sun.

He didn't do that when he was an assassin, and he certainly wouldn't do it *now*.

Ignoring the vibrating phone tucked into his pocket, Harlan stalked out of his kitchen. With jerky, aggressive movements, he swept his long fall of black hair into a high ponytail at the back of his head and jogged out of the manor.

The air was crisp, the wind biting, and his estate was wholly his. No one ventured past the gate after sundown, so he was free to spend his nights away from people — exactly how he liked it.

There was only one person he wished to see in the welcoming dark, but it was the thought of that very woman that compelled him to take off in a hard run. Perhaps if he burned enough energy, he wouldn't feel such a pounding need to track her down, hide her away, and sink his fangs into that soft tanned skin until she forgot the outside world existed at all.

So he ran. And he ran. *And he ran.*

Perspiration coated his bare chest and slid down his temples as he pushed himself to run the circuit of the estate's border as fast as he could. He hoped the strain of his screaming muscles would be enough to distract him, but it didn't work. It never worked.

Why did she matter so much? Was it the fact that he hadn't known a woman like he desperately wanted to know Zia in... decades, probably? Was it that awful quirk of vampiric biology that made them intensely covetous of potential anchors?

Was it simply that he wanted what she seemed to embody so effortlessly — sumptuous life, sunlight, and the kind of easy happiness he'd never known?

Or was it just that she looked like she tasted *really fucking good?*

At the farthest edge of his property, behind a garage that held all the various vehicles his staff used throughout the day, Harlan came to a slow stop. Breathing hard, he braced his hands against the cool brick wall and bowed his head. His eyes closed.

I'm so fucking hungry.

He hadn't had a satisfying meal since the day he laid eyes on her. It didn't matter how much synthetic shit he drank. It didn't even matter when he went through the trouble of importing real fresh blood from well-compensated donors. Nothing worked.

Harlan's claws bit into the pitted mortar between the bricks.

What is she doing right now? Is she safe? Is she on a date? Will she sleep at another man's house tonight?

Hot rage was a shot through his gut when he thought, *Is another vampire tasting her right now?*

Possessiveness, a hardwired evolutionary adaptation, wrapped its claws around his throat and *squeezed.*

No one was allowed to touch his anchor. No one was allowed to even fucking *look* at her. Instinct knew she was his, that her blood belonged on his tongue. It knew that his venom would work beautifully in her body, making her taste sweeter even as it bound her to him on a chemical level, made them a seamless unit.

Vampire and anchor. Anchor and vampire, one being — as nature intended.

It knew, and it screamed at him to act louder and louder every night, lest someone else claim the right to her first.

She could be with someone else right now. She could be smiling at another man, kissing him, letting him know all her secrets and desires.

Harlan choked, shoulders tightening, as if there really was a hand squeezing the life out of him.

Gods, he was a bastard for letting those things bother him. He had no claim on her, but the predator howled in outrage anyway. Vampires did not *share.*

They hunted. They sequestered. They jealously guarded. They pleasured. They *tasted*.

They *kept*.

So why is she out there on her own? Why isn't she here with me right now, waiting in my bed? Why am I torturing myself like this?

Because he was Harlan Bounds and... he wasn't fucking good enough for her.

His phone vibrated again. Snarling at the wall, he snatched it out of his pocket and held it to his ear. *"What?"*

It was the head of his small security force, a vampire soldier he had personally trained named Atticus Caldwell. "Sorry to bother you, Mr. Bounds, but I thought you might want an update on your... on Miss North."

Harlan's spine snapped straight. The roots of his fangs pulsed with red hot aggression when he demanded, "What's wrong?"

There was a curious note in Atticus's cool voice when he answered, "Well, nothing as far as we can tell."

Relief mingled with temper. "Then why are you *calling* me?"

"I just thought you might want to know that her car's still here."

That drew him up short. "What? Why? She went home."

"That's what the sensors said, yeah, but about an hour and a half ago she came speeding back onto the estate, parked with markedly less skill than usual, and ran onto the grounds like Grim's hounds were on her heels." There was a slight pause, then, with obvious amusement, "If you'd like me to hunt her down and—"

"You fucking take one look at Zia and I'll make your fangs into a pair of earrings for her, understood?" Harlan sucked in a breath through clenched teeth. *Calm.* "Where is she now?"

Atticus *definitely* hid a laugh under a cough before he answered, "Wards say she's in the rose garden. Gods know what she's doing out there. There isn't any light for her to work under."

Harlan was already turning away from the garage. Breaking into a swift jog, he cursed himself for not thinking of her. Of course he should have had lights installed. He should have had them installed all over the estate. She was a witch, not a vampire, and if she was going to stay on the estate, she'd need certain accommodations—

Forcing that train of thought aside, he snapped, "Why didn't you tell me immediately? She's been out in the dark this whole time. What if she's hurt?"

Why else would she stay past sundown, when she knew the gates closed? Certainly it wasn't to see *him*. He'd watched her skitter past the manor enough times to know that she was terrified of the very idea of him.

"She could have broken her ankle on the steps," he raged, moving faster. The icy wind buffeted his sweat-slicked skin like a wave of pinpricks. "She could have hit her head, or dislocated a shoulder, or had a seizure, and you waited an *hour and a fucking half* to tell me?"

"Boss, I've been calling you every five minutes since sundown."

"Well, you should have fucking come and gotten me, then!" Harlan ripped the phone away from his ear and shoved it back into his pocket. Breaking into a full sprint, he charged down the most direct path through the dense trees to reach the garden.

Fear was a deep, dark pressure in his belly.

He'd seen the very worst the world had to offer without so much as a flinch. He'd killed and he maimed and he had been left for dead on more than one occasion.

And yet the idea of Zia — beautiful, soft Zia — suffering for even a moment made bile churn in his stomach.

It was *wrong*. Everything in him rebelled against the thought of her coming to harm, of her sitting alone in the dark and crying out for help while he ignorantly continued on with his night.

If she was yours, this wouldn't have happened, the base part of him raged. *If you took what you wanted, she would be safe in the manor right now, dressed in silk and your bite.*

He ran faster, past the two circular fountains in the lawn and around the stout hedges.

The manor rose up in the darkness, perfectly visible to him in shades of blue and gray and violet. Harlan took the shortest route to the back — by running through the house.

Bursting out of the back door, he came to a sudden halt in the small landscaped sitting area attached to the kitchen to scan the patio. There was no sign of her, and the wind had swept away any lingering traces of her luscious scent.

Rose garden, he thought, vaulting over a decorative iron fence to land on the stone patio. *Please be in the rose garden.*

If she was hurt, he had a healer on call and could get her help in less than an hour. Everything would be fine. She would be fine. And after she was fixed up, he'd do whatever it took to convince her to give an old, worthless vampire a chance, because he was officially done denying the call of his anchor.

And I'll have some fucking lights installed!

Instead of bothering with the long flight of bisected stairs down to the gardens, Harlan grasped the railing and swung his legs over to drop himself down onto the gravel path.

How many times had he trod the path to the rose garden over the year, hoping to catch some fleeting feeling of closeness with her? Hundreds of times. He looked for her footprints in the soil, the beds she cleared, the new flowers she was studiously coaxing out of the ground with her skill and magic.

How many times had he stood at the entrance to the rose garden and scanned the area, hoping that she might be there even when he knew it was impossible?

His pulse jumped at the thought of doing the very same thing now, *knowing* that she would be there. For once, he would look out across the garden not simply see moonlit blooms, but *her.*

...Except she wasn't there.

Harlan stalked through the opening in the stone fence and down the gravel path between the beds.

The weight of fear increased until it felt like he could barely breathe under it.

There was no one in the garden. The only thing that caught his eye was a row of new rose bushes swathed in some sort of synthetic sheeting, insulating them from the cold night to come. His heart began to pound in earnest as he swept his gaze over the rows and rows of spectacularly tended bushes, hoping he somehow missed her. If she had collapsed somewhere, perhaps—

A flash of white caught his eye. Prowling toward the greenhouse, Harlan narrowed his eyes at the sight of what looked like some sort of gun-shaped tool laying in the dirt by the covered roses.

It was hanging just over the edge of the bed and angled slightly toward the greenhouse.

Turning on his heel, Harlan held his breath as he made his way toward the shadowy shape of the glass and metal structure.

It was old, and when he realized his new obsession spent most of her time there, he demanded Mr. Eisele purchase a new one for her use. Even in those early days, the need to give her the very best the world had to offer rode him hard. If she needed a greenhouse, his witch would get the finest, most state of the art one available.

But his groundskeeper had come back the next evening grumbling that she didn't want a new one, that it had historical significance, so would Mr. Bounds please allow it to stay?

Of course, he could refuse her nothing, even if he only wanted her to have the best, so he surprised Mr. Eisele by agreeing to keep it. What Zia wanted, Zia got.

Now, however, he wished he pressed the issue.

The interior of the greenhouse was obscured by over two centuries of discoloration and moss adhered to the thick, leaded glass panels, so it was impossible for him to make out any distinct shapes inside. Still, the sweaty skin on the back of his neck prickled when he reached for the brass handle.

She's here.

Hunting instincts rising in a wave, Harlan slowly turned the handle and pulled open the narrow door. The scents of green things and dirt and water and *her* hit him first. Luscious rose, vanilla, and the smallest hint of salt made his mouth water, the gland in the roof of his mouth aching with a fierceness he had never experienced. The scent of her burrowed into him. Combined with the sound of her rapidly beating heart, it worked to make him instantly, painfully hard.

And then he saw her.

Sitting on an overturned bucket in the far corner, she stared up at him with slightly unfocused eyes. In an achingly soft, tremulous voice, she breathed, "Mr. Bounds? Is... that you?"

Fuck.

Chapter Three

There was terror, and then there was "sit in a pitch-black greenhouse for an hour until the door slowly swings open to reveal two blazing, night-glow eyes and nothing else" *terror.*

Zia wasn't particularly fond of the dark when she had a nightlight and her favorite blanket. But *this?* This was fear on a level she had never experienced.

It was the kind that came directly from the oldest part of the brain — that fleshy stem that told the body what foods to crave, when to fuck, when to sleep. It was the part that saw snakes in fallen branches and faces in clouds and sweetness in bright colors.

It was the part that looked in the dark and saw death.

Zia sat perfectly still on her makeshift seat. Mere moments ago she was chilled to the bone and miserable. Now she felt almost outside of her body, entirely absent from the decision-making process that currently held her rooted to the spot.

She stared at those night-glow eyes — an almost electric green with candy-colored yellow centers, the hallmark of a predator — which could realistically only belong to one man, but... that really wasn't all that comforting.

Zia stared at the vague impression of his broad shouldered

shape, only truly given form by the placement of those eyes. Without them, she never would have seen him. Without the faintest whine of the old door hinges, she never would have heard him, either.

Her breaths puffed in front of her, hot and fast.

Gods, she knew he was just a man. He wouldn't hurt her. Only the worst kinds of vampires still hunted people for sport, and it was considered deeply immoral to take blood from the flesh without consent. *By most, anyway.*

But that animal part of her brain did not recognize that valuable context. It only saw a predator's eyes getting closer, closer, until they were barely a foot away.

Zia's heart pounded against her ribs so hard she felt dizzy. Why did it have to be so damn *dark*—

A blaze of light lit up the greenhouse.

She flinched, eyes closing against the sting, before she realized that she'd closed her eyes on a predator and snapped them open again.

Oh, she thought, quickly adjusting to what was actually a rather small light coming from the cellphone in his hand. Zia blinked. Her lips parted involuntarily.

Certainly she was not staring directly at a man's naked, sharply hewn abdominal muscles.

Certainly—

The muscles, thrown into stark relief by the little cone of light, bunched in front of her eyes. Zia let out a squeak of alarm as the man in front of her slowly crouched down to her level.

In the light, she could just make out a striking face — heavy brows over hooded eyes, a lush mouth, high cheekbones, and a narrow, rounded chin. His skin was a coppery brown and his hair, pulled back into a long ponytail, was black streaked with locks of gray. Sweat sheened his temples, curling the fine hair there into soft whorls.

Her breathing sped up.

Her imagination had filled in the gaps of his appearance over the last several months, padding the impression of wide shoulders, the relative certainty of towering height, and the suggestion of long hair with an idealized Mr. Bounds, but the real thing was nothing like she imagined.

He was *better.*

"Miss North?"

Her entire body jolted with surprise. *He... knows my name?*

Momentarily stunned, it took her a moment to grasp the position she found herself in. Mr. Bounds was in front of her. Mr. Bounds knew her name. Mr. Bounds was about to fire her. Mr. Bounds was *shirtless* and about to fire her.

Heart lurching, Zia shied away. Her back hit the cold wall behind her. "Ah, I'm— I'm sorry. Mr. Bounds, I didn't mean to trespass. I'm so sorry—"

"Miss North," he rumbled. The man had a baritone so rich, it damn near melted her bones. His gaze slid over her, scanning every inch of her face and neck with a dark, forbidding look. "Are you hurt? Did you have an accident? I have a healer on call. If you're in pain, tell me now."

Mortification threatened to choke the life out of her. *Gods, he thinks I hit my head or something.*

She had imagined meeting her mysterious boss a thousand different ways, but *none* of them were like this. Usually she'd grown a particularly gorgeous rose and he simply *had* to compliment her skill. Occasionally she imagined that they stumbled upon one another at a fancy party, have a torrid one night stand, and realize the next day that she was his estate's rosarian. Sometimes, she even thought of what it would be like to have him stumble upon her in the greenhouse, tear off her shorts, bend her over the workbench, and—

Zia flushed, her embarrassment building to catastrophic levels. "I'm fine," she croaked.

A deep, intense frown carved hard lines in Mr. Bounds's handsome face. It was perhaps the single most frightening expression she'd ever witnessed. That frown was pure menace.

"You don't sound fine." He canted his head to one side. His gaze dropped to her throat. Voice lowering to a murmur, he added, "Your heart is beating irregularly, Miss North."

Could a person die of mortification? She didn't think so, but she had high hopes. "I... Ah, you scared me?"

"Let me look at you."

Zia watched him settle his phone on the piled bags of soil to her left. Thick, corded arm muscle flexed under taut brown skin. Her mouth went dry.

She was so transfixed by the sight — Mr. Bounds, the shadowy figure of her fantasies, was *shirtless and a little sweaty in front of her* — that she didn't have time to worry before he skimmed his hands down her arms in one brisk movement.

Jumping at the sudden contact, she yelped, "What are you doing?"

"Checking to see if you broke any bones." The tips of his claws tickled the backs of her hands before he dropped his palms to feel the contours of her legs. With a completely impersonal mien, he ran his fingers down to her ankles, rotated both of her feet, and then moved back up to probe at her scalp.

Zia was so flabbergasted by the entire thing that she simply sat there, holding her breath, and tried her best to vacate her body.

Apparently finding nothing, Mr. Bounds sat back on his heels and braced his forearms on his bent knees. His frown deepened. One hand reached out again to just barely rest the tips of his claws on the curve of her knee. She could feel the tiniest prick of them through the fabric.

Danger, instincts wailed. *Danger!*

And yet, when his touch firmed, the pads of his fingers whispering against her knee, Zia didn't flinch away. Instead, her pulse found a new home between her thighs. A deep, luscious ache made her internal muscles contract.

Danger, instincts wailed again.

Danger, desire whispered back. *Gorgeous, delicious danger.*

Mr. Bounds's shoulders tensed. His voice was slightly rougher when he said, "I didn't find any injuries, but—"

Feeling her entire body flush with red-hot embarrassment and something much, much worse, she cut him off. "I'm really, *really* fine. I promise."

"Then why are you here? You should be... home." Those night-glow eyes moved slowly over her face, then down her body. One eyebrow arched. "And why are you covered in dirt?"

She swallowed, but the lump in her throat was a stubborn bastard.

Resigning herself to the impending loss of her dream job, Zia fought a reflexive prickling of tears to explain, "I... Well, I *went* home, but when I got there I saw an updated weather report that said we were going to freeze tonight. I came back to cover the new roses."

Fearing that he wouldn't understand exactly *why* she couldn't let them die, she rushed to add, "They're so rare, Mr. Bounds. All of them are heritage varieties that pre-date the war. I had to wait almost a whole year to get cuttings from the Rose Society, and the frost would have killed them if they weren't covered. I couldn't just let them die."

She bit her lip to stop herself from rambling on. Why would he care about her excuses? As far as she knew, he probably didn't even know what she did on his estate, or how important the rose garden was to her. It was a miracle he even knew her name.

He could find another rosarian with a snap of his fingers, and he almost certainly wouldn't have noticed if her prized new varieties died in the cold.

Curling her half-frozen fingers into her thighs, she dropped her eyes to the brick floor. "I know— I *know* no one is allowed on the grounds after sunset, so I tried to hurry, but I wasn't fast enough." She closed her eyes, bracing for the worst part. In a hoarse voice, she admitted, "I thought that if I just spent the night in here, maybe it wouldn't bother anyone. I understand that I'm definitely fired, but I just..."

Just what? Couldn't help yourself? Couldn't do your job? Couldn't think of a better way to explain why the roses matter?

There was no excuse for what she'd done. She broke the rule. The consequence was clear. That was it.

Except no scolding came. There was no upbraiding, no demands for her to get off his property. There was only the sound of wind and her own ragged breathing.

He was quiet for so long, Zia was actually forced to open her eyes and *look* at him.

Mr. Bounds was in the exact same position. He didn't even look like he had blinked since she began her pitiful little speech. Those vampire eyes were locked on her face, unreadable, while his expression was completely impassive.

Cold sweat dewing on the back of her neck, she worked up the nerve to whisper, "Mr. Bounds?"

That seemed to unfreeze him.

He cut his eyes away. His upper lip lifted to reveal a pair of prominent fangs as he made a distinctly perturbed clicking sound with his tongue.

Slowly, like he was trying to work it all out, he asked, "So you thought you should spend the coldest night of the year so far in *here* instead of, say, walking to the gatehouse to ask the guards to let you out?" He paused. Mr. Bounds's gaze snapped back to hers as his heavy brows lowered. *"Or* simply walking up the stairs to knock on the manor's door?"

Zia dropped her eyes. Gods, he probably thought she had mush for brains. A normal person would have done exactly that, especially when they realized they left their cellphone in their car and the temperature was dropping fast.

What could she say? *I know. I just really, really love my roses?*

He would laugh at her the same way people had always laughed at her. Or worse — he'd be *angry.*

Gods, Zia couldn't stand it when people got angry with her. She usually broke out into huge, embarrassing tears before they even opened their mouths.

"I'm sorry," she murmured, standing abruptly. Her hands fluttered around her legs. Useless. "Really, Mr. Bounds. I didn't mean to bother you. I'll go."

She'd go home to her lonely little house in the woods, which was too dark and cold all the time, and she'd have a nice, long cry about losing her job because she cared way, way too much. Then she'd call her *anne* in the morning and admit that she was right, Zia really should have just stayed home with the family and taken that job at the San Jose Botanical Garden.

When Mr. Bounds stood up in one smooth, almost catlike movement, the light couldn't reach his face. He was cast in shadow once more — only those terrifying predator eyes could be seen as she tried to squeeze past him in the narrow space.

"Miss North, wait."

Warm fingers curled around her wrist, halting her progress. Zia bit her lip and stared at what she hoped was the door. She hated the dark that waited just outside this tiny ring of relative safety he provided, but she preferred to lick her wounds in private more.

Still, she waited, horribly tense, for whatever it was he wanted to say to her. Would he tell her not to come back tomorrow morning? Would he scold her for how ridiculous she was? Would he *laugh?*

She would take almost anything over him laughing at her. It would cut so much worse coming from the man she'd nursed an impossible crush on for so long.

"Come into the house and warm up before you go."

Zia was so surprised, she actually swung her head back around to peer at the vague shadow of his face. "I'm sorry?"

In his deep, deep voice, he repeated, "Let me walk you back to the house. You're cold, you're upset, and you're not fit to drive. Let me... make you tea."

Without thinking, she blurted out, "Do you *have* tea?"

Zia wanted to melt into the floor. *For Glory's sake! Why can I not keep my damn mouth* shut?

Miraculously, Mr. Bounds didn't appear to take offense to her insensitive question. Instead, his brow furrowed. "I don't know. Sometimes I buy things that look nice, though, so we might get lucky."

Oh. Why did she find that painfully endearing?

"Okay," she breathed, momentarily dazed by the image of *Mr. Bounds* being so taken with a tin of green tea he could never drink that he bought it anyway. It was... kind of cute.

The warmth of his fingers vanished, leaving her somehow colder than she was before. She watched him scoop up his phone. He flicked off the flashlight setting before he turned to press just the very tips of his fingers against her back, ushering her forward.

Of course, without the light, she immediately stumbled over what she could only assume was a hose that hadn't been there a minute ago. "Shit!"

Mr. Bounds grabbed her arm, only just saving her from a nasty spill into her workbench. He cursed as he gently righted her. "I'm having this fixed tomorrow," he rumbled, turning the light on his phone back on. Stuffing it into her slack hand, he added, "I didn't realize this would be so hazardous. Forgive me, Miss North."

Something hot coiled in the pit of her stomach when he touched her back again, firmer this time.

"Really, it's fine!" She let out a high, nervous laugh. "I'm the one who shouldn't be leaving tools on the ground, or— or be here when I can't see them, I guess."

His entire hand rested on the small of her back now. Zia could feel the heat of it radiating through the layers of her sweatshirt and tank top as he guided her toward the door. The smell of soap, woodsy aftershave, and something richer, muskier, cut through the earthy scents of the greenhouse.

Her hand shook ever-so-slightly as she pointed the phone's light at her feet. *Calm, Zia. He's just a man.*

"I'll have lights installed. Not just in the greenhouse, but all over the grounds. I didn't realize it could be this unsafe for you."

"Oh, it's okay. It's not your fault I have weak human eyes."

His voice got somehow deeper, colder, when he said, "If I wasn't here tonight, you could have tripped on that hose and smashed your head open. By the time my guards would have thought to look for you, you could have been dead. That is unacceptable."

Chapter Four

THEY REACHED THE DOOR, AND MR. BOUNDS SHIFTED to the side to open it for her. That coil of heat in her belly got just a little hotter.

"Put that way, I agree that a light would have been nice, but *you* don't need them," she protested, stepping out onto the familiar gravel of the rose garden's path.

"No, but you do."

His fingers flexed on her back. With each step they moved slightly closer to her hip, until the palm of his hand molded to fit the curve of her waist.

Zia's fingers tightened around his phone. He obviously meant an expansive, all-staff-encompassing sort of *you,* but that dreamy part of her felt a little *zing! w*hen he said it.

However he meant it, she wasn't about to argue the point. She was in enough hot water without contradicting him.

Biting her lip, she tried very hard not to think about the fact that Mr. Bounds was carefully guiding her out of the rose garden, up the brick steps, and across the patio to his gorgeous manor house.

Or that his palm was firmly cupping her waist, his fingers splayed so every single pad touched her.

A few lights were on — one downstairs, in what she had always assumed was the kitchen, and another upstairs, in the room that overlooked the gardens. A part of her wilted with relief at the sight. Normally she was intimidated by the house and its mysterious occupant, but when it was lit up with warm light, beckoning her with the promise of warmth, she suddenly felt an acute yearning to go inside.

Gently pressing on her side when she hesitated at the threshold of the small garden attached to the back of the house, Mr. Bounds nudged her toward a narrow door with diamond cut glass panels. It was partially open. Again, he moved to one side to let her step in first.

Zia curled her fingers around the hems of her sleeves and ducked her head as she passed.

The air in the house was almost uncomfortably warm on her chilled skin, but she welcomed it. She *hated* being cold. Ruefully, she admitted to herself that there was no way she would have lasted the night in the greenhouse, though she struggled to imagine ever working up the courage to bother him.

As Mr. Bounds quietly shut the door behind her, she moved a little way into the kitchen, her wide eyes taking in the gorgeous furnishings as quickly as possible.

Though the lights were dimmer than she would have typically set them, she had no trouble making out the dark wood cabinets, the sumptuously veined marble countertops, or the polished copper fixtures that gave the entire space a rich, homey atmosphere.

It was gorgeous, but it was also... empty.

There were no gadgets on the counters, no magnets on the refrigerator. The fancy cooker looked like it had never been touched. The only hint of life at all was the single bottle of synth-blood on the counter by the sink. The cap was off and resting beside it, as if Mr. Bounds hadn't even finished his breakfast before he found her trespassing on his property.

Ugh, I probably ruined his entire night, and now he's going to sit me down for a long talk about why I'm fired.

Zia swayed back against the wall by the door. A heavy, antique clock ticked a steady beat over her head, counting down the seconds until her inevitable firing.

"Really, Mr. Bounds, I am *so* sorry," she said, glancing back at the door. If she left quickly, maybe it wouldn't be so bad. The damage was done, but she didn't have to make it *worse*. "I should go. You must have just been starting your day— *night,* and I ruined everything."

He turned away from the door to give her a piercing look. The frown was back. "Stop apologizing."

Zia gestured helplessly to him. "But—"

"No."

"But, Mr. Bounds, I broke—"

He turned from her to stride into the main kitchen area. "I said no, *Miss North.* I don't like it when you apologize, so you'll stop doing it."

Excuse me? Zia might have puffed up with a little indignation, but she was immediately distracted by the sight of his *back.*

Of course, she saw that he was shirtless in the greenhouse, but even with the light from his phone, her view of him had been distorted by harsh light and deep shadow. Now that they were in his house, dimly lit though it was, she could see *everything.*

He was gorgeous.

Wide shoulders slid into a neat waist and a delightfully sculpted backside, which was covered in dark blue running pants. Thickly muscled thighs ran into long legs. Beautifully tapered fingers drew the eye to rough knuckles and strong, rectangular wrists. Every dip of muscle, every strong sinew, every ridge of dense bone spoke of a life of action, movement. When he moved, even just to walk up to the cabinets above the cooker, it looked like *art.*

And yet, all of that was secondary to the scars.

Mr. Bounds's reddish brown skin was covered in them.

Slashes crisscrossed with bite marks. Two puckered stars of silver about the size of her thumb decorated his upper shoulder and right side. Clusters of jagged lines were the unmistakable legacy of claws.

Above it all, his inky black ponytail swung in a hypnotic wave — back and forth, back and forth.

Zia clutched his phone to her chest reflexively. *Gods, just who is this man?*

No matter how hard she tried, she couldn't imagine what kind of life left those scars. Clearly, they'd never been touched by a healer or they wouldn't be there at all. But why wouldn't someone see a healer? Even a regular doctor would have had equipment for scar removal easily available.

She tried to avert her eyes, but it was impossible. It was like trying to stop breathing. She could only manage it for so long before her gaze snapped back to that grisly network of old wounds.

Maybe he was a veteran? He was certainly old enough to have fought in the Great War.

Her heart squeezed, sympathy momentarily dulling the sharpest edge of her apprehension. *Poor man. No one should be put through so much pain.*

Mr. Bounds, ignorant of her study of him, opened a pair of cabinet doors and peered inside. After a moment, he said, "I don't know what you might like, so you should come see for yourself."

Feeling like she was in way over her head, she weakly demurred, "Oh, you know, that's okay. I don't want to cause you any more trouble tonight. I can just... go."

The ponytail swung slowly to the side as he turned his head, giving her an arch look over one sculpted shoulder. "I invited you in for tea, did I not?"

"...Yes."

"Then you'll have tea." He tilted his head toward the cabinet. "Come choose something."

Stalling for time, Zia slowly placed his phone down on the

lovely mahogany kitchen table to her left. *Don't make a fool of yourself.*

It was easier said than done. She often found herself doing or saying the wrong thing. That was why she never stood a chance in academia, nor in the higher levels of the Rose Society. She was, in the words of her eldest brother, Hasim, *just a little too silly.*

Zia nervously smoothed her thick, curly hair back behind her ears and inched her way across the kitchen. Standing as near to him as she dared, she clasped her hands in front of her and eyed the contents of the cabinet.

"Ah," she said. "Well, you certainly have an eye for powdered chocolate. And... salt."

She could feel his gaze on her profile but kept her focus studiously forward when he replied, "I appreciate their packaging."

"Well, yes, they do all look very nice." Zia tried hard not to smile. Gods help her, she didn't want to offend the man. There was just something deeply funny about the collection of goodies he stashed in the cabinet, never to be used.

There were at least four brands of expensive powdered, unsweetened chocolate — the fancy imported kind that came in tins and pretty jars. Salt in every color and style mixed with bottles of wax-stamped balsamic vinegar, paper-wrapped mustards, and what looked like many thousands of dollars-worth of saffron and whole vanilla bean.

It was a mess, but it was a *fancy* mess.

After daring to nudge things around a bit with the tip of her finger, she told him, "I don't think you have any tea in here."

Glancing at his face, she got the impression that the news somehow vexed him. "The other cabinets might have something. This is where I normally put things, though." A dark look settled on his face for a moment before he said, almost to himself, "I should have known to have something ready in case you needed it."

Zia's heart pinched. Mr. Bounds looked awfully scary, but that was very sweet. Unnecessary, but sweet nonetheless.

"It's okay. I think I can make something out of some of this." Her fingers closed around a can of — *goodness, is that Dutch canned milk?* — before she paused, uncertain. "Oh, I mean, I don't *have* to have anything, but if you'd like me to—"

"You will take whatever you like," he declared, a hard edge to his voice. "I will assist you if I can. If there's nothing here you want, I will have something delivered for you."

"That's *really* not necessary."

He turned the full force of his intensity on her when he said, "You *will* tell me if you need something, Miss North."

"I... Right." Zia had to shake her head. *This man sure likes giving orders.* "Can you reach that... I *think* that's sugar up there. In that snazzy blue jar with the... Japanese label, maybe?"

His arm shot up so fast, she squeaked and bounced to one side, the can of milk pressed to her chest. Breathless, she exclaimed, "Man, you're *fast.*"

Mr. Bounds plucked the jar off of the high shelf and made that strange, agitated clicking sound again. His voice was calm, almost flat, but she still got the sense that he was sincere when he said, "I apologize. I shouldn't have moved so quickly."

"It's fine, I'm just easily startled."

It wasn't normally *quite* so bad, though. Being near Mr. Bounds had her fight or flight instincts in a tizzy. Adrenaline pumped through her veins. She honestly couldn't tell if she wanted to lick him or hide from him.

Best not to do either, I suppose.

She reached out to grasp a tiny jar of vanilla bean and one of the tins of chocolate. Setting them all on the counter, she babbled, "My brothers say I'm flightier than a hummingbird and twice as silly. They used to love scaring me half to death when we were kids. Mostly at night, when they'd hide in closets and jump out from behind dark corners. Pretty sure that's why I still get really jumpy in the dark, but what are you gonna do? Brothers are brothers."

She sucked in a deep breath and forced herself to stop. *Quiet, Zia! He doesn't want to hear about your family, or your ridiculous fear of the dark. He's a* vampire. *You've made a bad impression already. Don't make it worse!*

Clasping her hands together, she croaked, "Now, do you have a small pan, a spoon, and a mug?"

Mr. Bounds stared at her for a handful of seconds before he slowly turned his eyes to the wall behind her. "Do those count?"

Zia spun around. "Oh, that'll do nicely!"

Someone had used several brilliantly polished copper pans as wall decoration. When she stretched up to pull the smallest saucepan off the wall, she was surprised by the weight of it. Normally she used the regular lightweight, indestructible ones from orc-owned brands. "Are these antiques?"

"They came with the house."

So the answer was yes. The manor house pre-dated the Great War, so the pans likely did as well.

Zia stared at the pan, considering its worth as an antique versus its purpose as a kitchen utensil, before she shrugged and trotted back to the cooker. After hunting down a similarly decorative teacup and spoon, she set out to use her well-honed cooking skills to whip herself up a luxe cup of hot chocolate.

As the milk heated in the pan, she carefully scraped at the gooey center of the vanilla bean and tried not to feel Mr. Bounds's gaze burning a hole in the side of her head.

"I didn't know hummingbirds were silly."

The tip of her spoon skipped off of the long vanilla bean. It *tinged* against the marble counter as her eyes skated back to her host. He was leaning against the countertop, arms crossed over his naked chest. A frown puckered the skin between his brows.

It was hard to look at him for too long. Every time she dared to glance his way, she spotted something new and alluring, like the hint of crow's feet, or his widow's peak, or the way his pupils still glowed faintly green in the light, or how his streaks of gray looked more like ribbons through his long hair—

"I suppose they're not, but they do move around very fast and do all sorts of funny things in the air." She shrugged and forced her eyes back to her task. "Could be worse. They could have compared me to a shoebill."

She dipped the spoon into the milk and began to stir.

"I don't know what a shoebill is."

Peeking at him through her lashes, she shot him a bashful smile. "A shoebill is another type of bird. They look like perpetually pissed off old men. Not what I'd like to be compared to, if I had the choice."

She could almost *hear* his frown deepening as she stirred in the sugar and powdered chocolate. A glance at the sugar told her even *it* was fancy, though the Japanese label shot down any chance of her figuring out why. She fought the urge to shake her head.

This would be perhaps the most sumptuous cup of cocoa she ever had, in the company of the strangest, most intense man she'd ever met.

"You are *not* a shoebill," he declared, low and serious. When she moved to turn down the heat on the cooker, Zia was surprised to see him gripping the edge of the countertop, his knuckles bleached white.

Every single knuckle was decorated with star-shaped scars.

"And if you *are* a hummingbird, it's not because you're silly. It's because you spend all day with your flowers." He paused, then, in a voice that was almost reluctant, added, "And it's because you're beautiful."

Zia's heart stuttered. "That... that is a better way of looking at it, yes."

Trying to calm herself down and not read into whatever that meant, she delicately poured her cocoa into the lovely, filigree-encrusted teacup. Steam curled in the air. The scent was heavenly. Raising the cup to her lips, she took a tiny sip.

Goodness gracious gods in the sky, that's a damn good cup of cocoa!

"Oh, you really do buy fantastic chocolate," she praised. A soft moan of delight hummed in her throat. "I think this is the best cocoa I've ever had."

Mr. Bounds looked at her for what felt like a long time before he gestured stiffly to the kitchen table. "Will you sit with me while you drink your... cocoa?"

She sent the table a nervous look. "Are you going to have something? It'll be strange if it's just me..." Too late, she realized what she said. Flushing hot enough to make her ears red, she tried to backtrack. "Ah, I'm sorry! I don't know the proper— I mean, I *didn't* mean to— Damn."

If she wasn't so busy staring at her cocoa in abject mortification, she might have caught the way Mr. Bounds's lips curled up at the corners.

Padding a few steps to his left, he swiped the open bottle of synthblood off of the counter. She recognized it from ads and a small section of the big grocery store she sometimes made the long trip to. The brand he apparently preferred came in a sleek chrome bottle with a blue label that read, *SIPIRON - Tastes real because it's made real! Now in our new self-heating bottle!*

Mr. Bounds used the bottle to gesture toward the table, saying, "I didn't finish my meal earlier. I can finish it while you drink your cocoa."

That solves that, I guess.

Willing her hands not to shake with nerves, Zia carefully walked with her mug over to the table. Before she could use her foot to nudge her chair out, Mr. Bounds grasped the back and pulled it away from the edge for her.

"Thank you," she murmured, sitting down.

He settled into the seat across from her. Those vampire eyes never left her face even when he slowly raised the bottle to his lips. It must have been a trick of the low light, but she swore his pupils expanded impossibly larger. "You're welcome."

Trying very, very hard not to stare at his mouth, she dropped her gaze to the table and sipped at her cocoa. Silence settled over them for several minutes before she finally worked up the courage to ask, "Mr. Bounds, you've been very kind, but I need to know... am I fired?"

"Fired?" He arched one dark brow. Besides his near constant frowning, it was the most expressive she'd seen him. "Why would I fire you?"

Zia held the teacup close to her chest. "I... Because I broke *the* rule? The one that's a non-negotiable, termination-on-the-spot kind of rule?"

He made that clicking sound again, but this time she thought she caught what he was doing. When he was agitated or annoyed, it appeared he flicked his tongue against the back of his fangs — which were two razor sharp, semi-hollow blades perfectly designed for piercing flesh.

She would know. She'd done plenty of research on vampires. Very, *very* thorough research.

Setting his bottle on the table, he told her, "You are not fired."

"But... why?" She swallowed thickly, the taste of rich chocolate and vanilla souring in her mouth. "Not that I'm not relieved, but I *am* confused. Mr. Eisele was *very* clear about what would happen if I got caught on the grounds after dark."

Mr. Bounds tilted his head slightly to one side. She got the strangest impression that he was struggling to figure out how to talk to her. "And yet you did it anyway, knowing you would almost certainly be caught?"

She thumbed the handle of the teacup. Her treacherous cheeks heated again. "Yeah."

"Why?"

"Because I *love* that garden, Mr. Bounds," she told him. She didn't care if she sounded crazy. He wouldn't be the first person to think so.

Pressing her hands onto her dirt-streaked thighs, she explained, "You've got some of the rarest pre-War varieties in the

UTA in your rose garden — ones that are almost extinct, or so obscure even the Society only has one or two examples in their archive. I've spent a year trying to bring everything back to its original state, and I've poured my magic into that soil. I couldn't let those roses die when I knew that it would be so easy to save them."

He was quiet for a moment, assessing her. She thought she spied some strange emotion in his fathomless eyes — surprise, or perhaps a shadow of longing — when he murmured, "And that is why you are not being fired."

She blinked several times in quick succession. "Really?"

"Yes. Why would I fire someone so passionate about what they do?" Behind him, the clock on the wall dinged a doleful note. Mr. Bounds's lips pressed together in a hard line. Eyes dropping to her cup, he said, "You should finish your cocoa. It's getting late and you still have to drive home."

She was almost too dizzy with relief to hear him. "R-right."

I don't have to leave the garden. Gods, it was a damn miracle.

A greenwitch bonded with land she worked on consistently, and Zia had poured more of her magic than was probably advisable into Mr. Bounds's rose garden. Being forced to leave it would have broken her heart in too many ways to contemplate.

She finished her cocoa in a daze. They spoke more, but she couldn't rightly recall the specifics of what was said. Something about calls he would make, and how he didn't want her driving late. He was no gifted conversationalist, Mr. Bounds, but she was too relieved to feel any awkwardness.

If he was even slightly less intimidating, she would have given him the biggest, most grateful hug. It wasn't about the money, or the hassle of moving back in with her family. It was about the garden and, if she were being honest, *him.*

When Mr. Bounds insisted that he would take care of the dishes and then would not be dissuaded from escorting her through the awful dark to the staff parking lot, she could only follow his lead with a big, dopey grin on her face.

I don't have to leave, she thought, catching sight of him standing tall and stiff by the gate as she slowly pulled out onto the road. *I don't have to give up my roses and... and Mr. Bounds knows who I am.*

Her heartbeat was still uneven by the time she made it to her lonely little house. The taste of rich chocolate lingered on her tongue, as deep and dark as the sound of his voice. *He called me beautiful.*

CHAPTER FIVE

Z<small>IA</small> HAD NEVER NEEDED AND ALSO RESENTED A weekend more.

On one hand, she was grateful for the space. She wasn't sure how she was going to handle walking by the manor every day, knowing what her boss's abs looked like, or how he must think she was nothing but a flighty, silly little gardener he let off the hook.

Or worse, that he called her *beautiful.*

It was good to take the weekend to gather her wits again.

On the *other* hand, it gave her two days to replay every single second she spent in his company until she couldn't tell up from down anymore.

She found herself staring at food burning on her cooker as she got lost in the memory of his voice and how he looked at her with those disconcerting eyes. Her showers stretched longer and longer as she rehashed every word and glancing touch they traded. There were so many things she could have said, so many opportunities she missed, and each new realization made her confidence shrivel.

If she were wittier, more sophisticated, would she have said the right thing to charm him? Did she even want to?

The image of those eyes appearing in the pitch black greenhouse would probably haunt her forever. Despite his kindness, deep in her gut, she still felt that anxious tension when she thought of him.

It was one thing to know vampires were predatory. It was quite another to stumble upon one in the dark. She'd woken up several times in the nights since, thinking he was there, hidden in the shadows. Her heartbeat was always a thunderous rhythm in her ears, her skin slick with cold sweat, and a deep, hollow ache pulsing between her thighs.

She wasn't sure she would ever be free of that instinctive fear she felt when he trained those night-glow eyes on her. She wasn't sure she would ever be free of the lust lurking under that fear, either.

Not that it mattered.

There was no way Mr. Bounds would cross her path again any time soon. He wasn't one of her fantasies. He was a man. An *important* man. He probably wouldn't spare another thought for his silly little gardener who drank cocoa with him in his kitchen. Another year might pass before she shared another moment with him.

She was torn over whether that was a blessing or not.

Though she felt hideously awkward and unrested, Zia didn't dawdle on Monday morning. Well before the sun began to rise over the sharp treetops, she left her little house and trudged to her car. Now that winter was on its way, she took no chances with the weather and kept herself thoroughly bundled in a down jacket, knit hat, and scarf.

Her boots crunched on the sparse, frosty grass that speckled her unpaved driveway. She climbed into her car with a foggy sigh. The winter was her least favorite season, and the first frost of the year always hit her hard.

Winter means less time in the garden and this godsforsaken cold, she thought, hitting the button on her dashboard for the automatic window defroster.

When she could see, Zia cranked up the heater and grasped

the steering wheel. She had to breathe several times before she worked up the courage to reverse out of her driveway and onto the narrow road.

He won't even be awake. And even if he is, he won't notice you. Stop thinking about how pretty your boss is and focus on winter-proofing the garden, Zia.

There was comfort in work. Although the winter would steal much of it from her until the spring, there would be plenty to do until late November, when the ground would become too frozen for even a greenwitch to work.

Forcing herself to focus on what she needed to get done before then, as well as what she would do with her time off in December and January, kept her reasonably distracted until she pulled through the gates.

The fact that her rental house was only about fifteen minutes from the estate was the entire reason she chose it. Nothing else about it appealed to her, really, most especially not the dark woods that seemed to creep closer around her home every night.

As a greenwitch, she loved the old trees, the loamy earth, the rich, wild foliage that filled the gaps between root and rock. As a person, she didn't necessarily enjoy the solitude the forest provided.

But it was close to work, which allowed her to start her day as early as possible. That meant she could usually get home before sunset and avoid the heart pounding anxiety that came with driving at night. It didn't matter that her mechanically inclined brother Arif had installed all the latest night driving safety features in her car. She *hated* being out at night by herself.

The sun was barely illuminating the sky when she parked her car — properly this time — in her usual spot. Girding herself for what would surely be a day of stewing in her own awkwardness, Zia adjusted her hat and forced herself out of the car.

It was one of the rare days when she would have preferred not to see Mr. Eisele and his trusty golf cart, so of course he was waiting for her by the gatehouse.

Her pulse jumped. *Oh gods, maybe Mr. Bounds changed his mind. Did he send Mr. Eisele out to fire me?*

Nevermind the fact that most days he parked his cart there to speak to the guards in the gatehouse, who would be switching from vampires to a mix of diurnal people for the day shift. Zia had only ever exchanged a few cursory greetings with the vampires, and generally steered clear of the ferocious-looking Caldwell if she could help it.

Unfortunately, that was exactly who the groundskeeper was speaking to. Standing in the shadow of the gatehouse's doorway, Caldwell had his powerful, tattooed arms crossed over his chest as he relayed something to the other man. Pale, covered in terrifying inked skulls and daggers and Grim imagery, he was just slightly less intimidating than Mr. Bounds.

Caldwell made Mr. Eisele look like a brittle turkey bone in comparison.

Seeing as she was also trying to avoid talking to Mr. Eisele, Zia tugged her hat down low over her eyes and made to scuttle around the back of her car. She didn't care about the long walk today. There was no hope of not looking guilty, so she didn't try. Avoiding *everyone* was of paramount importance.

At least until her mortification cooled a little, anyway.

Luck was not on her side, however. As soon as she rounded the left side of her car, Caldwell's smoky voice called out, "Miss North, a minute."

Shit.

Zia's stomach rolled with nerves. Could Caldwell fire her? No, not if Mr. Bounds didn't want her fired. But what if he really did change his mind? Even if he hadn't, perhaps Caldwell intended to upbraid her for breaking the rules anyway. Certainly the guards would all know she stayed after dark, and he was in charge of security, so it wasn't out of the question.

Ugh, she thought, forcing herself to turn around and walk toward the gatehouse. *I hate being scolded.*

Not because she didn't deserve to be, of course, but because she was a damn *crier*. It didn't matter how light the scolding was. The tears always came.

Forcing her spine to straighten, she avoided both men's eyes as she crossed the small parking lot. Her throat was painfully dry when she asked, "What can I do for you this morning?"

She could feel those unnerving eyes on her when he said, "I was just about to head to bed, but I wanted to be sure you knew about the changes."

Dread, thick and syrupy, gathered in the pit of her stomach. She dared to peek at Caldwell's hard face. There was no hint of feeling there. His features were cut from stone, handsome, and terribly intimidating. "Changes, sir?"

"Mr. Bounds is having lights installed around the estate this week, so there will be a small construction crew moving around. They'll take over the garden for a day or so, unfortunately."

...Lights?

Zia's eyes flickered between the two men's faces. Mr. Eisele looked bemused, his reedy arms crossed over his chest, and Caldwell looked... impassive. "Ah," she managed. "I see. What— what day will that be?"

Caldwell's expression didn't change even one iota, but she *swore* there was amusement in his voice when he answered, "Today. They're starting on the garden first."

Her breath left her in a steamy puff of surprise.

"I don't understand," Mr. Eisele complained. He shook his head, making the symbol of Burden he wore on a thin chain around his neck sway. "Why in the world would they start in the garden? If we're putting lights up, shouldn't we start here, or on the main driveway? Around the house, even?"

Caldwell shrugged and took one step back into the deeper shadows of the gatehouse. His gaze settled on her for a moment before flicking back to the groundskeeper. "Mr. Bounds's orders. I don't question them. If I were you, I'd give that a try, too."

Mr. Eisele closed his mouth with an audible clack.

"Is the work going to be extensive?" She glanced over her

shoulder, toward the path that led to the manor and its garden. She was strangely breathless. "If I can't work today, should I go home?"

"You should be able to work today," Caldwell assured her. Gesturing to someone over his shoulder with a quick flick of two clawed fingers, he continued, "However, since there will be strangers on the grounds while the work is being done, Mr. Bounds has assigned you a guard."

Zia shared a perplexed look with Mr. Eisele as one of the guards, a stern-faced demon she'd only met once or twice, squeezed out from around Caldwell. He settled himself to her right, a half step back, and didn't say a word as she gaped.

"I *hardly* think that's necessary, Caldwell," she protested.

"Mr. Bounds's orders, Miss North. Strangers on the property mean extra security." Tipping his head at them all, he began to close the door. "I'm going to sleep. If there's an emergency, try not to need me."

As the door clicked shut, Zia rounded on the groundskeeper. "Mr. Eisele, what in the *world*—"

He threw up his weathered hands. "You think *I* know what's going on? I'm as clueless as you, Zia."

"I do *not* need a guard!" She shot a quick, abashed look at the demon. "Sorry, it's not personal."

"Mr. Bounds's orders, ma'am," he rumbled, those unsettling amber-on-black eyes entirely unsympathetic. He was huge, with great black horns that curled around the sides of his head, and his clear disinterest in her plight made him her current least favorite person.

Mr. Bounds's orders, my ass!

The subject of lights made her heart flutter, foolish as that almost certainly was, but having a guard assigned to watch her every day until they left was downright silly. *Unless...*

Zia pointed at Mr. Eisele. "Do *you* have a guard?"

"Apparently not," he answered dryly.

She paled. Had he assigned someone to watch her because he

didn't trust her now? Surely no one actually thought something might happen to her because a construction crew came in to do some work. There had to be another reason for this, and she couldn't think of anything more logical than what she'd done on Friday.

Shit.

"I... Fine. Let's just— Maybe you can talk Mr. Bounds out of this?"

Mr. Eisele shook his head and turned around to climb into his golf cart. "Not likely. The boss isn't the *changing his mind* type. Not usually, anyway." He waved her over. "C'mon. I have enough shit to worry about today without being late. Get in, both of you."

Feeling increasingly uneasy, she gestured for the demon — whose name she *really* needed to remember — to get in the front passenger seat and then climbed onto the bench in the back.

Hunching her shoulders, she endured Mr. Eisele's grumbling as he drove them down the path to the garden. By the time he slowed to a stop by the edge of the patio, the sun was beginning to crest the tops of the trees.

Zia barely had both feet on the ground before he was speeding off again. That left her standing alone with the demon.

Oh, what a mess, she thought, turning to look at the manor. Motioning for her guard to follow her, she walked toward the little landscaped porch that hid the kitchen door. Her stomach was twisted into anxious knots. She couldn't believe she was willingly approaching the manor, but if he happened to still be awake, maybe she could—

"Miss North."

Zia jumped at the sound of Mr. Bounds's baritone. Biting back a squeak of alarm, she swung her gaze around, toward a tiny wrought iron table nestled in the shade of a massive climbing honeysuckle bush.

Mr. Bounds sat in a small chair, swaddled in blue shadow. He wore a shirt this time, though she wasn't sure that was a good thing. He looked just as devastating in a crisp white button down, his long hair loose around his shoulders, as he did half naked and sweaty from a workout.

Curling her fingers into fists, she said, "Mr. Bounds! Ah, good morning. I didn't expect— I mean, I was hoping to see you."

One dark eyebrow arched. His eyes made a slow perusal of her face. "Were you?"

Zia flushed. "No. I mean, *yes*. I wanted to..." She waved at her guard. "Can I ask why I have a guard? If it's because of Friday, I really am sorry. I won't do anything like that again. I promise I don't need someone to keep an eye on me."

A look of surprise flitted across his face before he stood up from his seat. Tucking one hand in the pocket of his slacks, he murmured, "You are not in trouble, Miss North."

"Then why..."

In an instant, his baritone hardened, sending every survival instinct in her body into overdrive. "Because I've lived too long to blindly trust strangers with precious things."

Though he stuck to the shadows, Mr. Bounds came close enough to touch. Only the low, decorative iron fence that marked the edge of the tiny garden and the patio remained between them when he added, "You will have a guard as long as there are people I don't know on the property. It is not a punishment, but it is non-negotiable." His eyes flicked to the demon standing a few paces behind her. "Michael will watch over you until the lights are installed and the crew leaves the estate."

She floundered. "But... why am I the only one who needs a guard?"

Mr. Bounds blinked slowly, once, before he answered, "Because I won't be able to sleep otherwise."

CHAPTER SIX

HARLAN STARED AT HIS CEILING. WITH THE SPECIALLY designed shades pulled over his windows, it was pitch black in his bedroom. The sun had been up for two hours. It was well past time he should have gone to sleep.

And yet, like the two days before this one, he struggled to find the inner stillness necessary for rest.

Zia is out there.

It was singularly exquisite torture, knowing she was within reach and yet unable to touch her.

It wasn't easy to ignore her presence before their encounter, but now it was impossible.

She was in his lungs, his pores, on his tongue, and burrowed so deeply in his mind that he lost all hope of ever getting her out. His thoughts spiraled around and around. The craving for her was merciless, but so too was his doubt.

How could he possibly hope to win her?

It was no easy sell, asking someone to become an anchor. It required enormous sacrifice on his partner's side — and an equal amount of blind trust.

That was part of the reason vampires were so ferally protective of them. An anchor gave up so much to sustain their vampire.

Pleasing them, protecting them, was the least a vampire could do in return.

Of course, the other reason was a much more fundamental, selfish one: no creature willingly relinquished their source of sustenance, of pleasure, of connection.

Harlan strained to listen to the muffled sounds of workers setting up lights in the garden. Why didn't he install surveillance equipment in the greenhouse? He cursed himself for his restraint. It would be such a relief to hear her even as the raw, hungry part of him gnashed its teeth at the thought of her speaking to someone else.

It wasn't fair, and he would never act on the impulse, but it was *there*.

For thousands of years, vampires kidnapped their chosen anchors, hiding them away in caves, in fortresses, in castles. There, they could lavish them with gifts, with fine foods, with pleasure, seducing them slowly. With every bite, every injection of venom, the vampire would grow more possessive and the anchor more attached.

The anchor's body would change, priming it to support its vampire. Their sleep cycle would shift. If they could bear children, their internal chemistry would alter such that they could carry a vampiric child to term. Once the venom had settled into their blood, no other vampire could claim them without being poisoned.

It was a slow, sensual process of possession, perfected over many thousands of years.

In the modern day, he could not get away with kidnapping his chosen anchor and sequestering her in his manor.

Well, I could, he thought, imagining her in his bed, a pretty shackle around her ankle. *But I'd rather she beg me for it.*

He was not trying to be a better person than he used to be. That was a dream he abandoned in his twenties.

But he didn't want the trouble kidnapping her might bring. He didn't want her to hate him. He wanted her to bare her throat to him freely. He wanted her to welcome him into the wet heat of her cunt with his name on her lips. He wanted her to smile at him when she saw him, not freeze like a startled deer.

I could still get her the shackle, though.

She would look so very pretty in his bed, at his mercy. While he took his fill of her, he would give pleasure back. Always.

His breath shortened as he imagined it. Zia was all soft, suntanned skin and tight, mink brown curls. She was strong but shapely, with a gently curved stomach, lush hips, and generous breasts. When he pressed his fingertips into her skin, she would be plush and sumptuously made.

And she'll taste so fucking sweet.

Harlan kicked off his sheets and palmed his aching cock. The thought of licking her until she came and then sinking his fangs into the delicate skin of her thigh made his spine lock.

His fantasies had been intense before, but ever since he touched her, tasted her scent on the back of his tongue, they had been almost excruciatingly vivid.

Harlan had fucked his fair share of women in his lifetime, all of them faceless and eager, ready to ease the ache in the moment he needed it. He'd even sipped from the flesh of more than a few of them, but he never returned, never felt the compulsion to bite again and again, until his venom took hold.

With Zia, the need was an almost physical pain.

In an attempt to relieve the pressure, he stroked himself hard and imagined it was her deft hand on his cock, her big brown eyes fixed on his face, hungry for his approval. He pictured her dipping her head to sip from *him.* Those lovely, plush lips would look so much prettier when they were wrapped around his cock.

"*Fuck!*"

His pulse pounded in the roof of his mouth. Gods, he needed relief. He needed to sink his cock into his gorgeous little witch until she came, and then he needed to plunge his fangs into her throat and fill her with his venom until he blacked out.

Imagining the sweet release of it, Harlan stroked harder,

faster, until the pressure became too much. Electricity danced up his spine as his muscles tensed. His orgasm was short, brutal, and yet unsatisfying.

Even as he lay there in the dazed aftermath, his stomach splattered with his release, his fangs fucking *ached* for her.

Harlan dug his claws into the mattress and arched his neck, his fangs bared in a hideous, desperate snarl. He couldn't survive this any longer. He *wouldn't.*

He could give her more than pleasure. He could give her wealth, safety, and the unwavering devotion of a bonded vampire.

The problem was that he couldn't quite figure out how to make that happen.

Mind churning and sexual hunger only momentarily sated, he got up from bed and cleaned himself up. When he climbed back in, Harlan turned on his side and folded his pillow under his head, his gaze locked on the shuttered window overlooking the rose garden.

How could he entice a soft creature like his witch into his arms?

She came from a good, loving family. Her parents had been married for over a century and lived in a Turkish enclave in San Jose. She had five brothers, all of whom were successful in their own ways. Once a month, she drove back down to San Jose to spend the weekend with her family.

She got perfect grades in school and studied botany at San Jose University. Up until she got the job as his rosarian, she lived at home. Her social feeds were full of flowers and family vacations.

There was not one smudge on her record, no hint of anything illicit in her online activity. The witch didn't even have a ticket or citation to her name.

She was infuriatingly unblemished by the world, while he was... not.

Doesn't matter, he decided. *I don't have to be a good man to treat her well. If she were my anchor, she'd want for nothing.*

If anything, he was the *perfect* partner for her. He was retired, but still feared by much of the criminal underworld of the UTA. No one could touch what was his. That shining, untrammeled warmth she radiated would not be smothered. He would cup her light in his hands, insulating it from the cruelties of the world he knew too well.

In an instant, the mental dam that he had erected to keep his instincts in check disappeared. They flooded his system in one huge rush — adrenaline and desire, possessiveness and a deep, terrifying tenderness.

Harlan's gaze sharpened on the window. The roots of his fangs, connected to the gland that produced his unique venom, ached with renewed ferocity.

I've been a fool.

So what if he knew he wasn't good enough for her? The year of pining after her was more than enough to consider his payment to the universe made. He would take what he wanted, and in exchange he would give his witch the world.

That night, he inspected the work in the garden. His shoulders were tense, his eyes narrowed on every bootprint in the dirt, every little trace of the strangers. He fucking *hated* that there were unknown people coming and going through his anchor's space.

"They worked fast," Atticus informed him, nodding to the thin, beautifully designed lamp posts that had been installed at regular intervals around the garden.

Harlan crossed the distance to the greenhouse. Putting a possessive hand on one of the glass panels, he growled, "Not fast enough."

His protégé didn't need to ask what had him so riled up. "Michael was with her all day. None of the workers even spoke to her."

"Good." His fingers skated down the cool, uneven glass. "I would prefer if they didn't look at her, either."

Atticus crossed his arms and arched a brow. "How bad is this going to get, boss?"

Harlan sent the bodyguard he'd practically raised a narrow-eyed look. "What are you talking about?"

"Miss North. Are you going to actually do something about her, or are you going to keep torturing yourself?"

He flicked a fang with his tongue, annoyed by his protégé's attitude. "Since when are you allowed to question me, boy?"

"Since the day you taught me how to use a bolt gun," Atticus grunted. "Answer my question, boss. You can't keep going on like this. If you do, you'll either do something you'll regret or be forced to send her away."

Harlan lifted his lip, snarling without much heat, before he ran his fingers through his loose hair. "I'm keeping her."

Atticus arched one red brow. "Are you, now? How are you planning on making that happen?"

"You don't think I know how to seduce a woman? I'm a hundred years your senior." He stalked away from the greenhouse and shouldered past his most loyal companion.

Of course, Atticus fell into step behind him. "Exactly. How long has it been since you pursued anyone? What's your plan of attack here?"

He had absolutely no intention of admitting how long it had been since he sought out companionship, fleeting though it always was. Taking an anchor had never been something he considered before. There was too much risk to their lives, and he'd never wanted someone enough to make it worth the trouble.

But it's been two years since someone came after me. The Families are moving on. I don't have to worry so much about her safety.

Even if he did, Harlan wasn't sure he would be able to keep himself away from her.

Ignoring the question, he announced, "I'm going to give her a gift so she knows my intentions."

And because my instincts are driving me fucking crazy.

If he didn't provide her with something soon, he was fairly certain he would combust.

Atticus's tone, lightly teasing before, lowered into something more cautious, "What kind of gift?"

"I don't know. A diamond bracelet or a car or something." Harlan ground his molars as he inspected the tiny lights the workers had installed in each step of the bisected staircase. *If they chipped even one brick, I'm going to start ripping throats out.*

"Ah, maybe something smaller would get your point across."

He lifted his head to glare at his companion. "Why would I do that? My anchor should have the very best things this world offers. If she wants diamonds, she *gets* diamonds."

"Right, sure, of course." Atticus rubbed the back of his neck, his expression pinched with discomfort. The tattoos on his hand, a gaping vampiric skull, looked particularly ghoulish in the warm light of the lamps. "But does she *want* those things from you right now?"

He waved the question away. "She doesn't know what she wants because I haven't declared my intentions yet."

"You assigned her a personal guard today, boss. I'm pretty sure she's going to get the picture soon, if she hasn't already. A gift like that might scare her off." Tucking his hands into the pockets of his black cargo pants, he offered, "Why not forgo the gifts for now and instead ask her to do something with you? You know, date and shit."

Harlan had begun climbing the stairs, but stopped to level a speculative look at the rugged vampire that had grown out of the underfed, beaten down boy he took under his wing. "Why would diamonds scare her off?"

"Because Miss North doesn't seem like the *accepts-diamonds-from-virtual-strangers* type, boss. She's too earthy for that sort of thing."

He did not enjoy learning that Atticus had been paying such close attention to his witch. Luckily for his protégé, he also knew that was instinct talking, not good sense. Of course he paid attention to her.

Atticus Caldwell was, for all intents and purposes, his son. He was violently devoted to Harlan — and therefore equally devoted to whomever he chose as an anchor. In Atticus's position, he would have done the same thing: gathered information on the target prior to making a move, so his team could go in informed and ready to dismantle any obstacles.

With an uncomfortable little jolt, Harlan realized that Atticus might actually have more insight into Zia than *he* did.

Jogging back down the stairs to join the other vampire by the edge of the koi pond, he demanded, "How often do you speak to her?"

Aware that he was treading on dangerous territory, Atticus kept eye contact and loosened his posture when he answered, "Maybe once a week. Usually only in passing. I rarely talk to her, but I see her almost every day when we change shifts."

Grim give me patience.

He loved the boy. He would not throttle him out of jealousy. It wasn't Atticus's fault Harlan had stupidly decided to torture himself over the past year. If he claimed her like he should have, it wouldn't have bothered him that the other man exchanged regular *hellos* with his anchor.

At least not after a while, anyway.

Forcing the acidic jealousy back down, Harlan tried to get his thoughts back in order. Once, he was the most feared assassin in the New Zone, if not the entire UTA. He could plan. He could use any resource available to him. He could hunt. He could take down any target.

He had to think like the assassin, not the possessive vampire, and take advantage of whatever it was Atticus knew.

"Tell me what you think she would like," he bit out, fingers clenching and unclenching by his thighs. "If not gifts, then what? How do I make it clear I want her?"

"Without making her uncomfortable, boss. That's the key."

Atticus shrugged. "She's real sweet, that one. Never has a bad word to say about anyone, does her work with a smile, and gets flustered when anyone pays too much attention to her. I thought she was going to start crying this morning when I told her she needed a guard. A woman like that will get spooked if you come on too strong."

Harlan's chest constricted so hard, it nearly knocked the wind out of him. "She *cried?*"

Panic blasted through him.

Zia wasn't allowed to cry. He was just trying to keep her safe. Why would she think that was a bad thing? Did it scare her? Why didn't Atticus fucking *say* something—

"She didn't *really* cry," Atticus rushed to assure him. "She just got this big, wet look in her eyes. Adriana is like that, too, remember? When she was a kid, any time she thought someone was mad at her, or upset *around* her, she would start crying. Didn't matter if she actually felt bad or not."

Harlan paled. He vividly recalled Adriana, Atticus's little sister, crying every time he looked at her wrong. It didn't matter that he treated her like a princess, nor that she frequently sought him out when she needed to feel secure in her brother's absence. He'd taken countless lives over the years and yet he never felt more like a monster than when the tiny vampire stared up at him with tears in her eyes.

Voice hoarse, he asked, "How can I court a woman like that? I'll terrify her."

Atticus shook his head. "Nah, not if you go slow. People like that aren't made of glass, they're just sensitive and easily spooked. You have to know how to get them to trust you."

"How do I *do* that?"

The other vampire nodded in the direction of the rose garden, lit up by soft lamp light. "Have you asked her for a tour?"

He blinked. "A tour of my own garden?"

Atticus's lips curled. "Not to overstep, but I'm gonna go ahead and say that it's much more *her* garden than yours."

Fair enough. "So I just... ask her to walk with me in the rose garden? Then what?"

"Then you keep making excuses to see her." Atticus propped his hands on his hips. Nodding decisively, he added, "And *then* you buy her the diamond bracelet."

CHAPTER SEVEN

"*ANNE*, IT'S TOO EARLY FOR YOU TO BE UP."

"The day I decided to have children, I made peace with waking up before sunrise, *gülüm.*" Her mother's smooth voice, lovely even at the early hour, filled Zia with warmth. At least, it did until she demanded in rapid-fire Turkish, "Where have you *been?* You haven't called in a week. Your father and I were worried something happened to you."

Shifting in the driver's seat of her little car, Zia tried not to sound guilty when she replied, "Nothing happened to me. I've just been busy with work, that's all."

Yes, busy breaking rules, almost getting fired, and then...

Well, she really couldn't explain the rest. Being assigned a guard for days was bizarre enough, but coming into work yesterday to find a note from Mr. Bounds on her workbench, requesting an early morning tour of the rose garden, was utterly beyond her ability to explain.

She glanced at the time. He asked her to meet him at five-thirty, giving them almost two hours before it became too bright for Mr. Bounds to tolerate.

Ten minutes.

"It's almost winter. Shouldn't you be wrapping things up

there?" Before she could answer, her mother pressed, "When are you coming home? I want to make sure everything is ready for you. Your brother has started putting his junk in your room, you know. He'll have to find a place to put everything if you're going to stay until the spring. I need to know when I should start forcing him to move everything."

Zia rolled her eyes. She didn't bother asking which brother was putting his shit in her room. Three of her five brothers lived at home. It could have been any one of them — if not all of them. Her mother did have a habit of referring to them collectively to save time, after all.

"I'm not sure when I'll be home, *Anne,*" she said, steering the car around a sharp bend in the mountain road. "I'm on my way to the estate now. There's a lot I have to do to prepare for the winter, and then I want to start working on my paper."

"Why can't you do that at home with your family? We miss you, *gülüm!* And it's going to freeze up there in those awful mountains. You need to come home soon. I don't want you driving in the snow." Again, as she barely took a breath before she continued, "Why are you going to work so early? It's barely even five! You are working too hard again, Zia. I can feel it."

She tried to ignore the way her stomach dropped when she thought of being away from the estate for three months. The rose garden wouldn't be accessible to her until the ground thawed, so there really was no reason to stay in her lonely little house for the winter, but...

Her gaze flickered to the time on the sleek dashboard. *Six minutes.*

She took a quick breath before she answered, "I can't concentrate with all the noise. Besides, when I visit, I want to be able to spend time with you, not hide away on my tablet doing work."

"You concentrated just fine for the first hundred years of your life. Why is it such a problem now?"

Because even though I hate how lonely my house is, it is nice to have my own space. There was no way she could say that to her mother, though. She'd throw a fit, thinking her daughter didn't like being with her family.

Instead of addressing the question, Zia said, "I'll come home for the Moon and help you cook. By then I'll be done with work. Won't that be nice?"

"*Only* the Moon?" her mother balked. "That's a month!"

"I know, *Anne,* but I have a lot of writing to do." Zia spied the turn off to the estate. Her pulse fluttered in her throat. "I have to go soon. I'm almost at work."

Exasperated, her mother pressed, "Why are you so *early, gülüm?* It's still so dark." Her concern bled through the speakers, making Zia's chest ache with homesickness. It was a small thing, but she was grateful that her mother had never once made her feel silly for her fear of the dark. "Aren't you worried about being out there on your own?"

Maybe a few days ago, sure. Zia liked to get a head start on things, but was early even for her. Normally she left the house at a much more reasonable hour, which got her to the estate just before sunrise. But things were different.

He wants me to give him a tour of the rose garden, she thought, breath quickening.

In sharp, jagged scrawl, Mr. Bounds requested her company. She had no idea what it meant — probably nothing — but seeing as she had resigned herself to going back to only catching glimpses of him through windows, she was almost beside herself with giddiness at the prospect of spending more time with Mr. Bounds.

And nerves. Definitely nerves.

"Mr. Bounds installed lights," she explained, only barely holding back the *for me* that almost slipped out at the end.

"Oh, it's about time. Did he just figure out not all of his employees are vampires?" her mother said, sniffy on her daughter's behalf.

Feeling defensive, Zia replied, "It was a very nice gesture."

Her mother scoffed. "To provide light for his employees to

work under? Certainly. I wonder what prompted him to be so very generous."

Not wanting to get into exactly why Mr. Bounds decided it was time to put lights on his property, nor the very strange few days that had passed since then, she tactfully chose not to reply.

Zia pulled onto the road and slowed her speed, approaching the closed gates of the estate with a nervous swallow. "I'm sorry, *Anne,* but I have to go. Mr. Bounds asked me to give him a tour of the garden this morning and I'm nearly at the gate."

"What? Zia, will there be other people with you?"

I hope not.

She bit the inside of her cheek to suppress a nervous smile. Voice pitched high, she said, "I have to go. Love you!"

Before her mother could demand to know anything else, Zia reached over to swipe her finger over the call button on the dashboard.

Jittery with nerves, she pulled to a slow stop in front of the intimidating gates. The workers had just finished putting in lights around the employee parking lot on the other side. They were slightly dimmer than a normal street light, but they still threw shapes through the bars of the iron gate.

Zia held her breath as she waited. Would she have to get out of the car and go up to the intercom built into the massive stone fence? Surely Mr. Bounds would have informed the guards that she was coming early, right?

Only a handful of seconds passed before there was a quiet beep from the tiny device on her dashboard one of the guards installed when she first got the job. A small green light flashed on the box built into the fence, and then there was a brief, blinding flash of magic as the intricate wards that sealed the property at night were momentarily lifted.

Whoa, that's some serious firepower.

She was not quite a gloriana, but Zia was not powerless. She never liked doing too much spellwork, but she had a knack for sigils and enough power to open up a lot of lucrative paths after high school. Greenwitches weren't in incredibly high demand, common as they tended to be, but sigilworkers were. There were endless uses for them — in particular those who could channel some really heavy duty magic.

Her father was a sigilworker, and two of her brothers had gone on to work for the Elvish Protectorate's government, doing gods knew what in secret labs and research facilities. Her father had always been vague about the specifics of his job, and now her brothers were, too.

Zia wanted no part of that life. She took no joy in staring at sigils every day, trying to get them to do as she wished, and she would have withered under the watchful eye of the government, telling her what to do and when to do it and who to talk to about it.

That didn't mean she couldn't appreciate a good, nearly impenetrable ward, nor the power that went into creating something of the sort that surrounded the estate.

Whoever crafted the ward built into the fence must have been almost mind-bogglingly skilled. Not only was it layered with enough power to blow her hair back, but it was nearly undetectable until it was altered for her sake — allowing her to drive through the gates.

It was marvelous work, but as soon as she stepped out of her car, Zia had to let all thoughts of wards and sigils go.

Caldwell was waiting for her.

A black golf cart was parked beside her usual spot, and the massive vampire was casually sprawled behind the wheel, one leg out and his tattooed arms crossed over his chest.

When she closed the door of her car, he tilted his head in her direction. "Morning, Miss North."

"Good morning, Caldwell."

Goodness, it was hard to shake the feeling that she was in trouble when he looked at her. Caldwell had such a stern, intense expression, he looked like he was about to either ignore her completely or give her the scolding of her life.

Even more nervous, she adjusted the fit of her knit hat over her curls and said, "Mr. Bounds asked me to come early."

"I know."

Of course he knew. He was head of security for the entire estate. *Ugh.*

"Right, okay, well... I should probably get going." Feeling awkward, Zia shoved her hands in the pockets of her puffy coat and turned towards the dark path through the trees, her pulse thumping. The workers hadn't gotten to the path yet, as they had mainly stuck to the areas most frequented by staff, but she wasn't about to ask Caldwell for a ride.

There was a low humming noise, then the peculiar crunching sound of rubber tires over gritty asphalt. Zia glanced up in time to see Caldwell pull up just ahead of her.

One hand resting on the wheel, he jerked his chin toward the passenger's seat. "Hop on, Miss North."

She glanced at the path again and swallowed. "Oh, you really don't have to—"

"Boss's orders." Caldwell's expression was utterly impassive when he added, "He doesn't want you walking by yourself in the dark."

Mr. Bounds asked him to pick me up?

Zia felt her cheeks heat. It meant nothing, of course. He was just being courteous, but that deep coil of heat refused to cool down. The knowledge that Mr. Bounds *thought* of her at all was strangely heady.

Fighting the urge to hide herself in her thick scarf, she muttered, "Okay, I guess."

She gingerly climbed into the golf cart. Caldwell made sure she was completely in before he set off. It was notable only because Mr. Eisele rarely did the same. She'd lost track of the number of times she nearly fell out of his cart when he put his lead foot on the gas.

Caldwell was incredibly intimidating, and she sometimes got

the feeling that he was laughing at her behind that hard face, but he wasn't any worse than the surly groundskeeper.

Peeking at her escort from under her lashes, she somehow found the courage to ask, "How long have you worked for Mr. Bounds?"

"Pretty much my whole life." Caldwell had a deep, husky voice — almost *too* husky, like he smoked way too much. She never picked up any traces of smoke in his scent the rare times she was close enough to do so, though, so perhaps it was natural.

"Your whole life?" Her brow furrowed. "What did you do as a kid? Shine his shoes?"

The corner of Caldwell's lips kicked up as they passed out of the range of the lights and into the long, dark tunnel of the forested path. "Nah. Mainly errands and things. He picked me up off the street when I was thirteen, so I wasn't good for much."

Mr. Bounds helped him out when he was just a kid? She tried to imagine the terrifying vampire bringing a boy under his wing and struggled. While he was kind to her the night she broke the rules, Mr. Bounds carried an air of such tightly restrained menace, she wondered how a child didn't wilt under his gaze.

Zia curled her fingers into her thighs. It took an incredible amount of willpower to restrain her mouth, which wanted to ask a million inappropriate questions about what Caldwell knew of Mr. Bounds, what their relationship was like.

Why have I never thought to ask Caldwell questions about Mr. Bounds before?

A furtive glance at the hard planes of his face in the blue-black, pre-dawn darkness reminded her. Perhaps the reason he didn't melt under Mr. Bounds's gaze was because Caldwell also carried that air of... something around him. A dangerous, sinister sort of something.

She didn't think it was just because they were vampires, either. It was in the way they carried themselves, how they moved, in how their eyes moved around them, missing nothing even when they were focused on her. It was almost like they were always waiting for someone to go for their throats.

It was like they *wanted* someone to try.

Painfully aware of the fact that she was sitting mere inches from a predator, Zia made a small, noncommittal sound in the back of her throat and watched as the path began to open up. Though her curiosity was strong, her sense of self-preservation was stronger.

If that's really the case, she thought wryly, *then why have I spent a year fantasizing about my terrifying boss?*

Moreover, why was she so excited to spend time alone with him?

The light of newly installed lamps glowed like a beacon beyond the trees. As they got closer to the patio, Caldwell told her, "Michael will find you after sun-up."

Her heart was beating so loudly, she almost didn't hear him. Frowning, she replied, "But the workers aren't going anywhere near the garden. I don't think I need a guard anymore." *Or at all.*

Those first two days were so unbearably awkward, she still cringed when she thought about them. Not only was she used to working completely alone, but she couldn't even talk to the people around her if she *wanted* to. Michael glowered with so much menace that not a single worker dared make conversation with her.

"Non-negotiable, Miss North." Caldwell pulled the golf cart to a stop by the bisected stairs. Resting his right wrist on the wheel, he turned his body slightly to pin her with an indecipherable look. "I know it's a change, but it's the way things are. Mr. Bounds wants you safe — and it's my job to make sure he gets what he wants."

Lifting his hand, he made a quick, impatient grabbing gesture with impressive claws. "Give me your phone."

"Why?" she asked, already handing it over.

Caldwell waited for her to unlock the screen before he began swiping his thumb across the razor thin device. It lit up the hard angles of his face from below, making him look even more sinister. "I'm programming my number, Michael's number, *and* Mr. Bounds's number in here. All you need to do is call one of us and we'll come running."

Mystified, she could only stare as he programmed one number after another into her contacts. "But... *why?*"

"If you're in trouble," he clarified, handing it back to her. A small, sardonic smile tilted one corner of his lips up. "Call Mr. Bounds first."

When he handed the phone back, she stuffed it into her pocket. Zia shook her head. Sliding out of the cart, she said, "I never get in trouble."

And even if she did, she couldn't imagine calling her intimidating, painfully attractive boss for help. Her first call would be to Patrol. The elves weren't exactly the warmest people, but they always did their jobs — particularly when it came to protecting their citizens.

Caldwell's expression darkened. As if he could read her mind, he leaned forward and firmly instructed her, "You only call us, understood? Don't want to call the boss, then you call me. If you're in trouble, we'll be the ones to fix it. Your safety is right up there with the boss's, Miss North. Number-fucking-one priority."

Utterly bemused, Zia could only nod. "I... okay?"

Apparently satisfied with that, Caldwell relaxed back into the driver's seat and flicked his claws in the direction of the stairs. "Go on."

Right, she thought, shaking herself, *Mr. Bounds is waiting for me.*

Adjusting her hat again, she turned on her heel and walked away from the golf cart. Caldwell's eyes lingered on her, raising the hair on the back of her neck, but she tried to push aside her lingering unease. There had to be a good reason for the sudden interest in her safety, but she couldn't for the life of her guess what it was.

Zia had never thought too hard about why security on the

estate was so tight. She just assumed that it was because Mr. Bounds was — presumably, at least — incredibly wealthy. Perhaps there was something going on she couldn't see, and that was why she was suddenly getting so much attention.

Maybe they're just upping security on all the staff?

That explanation didn't hold an ounce of water and she knew it. No one else got a guard, and she doubted anyone other than Mr. Eisele had Mr. Bounds's phone number in their contacts. But if it wasn't about the estate on the whole, then what *could* it be about?

Mr. Bounds made it clear that she wasn't in trouble for her stunt in the greenhouse. Other than that, there was only...

Zia almost missed a step.

No, he doesn't even know you. Why would someone like Mr. Bounds have an interest in you, anyway?

She was unsophisticated, silly, and obsessed with gardening. More often than not she had dirt under her fingernails and had never even been to an opera or a fancy museum gala. Goodness, she never even *traveled.*

Still, her heart lurched with giddy hope as she navigated the brick staircase. A soft, shy part of her whispered, *But he installed lights for you, Zia.*

When she learned they were installing lights, she assumed they would be the harsh white kind — the ones that offered maximum glow but unfortunately made everything in their reach look washed out and cold.

She should have known that Mr. Bounds would only allow modifications to his estate that *enhanced* the beauty of it.

Instead of floodlights, each lamp was crafted of beautifully designed wrought iron. The lights themselves were encased in milky glass designed to look like the buds of some lovely flower. They glowed with soft warmth, illuminating only enough for her to see by without washing away the intimidating majesty of the night.

Tiny lights illuminated each step she took, and down below,

the golden lamplight glittered on the wide koi pond, guiding her toward the man that made her heart skip a beat — or several.

Reaching the bottom of the stairs, Zia bit her lip and turned left. She barely made it to the entrance to the rose garden before she stumbled to a stop, her breath caught in her throat.

Mr. Bounds stood in the shadows between two lamps. He was a figure cut out of velvet darkness — broad shouldered, arms tucked behind his back, and powerful legs spread in a ready stance. His eyes, reflecting with that predator's night-glow, were fixed on her.

Her heartbeat stuttered and she swore she saw his eyes narrow.

Gods, she thought, stomach bottoming out with that dizzying, fearful thrill. *It's like locking eyes with a jaguar about to pounce.*

Chapter Eight

"Good morning, Miss North." His voice was a silky caress from the darkness.

Zia could feel her pulse racing in the hollow of her throat as she forced herself up the single brick step and into the garden. Her voice was embarrassingly husky when she replied, "Good morning, Mr. Bounds."

He took one long stride into the light. It was suddenly even harder to catch her breath.

Mr. Bounds was just... so *much*. Dressed in a thin gray sweater, black jeans, and a long black overcoat, he looked like a runway model straight from the underworld. Beautiful, but terrifying.

His hair was pulled back in another high ponytail. It tightened his features, giving his already cutting beauty an even sharper edge. The light from the lamps gilded his bronze skin and highlighted his heavy-lidded gaze. His lashes struck long, thin shadows across the high planes of his cheekbones. Like little knife slashes, they slid over his skin with every slow blink.

While his facial expression was impassive, his eyes... If she didn't know any better, Zia would have said he looked like he wanted to eat her up in tiny bites.

Her mouth was painfully dry when she said, "So... so you wanted a tour?"

"Amongst other things." He walked toward her, fine leather shoes making hardly any noise in the gravel, and extended a crooked elbow. "Walk me through your rose garden and tell me about your work."

Breathing hadn't become any easier. Being so close to him was overwhelming, heady. It felt like he was sucking the air out of her lungs when he looked down at her expectantly. Worse, she was pretty sure she liked the idea of him taking her breath, her blood, and maybe even her *heart* from her.

Again, she imagined the jaguar. Putting her trembling hand in the crook of his elbow felt more like reaching out to pet a hungry big cat. Would he snap his jaws around her delicate fingers or would he tilt his head into her hand, begging for more?

The thought of Mr. Bounds begging for anything made Zia go instantly molten. Gods, it was an erotic image. Having a man as powerful as him at her beck and call, eager to please?

A sharp ache took up residence between her thighs as her fingers flexed on his forearm.

Zia was so disoriented by the sudden flash of overwhelming desire that she found her mind going momentarily blank.

A silky murmur slid against the shell of her ear. Warm breath puffed against the sensitive skin of her throat, chasing away the chill. "Are you well, Miss North? Your heart is beating faster than normal."

Embarrassment took a hard swipe at arousal. *Shit. Why is it that every other race has super senses and us witches are left to fumble around?*

Not only could he see her clearly in the dark, but he could also hear every stuttering heartbeat, every hitched breath. Stricken, Zia stared at her shoes. *Does he know?*

"I'm fine," she lied. "Just nervous."

Mr. Bounds straightened. The movement drew her eyes back up to him involuntarily. His brow furrowed as he looked down his nose at her, but there was no judgment, no laughter there. "Do I make you nervous?"

Zia tried not to fidget. "Ah, well... a little."

She felt the muscle under her fingers tense. "Don't be nervous." Another command.

Daring to glance at him, she noted, "You give a lot of orders, Mr. Bounds. Not so sure that one is going to be easy to follow."

"Why?"

She raised her eyebrows. Swallowing, she answered, "You're awfully intimidating."

He was quiet for a moment before he said, "I don't want to intimidate you. I want you to be comfortable with me."

It was on the tip of her tongue to ask *why*, but Zia held the word in with a swift bite of her tongue. Whatever the answer was, she wanted to bask in this moment for as long as possible. She didn't want to know that he only wanted her to be comfortable because he wanted to be a better boss or something. She wanted it to be because he *liked* her.

Impossible, she thought wistfully, *but a girl can dream.*

Clearing her throat, she gestured to the flower beds with her free hand. "Should we start?"

Mr. Bounds inclined his head.

Zia gently tugged his arm in the direction of the bed on the right, which was the oldest of them. "Okay, so what do you know about your roses?"

"Nothing other than they came with the property," he answered, stepping with her. She could feel the heat of him permeating through her coat as he angled his body closer to hers. Only a scant few inches separated them when he leaned over to inspect the last bloom on the first huge rose bush.

When he stood so close, she was forced to come to terms with the fact that her height put her squarely at Mr. Bounds's collar, and that said collar was exposed by the v-cut of his sweater's neckline, showing off the hard lines of his clavicle and throat.

Desire was a slow drip in her veins.

It would take so little to simply lean forward and press her lips to that delicious, lickable hollow—

Focus, Zia!

Breathless, she asked, "So, my guess is you don't know how seriously some people take rose cultivation?"

Mr. Bounds slanted a look at her, but he didn't move back. "I know how important it is to *you*. That is all that concerns me."

If her heart beat any faster, she was pretty sure it was going to crap out on her. Knowing he could hear how every word out of his mouth affected her only made it worse.

Desperate to defuse some of the growing tension in the air, Zia said, "Oh, well you should know that you have some of the rarest varieties of roses in the West Coast in your garden. Some of them — like the one in front of you — were brought over from Europe and the Middle East before the war. I had to track down all the records to verify their provenance, but when I did, I found out two of them were on record as being no longer propagated in their home countries."

Mr. Bounds flicked his gaze back to the rose bush for just a moment before he turned his eyes back to her. "So they're rare."

"Yes, very." She reached out to brush her fingers over the leathery leaves and felt the plant reach back with a familiar *hello*. It didn't physically react to her, but she felt its recognition, its pleasure at being stroked and cared for after so long.

Affection buzzed between them, as real as the magic in her veins.

"It's a miracle that so many of the bushes survived being abandoned for so long," she added, quieter, as she skimmed her fingertips over the last pink-streaked bloom. "Roses can be hardy. They grow wild, you know, so it's not like they don't know how to make unfortunate conditions work, but..." She shook her head and sent her companion a rueful smile. "They're precious. I'm extremely grateful so many of them survived long enough for me to bring some life back into this place."

"That makes two of us."

Zia flushed to the roots of her hair. "Thank you, Mr. Bounds."

Gently steering her back onto the main path, he began to walk with her. "Tell me why you chose roses."

Another command.

She wrinkled her nose, but not because she was offended. There was something... charming about his apparent inability to ask *questions*. Instead, he seemed to default to a demand. Did he think asking would get him a refusal, or was it because he was simply used to getting things he wanted?

"Oh, well, that's because of my grandmother," she answered, stopping to point out another bush. "That's a shot silk rose. When it blooms, it almost looks like a peony. It has the most gorgeous, ruffled petals you'll ever see. It doesn't grow from seed very well, so the previous owner of the estate must have gotten a cutting, though I haven't been able to determine from where yet."

Mr. Bounds tilted his head, listening intently as she rattled off her theories about where that cutting might have come from, before he pressed, "What about your grandmother made you want to specialize in roses?"

"My grandmother was from Turkey — specifically from a little town a few hours outside of Istanbul. When I was a kid, we used to visit twice a year. She was a greenwitch, too, and had the most incredible rose garden." Zia sighed, thinking wistfully of her golden summer days spent running barefoot with her older brothers in her *anneanne's* lush yard.

Smiling hard enough to make her cheeks ache, she continued, "Oh, you should have *seen* the roses she grew, Mr. Bounds! These gorgeous climbing roses covered half her house, and then in the back she had these massive white roses. I swear, they never stopped blooming no matter what time of year it was. Every time we visited, she would cut some and put them next to my bed so my room would smell like roses when we arrived."

She caught his eye and her grin fell. Realizing she was rambling,

Zia sucked in a deep breath of cold air and forced herself to stop. "Sorry," she said, looking down at her sturdy work boots. "That was more information than you probably wanted. The shorter answer is that my grandmother liked roses and she passed that onto me."

"I didn't know my grandmother."

Zia's eyes flew back up. He didn't look particularly bothered by his admission, but rather pensive. "Oh, I'm sorry. That must have been hard for your family."

Mr. Bounds shrugged. "I don't have any family. My mother left me on the street when I was a newborn."

Zia's fingers spasmed on his forearm. Horror tightened her chest. "That's *awful*. I am so, so sorry, Mr. Bounds."

He cocked his head to one side and furrowed his brow. Confusion flickered across the harsh planes of his face. "For what? You didn't do anything to me."

"No," she replied, even more horrified by his confusion over basic empathy than his past. "I just feel for you. That must have been awful. Were you picked up by government services or Patrol or something?"

Mr. Bounds guided her over to another bush. His expression had closed off again, and for a moment, she worried that her question had crossed a line. Before she could apologize, he said, "No. I was born at the start of the war. At that time there wasn't even a puppet government in the New Zone."

He kept them moving from one bush to the next, as if he struggled to stand still while he spoke of his past. Zia let him guide her without protest. Softly, she asked, "If there was no agency to step in, who took care of you?"

"The Amauri family did."

Zia felt like he'd knocked the wind out of her. She knew the name from newsfeeds, from salacious tell-alls and dramatized entertainment feeds. The Amauri family was a juggernaut of the vampiric Syndicate — a crime family so well known they were practically their own *state*.

Voice suddenly squeaky, she found herself saying, "I... didn't realize they took care of babies."

"They don't. They raise soldiers."

So Mr. Bounds wasn't just a businessman. He was a — or at least had been — a part of the Amauri crime family. Zia felt the knowledge settle in her mind. *That explains the menace, then.*

"Oh." She let out a shaky breath. "Why are you telling me this, Mr. Bounds?"

He used his other hand to cover hers. The skin of his palm was warm, insulating her from the bite of the pre-dawn air. "You told me your story. Mine isn't as happy, but it's the only one I have to give you."

Zia's chest squeezed. A sudden bubbling of affection for this strange, intimidating man made her look up at him with unconcealed warmth. Softly, she whispered, "Thank you."

Mr. Bounds cut a look toward her, frankly assessing her reaction to his blunt admission. "Are you afraid of me now, Miss North?"

She took a moment to think about it before she shook her head. The UTA was a dangerous place. Morality changed to fit the mold it was forced into. Who was she to judge a man whose past she barely understood? Maybe her answer would change when she learned more, but until then...

"No, I don't think so."

He arched a dark brow. "Shouldn't you be nervous around a man who just admitted he's a criminal? I could hurt you, or worse."

"Will you?"

"No." A single, emphatic negative, so dark and deep, it was like he tore it out of his soul.

Zia squeezed his arm and offered a small smile. "Then I don't have anything to worry about. So far you've been nothing but kind to me, even when I was caught doing something stupid."

She brought her free hand up to brush away a stray curl. Staring at the collar of his sweater, she added, with no small amount of self-deprecation, "Besides, you graciously put up with my rambling. If you were really so bad, you would have told me to shut up the moment I started talking about shot silk roses."

At some point they had stopped walking, but she didn't notice it until Mr. Bounds gently slid her hand out from the crook of his elbow. Startled, she looked up to find him standing in front of her. A clawed thumb reached out to touch the divot in the center of her chin.

"I love it when you speak, Miss North." A smile curved his mouth and crinkled the corners of his eyes. It was tiny, not even a true grin, but it rocked her world all the same. "If I had my way, I'd listen to you talk about roses all night."

Zia felt the brush of his thumb against her chin — barely a whisper, but unmistakably there — and found herself swaying toward him. Magic prickled under her skin as heat built. The thrill of standing so close to a predator, a man who just admitted he was a criminal, mixed with the burn of desire, creating a potent cocktail that she had never experienced before.

She'd had boyfriends before. She'd even had good sex before. Nothing compared to the attraction she felt for this vampire she barely knew. It was in every beat of her heart, every breath in her lungs. It terrified her as much as it tantalized her.

What would someone like him — wealthy, powerful, *dangerous* — want with her? Nothing good. Nothing like what she wanted, certainly.

And yet... and yet when he pressed his thumb against the curve of her cheek and stared at her like that, it looked like he felt the same way. When he took a step closer, nearly banishing the distance between their bodies completely, Mr. Bounds looked like he wanted to bend his neck and sip from her lips like a parched man drinks from a well.

Unable to stop herself, words tumbled out of her mouth. "I... I didn't know you liked roses that much."

Mr. Bounds bent his head. The tip of his nose skimmed over her cheek as his palm slid down to cup the side of her throat. The pad of his thumb pressed lightly against her racing pulse. "Roses aren't the part that interest me."

The faintest scrape of fangs against the shell of her ear made her gasp.

Gods.

Zia felt her stomach drop. In its place, a vicious sort of desire expanded in a great, rolling wave. It crashed against her common sense with all the power of a tsunami. A sharp ache accompanied the sudden warmth between her thighs.

One tiny scrape of his fangs and it was like she was tugged under water, pulled toward him by an invisible current. She couldn't fight it any more than she could tell her body to stop reacting to this man she barely knew.

Her back bowed, swaying her closer, until their chests brushed. Without thinking, she reached up to clutch his biceps, her fingers digging into the fine wool of his coat. "Mr. Bounds?"

A hot breath exploded over her skin. His voice was rough, strained, when he muttered, "I'm supposed to be coaxing you, but I am not good at it."

Zia blinked. Surely she heard him wrong. "Coaxing me to... what?"

Mr. Bounds pulled back enough for her to see his tight expression when he said, "Coaxing you to want me."

Zia stared at him for what felt like a long time, her mind trying over and over again to process what he said. Even when it felt like she managed it, she was certain she had misheard him. Desperate for clarification, she asked, "Want you for... what, exactly?"

His jaw flexed just before he made that clicking sound again. Fangs flashed in the lamplight, sending another nearly debilitating rush of heat straight to her cunt.

"I'm used to taking things — or buying them. I don't do *gentle* well. I don't do patience well, either." A wry expression briefly stole the heat from his gaze. "Atticus warned me that I might scare you off if I came on too strong, but it's difficult changing your tactics when you're as old as I am."

She swallowed hard. "You... Are you saying you want to date me?"

"No."

Hurt and a healthy dash of humiliation cut straight through her arousal. *Shit!*

Zia took half a step back as the blood drained from her face. "Oh, of course. I'm sorry— I shouldn't have—"

Large hands closed over her hips, drawing her back until she was squeezed against him from chest to thigh. Mr. Bounds's expression was dangerously forbidding when he bit out, "No, I don't want to date you. I've spent a year watching you, waiting for you to look my way, Miss North. I am so far past wanting you, it feels like I'm going insane. I want to fucking *own* you."

Electricity crackled down her spine.

It should have upset her. She knew that. No modern witch would let a vampire handle her like this, nor let him declare that he wanted to *own* her.

But her body didn't care. It had spent the better part of a year craving a nearly unseen vampire, and now that it was in his presence, in his hands, it demanded she melt under the force of his raw hunger, that blistering *want.*

It wanted to be owned by him just as much as he wanted to own her.

Gaze darting from one bold feature to another, she finally settled on a long, almost invisible scar down the side of his chin when she breathed, "What would that entail?"

Mr. Bounds pressed his thumb into the soft flesh beneath her jaw and slowly tilted her face up, forcing her to look him in the eye. His eyelids were lowered, his lips parted, and when he leaned in to breathe against her mouth, each exhalation was a quick, hot burst.

"Have dinner with me," he murmured. "Let me take you out and spoil you. I'll show you what being mine would mean, and you can ask as many questions as you want. There's nothing I won't tell you."

And because her brain and mouth were at war even then, she found herself blurting out, "But you don't even *eat.*"

Was it her imagination, or did Mr. Bounds's lips curve into a real, honest-to-goodness smile against her own?

"Not food, no." Fangs slid over the cushion of her lower lip. There was a slight sting, not enough to draw blood but certainly enough to make her shiver, and then her lip was gently sucked into the hot well of his mouth.

It wasn't quite a kiss, but it was a touch so erotic, it nearly unwound her.

Zia whimpered, her back arching as she sought more contact. Her eyes fluttered shut as she dared to press the tips of her fingers against the curve of his jaw.

A low sound rumbled out of his throat as those fangs pressed again, a little harder than before. There was a sharp sting, then a slow, velvety drag of his tongue. One swipe. A second swipe.

He made that sound again, harsher than before, and pressed his fangs in again. Zia tensed, waiting for a real bite — *wanting* one with every fiber of her being — but it never came. For a suspended moment, he simply held himself there, perfectly still, with his fangs hovering on the brink of piercing her flesh.

She felt the hand cupping her throat tense before Mr. Bounds slowly withdrew, letting her lip go with an obscene *pop!*

"Fuck patience," he muttered, pressing his damp lips against her ear. His voice was low and hoarse. Gone was the man who couldn't be read. This new person had desire etched in every ragged syllable. "Dinner. Tomorrow night. I'll pick you up. If you hate it, you'll never have to see me again. Your rose garden will be yours and I'll never bother you for more. It will be like I never even existed."

She heard him swallow. It was a deep, painful sound, as if he struggled to make the muscles of his throat work.

In a voice that was almost soft, he finished, "But if you want more, I'll give you *everything.*"

"Dinner," she breathed, eyes closing. "Dinner sounds— Yes."

"Yes?"

Damp lips skimmed over her cheek until they found hers once more. Still, he didn't quite kiss her. Instead, he hovered, mingling their rough breaths, until she belatedly answered, "Yes, I'll go to dinner with you."

Only then did he tighten his grip on her neck. He dragged her closer, bending her until her face was tilted up to his liking, and then gave her the best kiss of her life.

His tongue slid past her lips to caress her own. His lips moved, gentle but firm, and he tasted like something sharp and somewhat sweet — like cold river water, or the bite of fruit just beginning to ripen.

It only lasted a moment. Before Zia could dig her fingers into his hair and give back as good as she got, he ripped his mouth from hers and took three steps back.

She opened her eyes to find Mr. Bounds standing by the greenhouse, one hand braced on the glass wall, his expression—

Well, she'd never seen an expression quite like that before. It was almost *ravenous.*

Color rode high in his cheeks. The look in his night-glow eyes was wild. His lush lips were slightly swollen and wet. Most affecting of all was the way his chest rose and fell with each hard pant, and how the muscles of his shoulders rounded, as if he were holding himself back from lunging at her.

Prey, his stance said. *You're my prey.*

Zia pressed a hand to her chest, trying and failing to get her bearings. Unbelievably, her knees wobbled. It was just one kiss, but it felt like he did much, much more.

Fingers fluttering uselessly at her throat, she gasped, "Why did you stop?"

Mr. Bounds flashed his fangs at her in a snarl that was all

harsh need. "Because if I didn't, I'd end up fucking you in this greenhouse."

Zia trembled. Working up the last of her frayed nerves, she whispered, "That doesn't sound so bad to me."

He let out a huff of air, almost like she'd knocked the wind out of him. "Don't do this to me, pet. I don't want my first taste of you to be my last."

Her brow furrowed. "Why..."

He flicked his gaze to the greenhouse, then the sky.

Gradually, she became aware of the fact that it was getting easier to see him. Shooting a startled glance upward, she exclaimed, *"Oh.* Gods, I didn't even think about it! You need to get inside! The sun's coming up."

Mr. Bounds shook his head hard, making his long ponytail whip behind him. *"Fuck."*

Passing a hand over his face, he slowly straightened. When she caught his gaze again, his eyes were only slightly less wild than they were before. "Tell me again," he demanded, taking one menacing step closer. "Tell me you'll see me tomorrow. I won't be able to sleep if you don't."

Zia licked her lips. The instinctive urge to flee was almost overwhelming — and arousing.

"Eight o'clock," she answered. Zia cursed the sun for taking him away the moment she got what she wanted. Longing thickened her voice when she added, "I'll be waiting for you."

A vicious sort of satisfaction flashed across his face.

Taking one step backward, he kept his gaze locked on her when he rumbled, "Good, pet. Think of me while I sleep." He let out a harsh breath and scrubbed his hand over his jaw. "Gods know I'll be dreaming of you."

Chapter Nine

IT WAS HARD NOT TO SCOWL AT THE LITTLE COTTAGE Zia called home.

Of course, Harlan knew what it looked like. One of the first things he did when his obsession with the witch took root was investigate her home. It was second nature for him to dig up everything he could about a target — what their habits were, where they lived, what and who was important to them.

He knew Zia's house. He knew the floor plan. He knew what she paid each month and who her landlord was. He knew that there were seven sensors installed around the tiny wooded property and that she had recently asked the owner to fix a leaky sink.

But up until the night of their date, he did not allow himself to cross the line into *going* to her home.

The assassin he once was wouldn't have hesitated. He would have easily disabled her paltry security and waltzed right in, ready to learn every illicit and mundane detail about his prey's life before he struck in the darkest part of the night.

He didn't do that, though.

Harlan had been trying to leave that those habits behind him for four years. Besides, Zia wasn't a target. There were no bounties on her head. No one had anonymously contracted him to put a bolt through her brain in exchange for cash.

She was not a part of that world, and certainly not the kind of target he ever would have accepted.

Being the best meant he got to be choosy. The choosier he got, the more coveted his services became. By the end of his career, he made a point to only accept bounties for the vilest of the vile — feyrunners, flesh-peddlers, and those who wished to create their own cruel little empires out of filth and violence.

The only people he was beholden to were the Amauri family. When they asked him to kill, he didn't get to ask questions, or say no. It was only through a profound act of service to the matriarch herself that he had been allowed to walk away from them at all.

Zia could not have been farther from that life if she tried.

So he stayed away. For a year, he fought his fascination with her and resisted impulses ingrained in him after a lifetime of clawing his way out of the gutter. He didn't watch her home. He didn't track her car. He didn't monitor her communications — though he did keep an eye on her landlord, just to be sure she was being taken care of.

Even the planting of the sensors fell to Atticus. As much as it pained him, Harlan knew he couldn't be trusted so near her home.

Until now.

Even as he pulled to a stop in front of her cottage, Harlan wasn't entirely certain he should be allowed to.

Because now that he'd seen it in person, he didn't like it at all.

It was a plain, square little house with a sparse lawn and a gravel driveway. Light from inside blazed through the cracks in the curtains, throwing the looming trees that ringed the property into sharp relief.

And there *were* trees. Zia's cottage sat on a tiny speck of land carved into the dense Sierra Nevada mountain range's forest, almost like an afterthought. She had no neighbors within earshot and only one easily blocked route in and out. There was no fence or ward around the home, either. Even the sloppiest criminal could walk right out of the trees, break a window, and be inside her home without anyone noticing for the gods knew how long.

If they didn't trip the sensors, it wouldn't be until Zia skipped multiple days of work that anyone would even think to look for her.

Harlan's stomach turned as he hit the ignition switch. *Un-fucking-acceptable.*

Stepping out of the low-slung sports car, he braced one hand on the roof and buttoned his suit jacket with the other. The air was bitingly cold and spiced with the scents of pine and rich, red soil.

Harlan sucked in a deep breath and let it out slowly. A cloud of steam swirled in the air as he tried to rein in his initial impulses. Both the vampire and the assassin demanded he extract her from that unsafe little hovel at the first opportunity, but the man kept a stranglehold on the desire.

He could not waltz into Zia's life and completely demolish it, only to remake it in the image that best suited him. She didn't grow up in his world. There was no way she'd see his raging need to protect her like someone from the New Zone might. She was not used to the constant need for vigilance, nor the dance of seduction and protection that was the backbone of vampiric society.

Finding someone bigger and more powerful than you to act as a protector was expected, both in business and in more personal relationships. In the cut-throat world of the New Zone, where the families of the vampiric Syndicate were constantly at war, it was essential.

Either you were protected, you became strong enough to be the protector, or you died.

But this wasn't the New Zone. This was the coddled, soft-skinned land of the Elvish Protectorate, where danger lived in high towers and pretended to obey laws. The weak felt safe because they didn't expect a monster to live next door to them —

and if they did, they felt secure knowing that Patrol would keep them safe.

Harlan was willing to bet that *he* was the most dangerous person Zia had ever met.

And she doesn't even know it.

Keeping his anchor safe and ignorant of just how bloody his world was would be the greatest challenge of his life.

His stomach turned again, churning with unfamiliar nerves.

If she says yes.

He didn't know how he would cope if she turned him down. If the sacrifice of being his anchor was too much for her, if she simply didn't feel the same way he did, he wouldn't try to force her — but letting her go would gut him all the same.

Dress shoes barely disturbing the gravel of her driveway, Harlan strode toward her front door. A fetching little wreath made of dried wildflowers decorated the drab door, adding a splash of color to the otherwise plain structure. He took it in with a small, almost imperceptible smile.

Another thing he noticed was that Zia had thoughtfully left the light over the door off — saving his sensitive eyes from searing discomfort. Harlan's chest constricted with painful tenderness when he glanced up at the small light.

It was such a small thing, but for someone used to the world's cruelty and little else, it was painfully significant. He didn't buy that small gesture with money or intimidation. She did it simply because she was thoughtful. Because she *cared*.

If his craving for her was relentless before, it took on a new, uncomfortably desperate edge now. He didn't just want her. He wanted all her little acts of kindness, all her smiles, all her love. He *needed* those things.

I'll have them.

Sucking in a deep breath, Harlan raised his hand. The moment his knuckles touched the surface of the door for a swift knock, he felt a faint hum of magic all the way through his bones. His lips parted with surprise.

She has wards on the house, he realized, unexpectedly pleased. *Strong ones, too.*

Maybe she wouldn't be so easy to sneak up on as he thought. While they weren't enough to keep out someone like him, they would repel at least the lowest types of thugs.

He recognized the tenor of the wards she employed. They would cause severe disorientation and vomiting in any trespassers, giving her plenty of time to call for help. *He* could slice through the web of magic with ease, of course, but it was at least something.

A tiny trickle of relief eased some of the tension in his shoulders. If she didn't want to move into the manor right away, he could contact the man who warded the estate and ask him to lay down an almost unbreakable net of magic over the cottage, adding layers onto the wards she already placed. It would cost him another few million, and Shade wasn't exactly easy to work with — let alone get a hold of — but there was no amount of money he wouldn't pay to keep his anchor safe.

Harlan was already thinking ahead, his keen, action-oriented mind working at lightspeed to plan for how exactly he would look after Zia. That didn't mean he wasn't paying attention to the soft sounds coming from within the home, however.

Anticipation threatened to edge out his taut nerves as he listened to the beat of heels on thin carpet, the gentle brush of fabric swaying against a moving body. His heart rate spiked when the light from her living room window was extinguished.

The sound of her heels got closer, closer, until he could hear her breathing on the other side of the door. The thump of her heartbeat made it through, too, echoing his own.

Slowly, the knob turned and the door opened.

If he had been any other man, he would have staggered back a step at the sight of her. As it stood, all he could do was freeze, his breath stalling, as he stared at her backlit form.

Zia had pulled her curls up into a soft updo. Delicate ringlets of rich brown spilled out around her temples, ears, and the back of her neck. She wore a simple red cocktail dress with a deliciously curved neckline that enhanced the generous swell of her breasts. The skirt fell to her mid-thigh, giving him plenty of room to admire her shapely legs, which were swathed in sheer black tights. Little red pumps with straps over the top completed the ensemble.

She looks fucking delectable.

Harlan slowly raised his eyes back to her face and found her biting her red-stained lip. She had put on a dash of makeup for their date, which was unusual for her. He didn't think he'd ever seen her with makeup on before. The fact that she put the extra time in for their date made his chest swell with pride.

Of course, it also made his cock hard. He wanted nothing more than to see that lipstick and mascara smeared by the end of the night.

With his cock stiff and the gland in the roof of his mouth aching worse than it ever had, Harlan had to force himself to remember his manners. In a hoarse voice, he said, "Good evening, Miss North."

"Hi," she murmured, looking up at him through her lashes. He watched her throat move with a hard swallow. "You... you look nice, Mr. Bounds."

He glanced down at himself. There was nothing particularly noteworthy about his appearance aside from the fact that his suit was handmade for him. Like everything else in his life, he wanted the clothing he wore to be both beautiful and sophisticated, a stark contrast to everything his life had been in his youth. Sometimes that meant he wanted a flashy car, but other times it meant he simply wanted a suit that was perfectly made, with the best fabrics, by the most skilled tailors money could buy.

He looked like he had good taste, but Zia looked good enough to *eat*.

Harlan pressed his tongue against the roof of his mouth, desperate to relieve some of the ache, as he shook his head. "Not as good as you," he argued. He let out a hard breath that steamed between them. "You look gorgeous."

He watched, fascinated, as her olive skin turned rosy with a blush. Would all of her flush that pretty, dusky pink? *I hope so.*

"Thank you." Zia reached behind the door and unhooked a simple black coat and purse, her smile shyly pleased.

Harlan took a step closer to help her into her coat, seizing on any opportunity to be closer to her. When she looked up at him with surprise, he merely nudged her back, urging her to slip her arms into the sleeves. Her warmth filled the space between them.

The scent of her, lush and sweet, was a heady perfume he couldn't get enough of, no matter how deeply he breathed.

When she was tucked into her coat, he took a reluctant step back to allow her to lock the door. That done, he offered her his elbow. Zia's hand was small, the pressure of her touch as light as a feather, but even that contact was enough to stir dark instincts.

Take her away. Hide her in the manor. Sip and lick and fuck until she never wants to leave your side.

Harlan pressed his tongue against the roof of his mouth again. *Patience!*

"Pretty car," Zia noted, oblivious to his struggle as he carefully escorted her over the gravel. "My brother Arif would lose his mind if he knew I was riding in something like this."

Harlan opened her door and watched her slide onto the butter-soft leather seat. "Would he be as happy knowing there was a vampire driving it?"

Zia wrinkled her nose. "I don't think he'd care. My brothers have never been very interested in my love life."

Halfway through closing her door, Harlan paused. "Aren't brothers supposed to be overprotective?"

He knew she had five of them — a number of siblings that was absolutely unimaginable to him. All he knew about such things came from media and Atticus, who was himself a violently overprotective big brother. Even if he didn't have Atticus's example, he couldn't imagine anyone, let alone a herd of brothers, not wanting to swaddle Zia in cotton wool.

She shrugged. "They leave that to my mother."

"And how would your mother feel about you going on a date with a vampire?" Not that he cared, really, but he hadn't survived this long by not scoping out threats. If any of Zia's family objected to his place in her life, he would have to find a way to eliminate the obstacle.

Her lips puckered as she thought about her answer. "She probably wouldn't be a fan. She was dead-set on me marrying and bonding with one of my brother's friends for a long time. He was an *accountant*." Her nose wrinkled. "She thinks I can't handle stress, so she worries about me spending time with…"

"Predators?"

She flashed a bashful smile. "Yes."

Harlan dared to reach down to brush a curl from her forehead. "Did she ever consider that you might be safer with a predator who can protect you than someone who can't?"

"No," she murmured, eyelids fluttering, "I don't think she has."

Forcing himself to step back, Harlan hummed and gently closed the door. There was no escaping temptation, though. By the time he slid behind the wheel, the small cab of the car had already filled with her mouthwatering scent.

Gods help me, he thought, hitting the ignition with a little too much force, *I don't know how I'll make it to the restaurant.*

Harlan slanted a look over his shoulder, his jaw tight, as he pulled out of the narrow driveway and onto the main road.

Seeing a flash of light in his rear view mirror, he felt a little more of his anxiety over her safety ease. He was not ignorant of the risk he was taking, bringing Zia out into the open with him. Two days prior, he received word that the fierce and ancient head of the Amauri family, Dora Amauri, had passed away, leaving her grandson as her heir. Of course, as was the way with these things, a power struggle began immediately. Old friends and informants claimed that the family had split into three factions, sending ripples of violence out far and wide.

While he hadn't been disturbed in two years, he worried that eventually one of those ripples would reach him now that he had something he couldn't bear to lose. It was one thing to handle upstarts looking to make a quick name for themselves. It was quite another to take on Julius Amauri, the bloodthirsty bastard who once held the leash around Harlan's neck. Only Dora's favor had stopped him from hunting Harlan like a rabid dog when he left the family.

With the Amauris split and Dora's grandson Felix struggling to fend off his power-hungry cousins, there was nothing to stop Julius from seeking him out.

His only hope was that Julius would be too busy trying to win the Amauri war to think of his old protégé. If he got *really* lucky, the piece of shit would die early. *And bloody.*

Regardless, Harlan doubted he was being watched at that very moment, but he wasn't about to take any chances on an attack. A nondescript SUV of men followed them at a discreet distance, armed and ready, just in case.

"Am I allowed to ask where we're going?"

He glanced at her out of the corner of his eye. "You will ask anything you want to."

A small bubble of laughter filled the car. "You make everything sound like an order. Do you do that on purpose?"

Flicking his finger against the control panel, Harlan turned the heat up to a comfortable level and answered, "It's a habit. Someone in my position isn't supposed to *ask* for anything. Asking for something in a vampiric family is equivalent to begging. Making demands shows... status, I suppose. Power." He paused, looking at her again. "Does it bother you?"

He felt Zia's gaze on his profile as he steered the car onto the smooth road. "No, not really. It's just something I noticed. As long as you don't mind me pushing back when you get overbearing, it doesn't upset me. Sounds like it's sorta of a... crime family cultural thing."

"You can push back as much as you like." There was a dry note to his tone. The irony of the fact that Zia, sweet-faced and harmless, was perhaps the only being on the planet who *could* push back without consequence, was not lost on him.

Fabric rustled as she oriented her body toward him. The beat of her heart was loud in his ears, faster than normal, and her scent flowed with the currents of warm air blowing from the vents.

It was torture. He loved every second of it.

"So where are we going?"

"There's a small restaurant in Grass Valley I like," he answered, resisting the urge to rest his hand on the skin of her supple thigh, as well as the compulsion to add that he knew she had probably never been there. She so rarely left her little house on the weekends that he wondered if she even knew Grass Valley existed. This would hopefully be a low-key treat, which was just the sort of middle ground Atticus urged him to find when he initially suggested a five star restaurant in San Francisco with a side trip to a jewelry store.

Peeking at her, he added, "It's called The Gold Vein."

"Sounds vampirey. Do they serve fancy synthblood there or something?" Zia made a soft sound in the back of her throat. When she spoke again, her words were rushed. "Ah, sorry if that's offensive. I'm just curious."

Harlan couldn't resist any longer.

His right hand moved off of the wheel to rest lightly on her knee. The material of her tights was smooth and her heat blazed through the thin barrier to sear his palm.

Catching her eye, he said, "You can ask me *anything*, pet. You don't need to be afraid of offending me."

Certainly, he'd kept far worse company over the years. He struggled to imagine his Zia saying anything that could truly shock him.

Feeling the fine muscles under his hand flex, he continued,

"To answer your question: no. I agree it would be a good name for a vampire establishment, but unfortunately I believe it is a reference to the mining done in this area before the war."

"So if it's not a vampire bar, then why do you like it?"

He shrugged. The movement pushed his hand a few centimeters higher up her thigh. The sound of her breath hitching made him want to close his eyes and *revel* in her.

Voice lowering, he answered, "They have good wine and their diverse menu makes it easy for me to have meetings with business partners when I need to. I also like the way it looks."

"You can drink wine?"

He tilted his head toward her in a sideways nod. "A small amount. It's bad for me, but I like the taste."

He felt the fluttering brush of fingertips against his scarred knuckles — there and gone again in an instant. "Why not just take me to The Shack? We're not business partners, and I don't need to be wined and dined. I'm not very fancy."

Harlan inwardly balked. "I would never take you there," he answered, vehement. "They sell cheap food, t-shirts, and hunting gear. I'll pull out my own fangs before I take you out to The Shack."

Her laughter bubbled up again, the sound so light and pleasant it was almost foreign to him. The laughter he was used to was cold, cruel. It wasn't this full-throated sound of delight that shook him to the core. "Mr. Bounds, I happen to like their milkshakes. Besides, it's the only restaurant in Pineridge. It makes sense to go there."

Seeing as Pineridge was the closest town to the estate, he understood that many of his staff chose to go there in their free time. That didn't mean he would tolerate taking Zia to a place that thought decor should come in the form of stuffed animal heads and talking mechanical fish.

He didn't mind that it was a place where the average person could get cheap food. Harlan had simply spent way too much time creeping through the backs of establishments like that —

usually fronts for more illegal fare, but decent escape routes after a quick, public hit — to ever willingly take his anchor to *The Shack*.

Rats were the *least* of the horrors he witnessed in the kitchens of seedy restaurants, after all.

"If you want a milkshake, I'll have it delivered to you," he allowed, casting her a look that told her how great a sacrifice that would be. "Otherwise, I only ever want to see you eating in a place where I can be certain they at *least* clean their counters regularly, pet."

Zia's lips parted in a look of soft surprise before a slow, sweet smile curled her lips. Shyly, she asked, "Are you *worried* about me, Mr. Bounds?"

Harlan shook his head. "You have no idea."

CHAPTER TEN

THE GOLD VEIN STOOD OUT AGAINST THE OAK TREES that lined the sloped street. String lights looped around its wooden facade, casting a warm glow into the blue-black October night. The building itself was once a saloon built for the first wave of miners that came with the settlement of the territory, but it had been refreshed and redesigned in recent years to give it a sophisticated face-lift. Old wood beams and the antique bar were refinished, tasteful bespoke light fixtures dangled from the ceiling, and the furniture was an eclectic mix of velvet and vintage leather. The strains of soft guitar drifted through the air.

"Oh, it's so pretty," Zia breathed, her eyes darting from the silk wallpaper to the white table cloths to the twinkling lights like she couldn't take it all in at once. It took a moment for her brow to furrow. "Why is it empty? Are we early for the dinner service?"

"No," he answered. Harlan kept his eyes on the owner, a balding, jovial arrant who came to take their coats, his hackles raised. It didn't matter that he was familiar with the man. With his instincts in a tailspin, *any* stranger near his anchor made him bristle.

"Welcome, Mr. Bounds," the owner said, gesturing toward a set of polished stairs. "Your private dining room is all ready for you. Your server will be with you as soon as you're settled in."

As he guided Zia up the stairs, Harlan felt her lean in to whisper, "Private dining room? The entire restaurant is empty!"

And it would remain that way. He didn't want anyone to disturb them while he attempted to win his anchor, and the deeply vampiric need for isolation made it impossible for him to tolerate an entire room full of strangers just below his feet while he did so.

"I always get a private room when I visit," he assured her.

Zia cast him a sidelong look. "For all your dates?"

Harlan gave her waist a single, possessive squeeze. "No dates before you matter, but if it makes you feel any better, no, I've never taken anyone here before."

A little jolt of surprise moved through her body. It was followed by an uptick in her heart rate — the sweetest little stuttering beat he ever heard.

Breath quickening, he nudged her down the narrow hallway that led to what was once a gambling parlor. A single circular table had been set up for their use beneath a set of wide, gabled windows that overlooked the quaint street below. The lighting was soft and golden, provided by a series of artfully placed string lights and flickering candles in tall glass fixtures.

Zia looked dazed as he pulled out her chair for her. In the golden light, her dark eyes looked like melted chocolate.

Harlan settled in the chair across from her and only took his eyes off of her face long enough to watch their server fill up their glasses with wine. That done, he made himself scarce. The door closed with a soft click.

"This is... a lot," she breathed. Her fingers danced along the edge of the table as the look on her face changed from awe to uncertainty. "You didn't need to go to this kind of trouble for me."

Swallowing a sip of red wine in the hopes that it would soothe some of the raging ache in his mouth, Harlan eyed her over the rim of his crystal glass. "Why do you think that?"

Zia bit her lip and then released it. "I don't know. I'm just not used to this sort of thing. No one's ever..." She gestured helplessly to the table. "I'm not the kind of girl most people wine and dine, is all."

A bubble of fury burst in his chest. His voice was a whip's crack when he replied, "Don't say that. A nice date is the *least* of what a *girl like you* deserves. Tell me who convinced you that you aren't worthy of the bare-fucking-minimum and I'll correct their mistake *tonight.*"

Zia's eyes, already large and doe-like in her soft-cheeked face, widened to a comical size. "Oh, no, that's..." Her fingers fluttered over her cutlery as if they needed something to do. "No, really, that's okay, Mr. Bounds. I'm just— I'm not used to places like this."

Worry seized him. He aimed for low-key — as much as he was capable of, anyway — but it was possible he'd missed the mark. "Do you not like the restaurant?"

Startled, she gripped the edge of the table and leaned forward. "No! It's *lovely.* No one's ever taken me somewhere this romantic before. It's just different, that's all."

Lowering his glass, Harlan flexed his claws around the delicate stem. *Calm, Harlan.* "Tell me what your previous dates were like, then."

She shrugged one shoulder and reached for her wine. Speaking into the glass, she answered, "Movies. Coffee. Sometimes a picnic."

In other words, *low effort.*

He fought a scowl. "Do you prefer those things?"

"No, not really," she admitted, lowering her glass. "I've mostly dated academics. They aren't the most romantic sort, you know. I never minded it very much, but..."

Harlan tensed when a light knock interrupted them. The server was in and out, skillfully taking Zia's order and delivering a plate of appetizers for her before he vanished again.

When the door closed, Harlan announced, "That will never be good enough for me."

Zia looked up from her plate with surprise. "What won't be?"

"You not minding something *very much,*" he explained. Harlan's gaze was sharp on her expression, taking in every flicker in her eyes, every brush of her tongue over her lower lip. "Your satisfaction is all that concerns me, Miss North."

Her heartbeat jumped. A flush brought dark color to her cheeks. Her voice was soft when she noted, "You're... very intense, Mr. Bounds."

One corner of his mouth lifted. "You have no idea how intense I can be."

Zia sat back in her seat and folded her hands in her lap. Her eyes drifted over his face. He wondered what she saw there that made her look both uneasy and exhilarated. "Mr. Bounds, I... What exactly do you want with me?"

What don't *I want with you?*

Watching her with half-lidded eyes, he asked, "Do you know what an anchor is?"

"Only what I've seen in feeds and read online." She canted her head to one side, sending stray curls tumbling over a mostly bare shoulder. "It's sort of like a mate and a buffet wrapped up in one person, right?"

Harlan huffed. His smile, rusty and rarely used though it was, grew. "You could say that." Pausing, he ran the tip of his tongue over the ridges of the swollen gland in the roof of his mouth. A pulse of dull pain followed.

In a lower voice, he continued, "The myths say that Grim fashioned anchors for us after we were cast out from the rest of society. In her infinite kindness, she gave us companions who would sustain us, and who we could love in return." His small smile turned wry. "Science says that it's an adaptation meant to help spread the virus after blood to blood transmission began to fail. An anchor can produce offspring that will carry the virus, and so the chain continues."

There was a moment of silence before Zia sucked in a breath. "So... are you saying you want *me* to be your anchor?"

Harlan licked his lips. Should he have wooed her before this? Would knowing what he wanted scare her off? Perhaps.

But he was a direct man. He didn't play games, nor negotiate. When he wanted something, he took it. When he aimed at someone, he didn't miss a shot. He was honest in the only way he could be — by acting decisively.

"An anchor is the center of a vampire's whole world, Miss North," he told her. "They are more than a lover, more than sustenance. They are *everything.*" His thumb brushed the base of his glass, circling it slowly. "Yes, I want you to be my anchor. Yes, I want you to be the center of my world. *Yes,* I want you to be my everything."

Zia's heartbeat was a swift rhythm in his ears. Her eyes were wide and her expression dazed when she said, "But... you don't even know me." She glanced down at her plate of untouched appetizers and blinked. "We haven't even eaten dinner yet."

Nerves made a muscle in his jaw tick. "It's important for you to know that no matter what you decide, the rose garden is yours. Like I told you, if you choose not to pursue a relationship with me, I will never force the issue with you." He swallowed hard. The words were like glass in his throat, though he meant them wholeheartedly. "But it is equally important to me that you know I have wanted you every day since you stepped foot on the estate. If you choose me, I promise, you will not regret it."

She shook her head and pressed her palm against her chest, as if she could calm the racing heart that sang so sweetly for him. Almost to herself, she muttered, "This can't be real."

Harlan's eyes narrowed. "Why can't it be real?"

Her gaze flew up from her plate to meet his. "Because," she answered, breathless and baffled, "I've imagined this *exact moment* a thousand times. It— I never thought it could *happen.*"

It was his turn to be confused. Brow creasing, he took a moment to silently digest that admission while he took a long sip from his glass. His own heart thumped unevenly in his chest.

When he spoke, his voice was a deep, raw baritone. "What part did you imagine, Miss North?"

Zia's eyes followed his hand as he lowered the glass back onto the table. They lingered on his scarred knuckles for a moment before they traced a path up his arm, over his shoulder, and back to his face. A hot blush seemed permanently infused in her cheeks when she whispered, "That you would want me back."

The moment stretched between them, taut and increasingly warm. Their eyes were locked on one another even when the server returned with her meal. Perhaps sensing the tension, he didn't say a word as he placed her plate in front of her and then beat a hasty retreat.

She'd ordered a large, beautifully colored salad decorated with ripe tomatoes and curls of pickled carrots, as well as a small bowl of rich pumpkin soup drizzled with a swirl of cream.

Neither of them spared a glance for any of it.

Harlan sat back and braced his forearms on the armrests of his chair, every muscle in his body tense with the urge to spring. "You want me."

"I... yes." Zia licked her lips. Laughing softly, she added, "You scare me half to death, but it's like—" Her eyes cut away for a second before they flew back to his. "But it's like I *want* you to scare me."

Fuck. Harlan gripped the armrests so hard, the wood creaked.

"Being my anchor won't be easy," he warned her, desperate to give her one final out before the steel jaws of desire stole the last of his mercy. "You won't live in the sun any longer. I'll need you with me constantly. I'll be possessive, territorial, and overbearing." His jaw worked for a moment as pressure and pain pulsed in the roots of his fangs. Raggedly, he added, "I'll need to feed from you, Zia."

Her breath hitched. Slowly, as if she was testing the words as she spoke them, she replied, "There are lights in the garden now, right? I can still work at night. At least, I can give it a try. And I'm already on the estate five days a week. What's two more?"

Adrenaline rushed through his veins. Harlan planted his feet on the floor, bracing himself to stand at the slightest sign of her capitulation. "Is that a yes?"

"Would this be permanent?"

"Absolutely."

She chewed on her lip for a moment. He could see the sacrifices she would have to make weighing on her, battling with the yearning that was written so plainly on her face. "Do I have to decide right now?"

Harlan stiffened as the spicy scent of desire reached him. It was the thinnest thread in the air, but it was *there*.

"No," he managed to grate out. Sucking in a deep breath, desperate to get that scent in his lungs, on his fucking tongue, the great Harlan Bounds found himself begging, "What would it take to convince you? What do you need? I'll give you the world if you ask for it, pet. I'll give you fucking *anything.* "

He watched the dark circles of Zia's pupils expand. "I want to go on more dates like this. Romantic ones. Fancy ones, even." Her smile was small, fleeting, but so full of breathless delight it cut him to the quick. "I want to get to know you. I want to know more about your life, your... past, even if it's ugly. I want to know more about what I'm getting into."

"You want to know what you're getting into?" Harlan stood up slowly from his chair. The sound of her sharp gasp, the increasingly potent scent of her arousal, the soft, almost fearful look in her eyes as she watched him, were enough to make him lose his damn mind.

Fuck patience. Fuck the year he spent pining after her. He wanted a taste, and he was damn-well going to get it.

Prowling around the table, he first crossed the room to lock the door and then stalked back to her. In one quick movement, he grasped the armrests of her chair and spun it to the side. She let out a small *eep* of surprise, but the sound faded into nothing as she stared up at him with her lips parted.

Harlan shrugged out of his suit jacket and threw it onto the back of his chair. Next, he loosened his black silk tie. Eyes on her flushed cheeks, he gently but firmly used the toe of his dress shoe to nudge her feet apart with one swift tap.

That seemed to wake her up from her daze. Fingers curling around her chair's armrests, she squeaked, "What are you doing, Mr. Bounds?"

Dropping to his knees, he palmed her thighs beneath the hem of her skirt and slowly pulled them apart. "I'm going to show you what you're getting into," he answered, using his grip to drag her towards the edge of the seat. "Now, pet, when I make you come, I want you to call me *Harlan.*"

Chapter Eleven

Fantasy, Zia realized, was a hollow, sugary thing.

Her gauzy dreams of Harlan momentarily satisfied a craving, but inevitably left her hungrier than before. So she dreamed more, imagined being with that shadowy figure a hundred different ways, to chase that weak burst of satisfaction.

Fantasy built up a habit of taste and consumption, daydream and desire, until she thought she knew what it would be like to have him between her legs.

She was wrong.

When he knelt between her thighs, Zia realized that she had been living off of nothing but spun sugar. The real thing was as rich and heady as the wine in her forgotten glass. She wanted to drink and drink and drink until there was nothing left.

His hands were hot on her thighs. The thin barrier of her tights seem to somehow enhance the sensation of his firm touch, not muffle it. His fingertips pressed hard as he pulled her legs apart, making room for himself in the gap.

Her heart felt like it was beating too fast — spurred on by a potent mix of adrenaline, instinctive fear, and a desire so all-consuming, it edged on pain.

When he dipped his head to give the soft inner curve of her knee a searing kiss, she let out a whimper. Every nerve jumped. Her fingers curled into the armrests of her chair until the beds of her nails turned white.

He swept his tongue over the thin material of her tights, dampening it. Goosebumps broke out across her skin. His breath ghosted over the wet spot when he looked up at her, his gaze predator-sharp. "How much do you value these tights, pet?"

Zia could barely manage human speech. Breathing hard, she whispered, "Not very much."

A smile quirked the corners of his mouth. It was tiny, but she marveled at the sight of it. When Mr. Bounds — *Harlan,* she reminded herself — smiled, it took decades off of his face.

She rather liked his distinguished look, but Zia enjoyed that spark of humor far more.

"Good." Harlan flattened his tongue against her inner thigh and slowly dragged it up, leaving a cool trail from knee to cunt. Molten heat flowed through her veins and settled between her thighs as she watched his dark, gray-streaked head move ever-upward. "I want to bite holes in these damn things," he muttered, pausing to press another hard, sucking kiss to the softest part of her thigh. "But then other people might see your pretty legs, and I can't fucking have that."

Zia tried not to squirm in her seat. "Do— do you want me to take them off?"

His thumbs pushed her skirt up until it was bunched around her waist. "No. I'll just have to be strategic about where I tear." Nearing the gusset of her tights, he commanded, "Hold your skirt up for me, pet."

She hurried to obey him, her body moving without any thought of resistance or coquettish hesitancy. She wanted him to tear up her tights until they were nothing but ribbons. She wanted this terrifying vampire to pry her legs apart and lick her until she came. Zia *wanted* him to use those fangs on her.

Again, her mind reeled. *Is this really happening?*

A week ago, he was a faceless character in her most illicit daydreams. Now he was kneeling before her, his eyes locked on the damp fabric straining with tension between her spread thighs.

That feeling of being the sole focus of a jaguar about to pounce hadn't gone away. That deep, back of the mind terror remained, too, as if her instincts knew something about this man that she didn't.

But it was like the fear came into being only to immediately transmute into something else — a white-hot lust and the driving desire to be consumed by him.

This predator could be yours, the darkest part of her whispered. *Silly little Zia could have a dangerous vampire at her mercy.*

He was already kneeling at her feet. What kind of power was this man willing to give her? In yielding to a predator such as him, chasing that tantalizing fear, what power lay in wait? The possibilities thrilled her.

So even though her instincts screamed at her to back away slowly, Zia curled her trembling fingers into the thick fabric of her skirt and did as he asked.

Harlan's hands slid down over her soft hips. His eyes jumped from the damp seam of her tights to the sheer expanse that covered her mons and lower belly.

He let out a hard breath. "Pet... are you not wearing panties?"

Swallowing thickly, she answered, "I didn't want any panty lines."

"Fuck," he muttered, framing her core with his hands. The sharp tips of his clawed thumbs stroked the seam that ran over her cunt, only to part over the gusset in the center. "I'm going to take a thousand tiny sips of you and it still won't be enough."

His eyes flicked up to meet hers. "Will you let me?"

Zia couldn't imagine anything she wanted more, but to be sure, she asked, "Drink my blood?"

Harlan's pupils, naturally much larger than her own,

expanded such that they seemed to swallow up the soft brown of his irises. There was nothing left except a shallow pool of black — his signature night-glow dulled in the soft light of the candles.

"That too," he rumbled.

"Oh." Zia sucked in a shuddering breath. She swore she could feel her pounding heart in her throat.

Of course she had oral sex before, but this was a level of intensity and connection that defied all comparison. She was almost dizzy with anticipation. If he didn't do something soon, it felt like she might simply burst into tears from the all-consuming ache between her thighs, the hunger that made her grip the armrests until her fingers hurt.

"Yes," she finally answered, daring to spread her legs as far as the chair allowed. "Sip however you like. Just... please hurry."

Harlan's voice was dark, almost a growl, when he said, "Absolutely fucking made for me."

She jumped with surprise when his claws tore through the seam of her tights, poking holes in the taut material before he used his fingers to pull them wider. The cold air of the room rushed in to meet her flushed skin.

He didn't give her any time to be self-conscious. Harlan only spared a moment to mutter an oath — to which god, she had no clue — before he spread her with the pads of his thumbs and licked a stripe from core to clitoris.

Zia jolted, a flash of pleasure jumping up her spine. Magic bubbled under her skin as he began to devour her. It *burned*.

Greenwitches, like empaths, were natural connectors. Their magic looked for places to *go*, beings to touch, though the specifics of who and what varied from being to being. Zia's normally reached for plants for an outlet, but at that moment, it wanted nothing more than to sink into Harlan and make a new home for itself.

Power rushed through her as he slid his tongue into her hot core, stroking her from the inside as his thumb slowly swirled around her clitoris. Every touch was slow, almost decadent. It was *divine.*

Bunching her skirt into one hand, Zia used her free one to get a grip on his hair. He'd pulled it back into a loose braid tonight, but she didn't care. Her fingers speared into the thick, silky strands as he tasted her. A low, desperate noise hummed against her skin.

"Harlan," she breathed, rocking her hips into his mouth. "I need— I need—" Zia made a soft sound in the back of her throat, half a moan, half a cry of frustration.

He didn't increase the pressure or speed, but continued savoring her with his slow licks and swirling thumb. She panted as the pleasure mounted to almost unbearable levels. The steady strokes of his seeking tongue weren't enough. She needed *more.* Harder. Something *extra.*

Finally, he pulled back just enough to press a hot, open-mouthed kiss to her slick inner thigh. His voice was raw when he said, "And I thought *I* was the hungry one." Turning his head back to her cunt, he looked up at her through his lashes and warned her, "Remember that this is just a taste, pet. When you're mine, I'll fucking *debauch* you."

Goodness gracious gods in the sky. I don't think I've ever wanted anything more.

Zia opened her mouth to ask what exactly that meant, but the words were locked in her throat. She was too busy watching her vampire to try and get them out, anyway.

Harlan stretched out his tongue to give her a long, blissful lick, as if he wanted to savor the taste of her, before he sealed his lips over her clitoris.

The *Ten Fun Facts About Your New Vampire Boyfriend* article hadn't been good for much, but a few lines stayed with her. She recalled reading somewhere that vampire tongues were slightly "scoop shaped". It was an adaptation to help them quickly pull blood from the relatively small wounds created by fangs. She didn't think twice about it when she saw the anecdote however many months ago, but now it was deliciously relevant to her interests.

It turned out Harlan could do *impossible* things with his tongue.

Within moments, she was clutching his hair and rocking her hips in a desperate rhythm against his mouth, the pressure compounding.

"Harlan!" Zia arched and threw her head back when he gave her a particularly hard pull that flirted with pain. One leg made its way over his shoulder as she fought to draw him closer.

Her orgasm tumbled through her, end over end, like a swirling wave. She didn't know up from down. His tongue flexed hard again and again, creating a rhythmic pulse that prolonged the pleasure. She felt him gently, with expert care for his claws and her delicate skin, slip two fingers just inside her. There was a small flare of pain as her muscles stretched suddenly, then another burst of white-hot pleasure when the pads of his fingers expertly massaged her inner wall.

Just when her orgasm was beginning to fade, he moved his tongue faster, forcing another peak, and pressed harder.

Zia made a wild, raw sound in the back of her throat. It ended on a breathless scream when he ripped his lips away from her, turned his head, and plunged his fangs into the soft flesh of her thigh.

At first there was no pain. The high of her orgasm blocked out whatever initial pinch there might have been, and his fangs were so damn sharp, they glided through her skin without the slightest resistance.

It took a second for a dull, burning ache to register, but almost as soon as it did, a hot pulse of... *something* wiped it away.

Zia looked down just in time to see Harlan close his eyes in ecstasy, a low groan rumbling out of his throat. The muscle of her thigh went lax as his venom began to spread, loosening her for his gentle consumption.

Warmth — foreign, almost like the slight buzz of one too many drinks — suffused her. The lights took on a slightly foggy glow. Everything looked just a little bit gauzy as a new taste, almost as sweet as sugar but with a raw, earthy edge, bled through the thin membrane of her cheeks.

Read about that too, she thought, blissed out. *You can taste a vampire's venom when they bite you. Didn't think it'd be so yummy though.*

Slumping into her chair, Zia watched him from under eyes gone half-mast, her fingers slack in his hair and her breathing labored.

Slowly, almost reluctantly, Harlan extracted his fangs. There was no pain this time. Another neat vampire trick, she knew, was a perfectly calibrated venom that both held off clotting and ever-so-slightly numbed the wound.

You don't need to worry about pain, the article had assured her. *Vampire venom has been used as a pain reliever for thousands of years. Your fanged BF knows how to make a bite a good time, we promise!*

Rivulets of bright red blood began to flow from the two punctures, but Harlan didn't let a single drop go to waste. The look in his eyes was dazed, *hungry,* when he lapped up the streams.

Following them back to their source, he pressed his lips to the wound and slowly, almost reverently, began to draw from her. One hand wrapped around her outer thigh, supporting its weight, while his other one stroked up and down her stomach, every touch an act of worship.

Oh, she thought, trembling, *that's... Oh, that's so lovely.*

Zia pushed his disheveled hair back from his forehead, daring to stroke him back. When he leaned into her touch, she continued petting him with considerable delight. *This is why people say sex with a vampire is some of the best you'll ever have.*

It wasn't just the skill, nor the special tongue. It was *this.*

Harlan drinking her blood was an act of breathtaking intimacy. Never in her life had she felt more connected to another person. She felt precious, *needed*. She felt like she could cup this fearsome predator in her hands and hug him close, insulating them from the world.

It was just the two of them, wrapped up so wholly in one another, there was no telling where one ended and the other began.

While the endorphins of her orgasm bubbled through her, he reverently took what she so enthusiastically offered him. Zia sustained him, gave him the gift of something so personal, it literally coursed through her veins.

In that moment, he belonged *entirely* to her. Silly Zia, with her roses and her papers and her chatter, held a vampire in the palm of her hand.

"I like this," she found herself murmuring. "A lot."

Harlan opened his eyes. He looked sated, almost *drugged*, when he dragged his tongue over the wounds. For several long seconds, he simply lapped at her. It was like he couldn't get enough even when the blood stopped flowing and her skin glistened in the candlelight.

He met her gaze through the dense fringe of his lashes. Speaking against her wet, reddened skin, he told her, "Thank the gods you do. One taste won't be enough." A smile kicked up the corner of his mouth. The crows feet around his eyes crinkled. "And next time I come, I want it to be inside you, pet."

Zia's breath caught. He looked...

Well, she wasn't entirely sure how she ever thought he looked *stern*, almost emotionless. This Harlan looked like she'd torn him open, rearranged something vital inside him, and then sewed him back together again.

He looked... *soft*.

Her chest constricted. Seeing so much tenderness echoed in his dark eyes was almost too much for her to handle.

Zia lowered her gaze to where his lips rubbed against her

wound before she moved it back up to where her fingers were gently petting his hair. Following the origin of a lock of gray hair from his temple to his ear with her thumb, she whispered, "Agreed, Mr. Bounds."

Chapter Twelve

"I KNOW YOU CAN'T SPEND THE NIGHT, BUT MAYBE YOU could stay with me for a while? I mean, only if you want to, of course," Zia found herself suggesting a few hours later.

Dinner did eventually make its way into her stomach, though it took a while for them both to recover from their... interlude. Even then, Harlan was apparently reluctant to let go of her. She spent most of the evening sprawled in his lap, boneless, as he fed her bites of delicious food. He didn't seem to mind that there was a wet spot on his thigh from where he came, and she didn't either.

It made that drugging feeling of *power* all the stronger.

She did that. She made this powerful, fearsome being orgasm without so much as a touch. Was there anything more erotic than that?

But the night was ending. Her stomach was full, she was a tiny bit tipsy, and Harlan stood in the dark stoop of her cottage, his hair mussed and his eyes night-glow. At some point, he completely abandoned the braid.

Probably because she kept raking her fingers through it.

Zia didn't want to say goodbye. She craved more of that taste of closeness — if not from his fangs, then from the comfort of falling asleep in his arms.

She blinked, staring at the old thumb scanner by the door knob. In less than a week, he went from sensual boogeyman in the shadows to someone she desperately wanted to cuddle with.

Hold your horses, Zia. You don't even know if this man likes sharing a bed!

"I'll stay for as long as you want me to."

Her eyes flew back to his as her thumb met the scanner. Suddenly feeling shy, she backtracked, "It's okay. I don't mean to be pushy. I know you probably have stuff to do, so I wouldn't want you to waste your night."

There was a faint beep, and then Harlan reached around her to open the door. Instinctively, her magic reacted, bending the wards slightly to let him through.

She blinked again. *That's new.*

Normally she had to actively will the thick net of woven magic, anchored with advanced sigils on the house's walls, to bend. The only people her magic instinctively recognized as non-threatening were her immediate family. Everyone else rubbed up against her wards wrong, which was exactly their point. Strangers needed permission to enter.

Except Harlan, apparently.

"There is quite literally *nothing* I would rather be doing than spending time with you, Zia." To emphasize the point, he palmed the back of her neck and used his thumb to tilt her head back. Pressing a slow, skimming kiss to her lips, he murmured, "If I had my way, we'd be at the manor right now. I'd tie you to my bed and have my wicked way with you, pet. And then you'd *never* leave."

Pressing her palms against his chest, she teased, "Don't you think it's a little fast to be asking me to move in with you, Mr. Bounds?"

Slowly, he began to back her into the house. The fresh, earthy scent of all the greenery she so lovingly cultivated filled the air like a soft greeting. Her heels clicked on the cheap laminate of the entryway as the shadows closed in around them. She felt him reach back. A moment later, the door swung shut.

"You are *my* anchor. Living together is a given." He pressed a series of soft, seeking kisses to her lips, the corners of her mouth, and even the little dimple in her chin. "Your security and happiness is now my only concern, pet. When you move into the manor, I'll be able to spoil you every second of every day. More importantly, I'll know you're *safe* every second of every day."

Zia's mind was muddled by the kisses, by the hand roving over her waist to palm her backside, by the crisp, luxurious scent of him in her lungs, but still, she caught the words *security* and *safety.*

Greatly reluctant, she stalled his next kiss with a gentle press of her fingertips to his lips. Searching his expression in the shadows of the entryway, she said, "You told me that you worked for the Amauri family and the Syndicate for a long time. Is that why you're so... focused on security?"

She knew that the Syndicate was a sprawling network of wealthy vampiric families constantly at war with one another over whatever it was organized crime groups valued, but he told her he was retired. Besides, they were as far from the New Zone as people could get. She struggled to imagine any threat lasting more than a moment in the EVP. The elves wouldn't suffer any sort of organized crime in their territory.

...Right?

Perhaps it's just a vampire thing. Or maybe old habits, she thought, watching his jaw tense.

He stroked the swell of her cheek with his thumb before he took a step back. In an instant, that softness she had quickly become so fond of vanished like a puff of smoke. In its place was the inscrutable vampire who raised the hair on the back of her neck. "Go get changed into something comfortable."

"Why?"

He gave her hip a squeeze before he gently nudged her in the direction of her bedroom. "Because this is going to be a long conversation."

"Bossy," she muttered, without heat, as she crossed the short distance to her bedroom door.

The faintest amused huff reached her. "You'll get used to it."

Zia bit her lip, suppressing a smile. Even the low-burning unease in her belly couldn't stop the warmth that spread through her. She wasn't sure what it said about her that she liked his bossiness so much — who in their right mind found an inability to ask for things *charming?* — but she did.

Nonetheless, she was determined not to let him know that. If he suspected she was fond of his imperiousness, she had the suspicion that he would become utterly intolerable.

Not wanting to waste a second with him, she hurried to peel off her dress and ruined tights. The tights went into the tiny trash can in her bathroom, though she momentarily considered keeping them as an erotic momento.

That done, she pulled on a pair of stretch lounge pants, a comfortable sweater, and gave her face a good, hard scrub. Her curls were a mess, but at least her skin was flushed and her slightly smeared mascara nowhere to be seen.

Zia stood in the center of her bedroom for a moment, considering whether she should pretend, for a while longer, that she was more sophisticated and sexy than she was. Perhaps she could replace the sweater with something tighter? Maybe something with lace? The lounge pants would have to go, too, though she was at a loss as to what could possibly replace them. Her only other options were flannel pajama pants with schnauzers on them and *jeans.*

In the end, she forced the doubt and insecurity aside. For the gods sakes, the man had already put his tongue between her thighs. He had practically asked her to move in with him. What did she have to be self-conscious about? If he didn't think a woman could be desirable in comfy pants and a wool sweater, then he wasn't the man for her.

Tugging on a pair of fuzzy socks, she trotted back into the small living room to find Harlan seated on her couch. Her hundreds of houseplants — big and small, planted, purchased, rescued, and reclaimed — overflowed around him like a lush, living throne. He had turned one lamp on, casting him in a soft yellow glow, and sat in the way powerful men sometimes do: legs spread, one ankle propped on a knee, and arms stretched over the back of the couch.

He looked damn good.

As soon as she stepped into the room, his hungry gaze pinned her in place. A tiny smile curled his lips. Lifting his right hand off of the armrest, he curled two fingers in the air. "Come here, pet."

Her entire body flushed. There wasn't even a flicker of disappointment in his gaze. He wanted her just as much with her makeup scrubbed off and her fuzzy socks on as he did when she wore her best cocktail dress and heels.

Goddess, she thought, already walking, *he could ask me to jump off of a cliff and I'd probably do it.*

Her heart sped up with every step closer. When he planted both feet on the floor and reached for her, she felt it lurch in her chest, as if it was trying to reach him.

Harlan gathered her into his lap, arranging her so her legs were stretched over the cushions, and tucked her head under his chin. They were quiet for a long time. Zia listened to his steady breaths as he slowly stroked his knuckles up and down her spine.

Finally, he broke the silence. "I am not a good man, Zia."

She held her breath. Though a part of her wanted to explode with questions, she got the sense that he was working himself up to something, and she didn't want to interrupt him.

In his rich baritone, he haltingly continued, "I told you I worked for the Syndicate. I didn't tell you what I did. It's important that you know that before we... before we go any farther."

She curled her fingers into the lapel of his jacket. Whispering, she asked, "What did you do?"

"For nearly one hundred years, I was the best assassin in the

New Zone — the loyal hunting dog of the Amauri family. I killed, I maimed, I stole." Harlan threaded his fingers into her curls and gently pulled her head back, forcing her to look at him when he continued, "I am the most dangerous kind of criminal you can probably imagine, Zia, but if you choose me, you will have me on a string. There is not one being on this Earth who could defend you more fiercely than me."

She swallowed hard. In a hoarse voice, she said, "You told me you were retired."

Harlan's eyes darted about her face, as if he hoped to find something in her expression. "I am. I haven't accepted a contract in four years. The family let me go, and I made it clear that I wouldn't work for them ever again when I left."

"Did you *like* killing people?"

The lines around his eyes deepened. "No. It was a job — one I was trained for since the moment I could walk."

Relief helped soothe some of the nausea that climbed up the back of her throat. *Thank the gods.*

Zia was no fan of violence, and her stomach turned at the idea of someone being *paid* to take a life, but she was not completely naive. The UTA was a dangerous place. Even the EVP had its dark corners and shadowy deals. She knew that her brothers probably did things she would find morally repugnant in those secret labs, just as she knew that Harlan's life in the New Zone was something she probably couldn't comprehend.

It was a notoriously lawless territory. The Syndicate was the closest thing to a real government it had. She struggled to imagine what kind of brutality was necessary to keep control in a place full of exiles, criminals, and people desperate to disappear. It must have been particularly difficult when the people who *did* have enough power to do so were constantly at war with one another.

So though it disturbed her to imagine Harlan killing people — being the *best* at it, no less — Zia wasn't entirely surprised. She knew that it wasn't just his vampirism that made the hair on the back of her neck stand up.

Harlan was *dangerous*.

And deep in her subconscious, she knew that it was no small part of what drew her to him.

But more than that, Zia felt a bristling sort of indignation on his behalf.

She thought of the scars she'd seen. There were so many that she couldn't possibly count them at a glance: slash marks, bite wounds, and bolt holes. If he was trained to kill from the moment he could *walk*, it was no wonder he became the best — if he didn't, he would have *died*.

So while she was horrified to learn about his past, she wasn't selfless or morally upright enough to reject him because of it. Zia simply wanted him too much.

If he was waiting for her to freak out or run from him, Harlan was in for a surprise. Instead, she merely sucked in a shaky breath, let it out slowly, and then calmly asked, "Will you ever hurt me?"

His brows snapped down in a deep scowl. Claws pricked at her scalp. "No. Never. You are all that matters to me now."

"Do you plan on becoming an assassin again?" She peered at his face, her stomach clenching with unease. "I think I can be okay with your past, but not if there's death in your future, Harlan. I can't be part of that."

"I will kill to keep you safe," he replied, utterly immovable. "I will slaughter anyone who threatens you. I will defend what's mine, Zia, and I won't apologize for it. But no, I will not accept another contract. I never want to go back to that life."

Relief loosened her expression. "Is that why you're so focused on my security?"

Harlan shook his head. Leaning down to run the tip of his nose over the swell of her cheek, he quietly explained, "No one is supposed to retire from the Syndicate, pet. You live by it, you die by it. The fact that I successfully got out is... unheard of. It makes me a target for upstarts trying to make a name for themselves."

Zia slowly curled her arms around his neck. Tightening her hold until she could bury her face in his hair, she asked, "Make a name for themselves? Kind of like trying to take out an alpha so you can get a better place in the pack?"

"Yes, exactly." His voice dropped deeper, became colder, when he added, "And there are a few people from my past who would delight in putting a bolt between my eyes. *After* they made me suffer."

Zia shuddered. She pressed her nose into the curve of his neck and let out a soft sigh. *He's here. He's safe. No one can touch him.*

"That probably makes me a target too, doesn't it? If I'm important to you, then..."

"Yes." Harlan's arms tightened around her. "But I haven't seen a threat in over two years — and even if I had, there is not a chance anyone would hurt you."

Her lips curved against his skin. It was a shaky smile, though he couldn't see it. "Because you're the best assassin in the New Zone?"

"No." His voice was dark and full of promise when he murmured, "Because I'm *yours.*"

Harlan left just before sunrise, though it pained him to do so.

Each step he took away from her little home felt wrong, like he was stepping across the deck of a heaving ship.

His breathing sped up and cold sweat broke out across his chest and neck. Instinct demanded he turn right back around, barricade them in her bedroom, and sleep the day away with her locked in his arms. Maybe he'd bury his fangs in the soft flesh of her throat and keep them there for good measure.

It was too soon for that, though.

Not that Zia would mind. She had been shockingly accommodating to his needs — and his past — but some things took time. As his venom worked, she would gradually change sleep cycles, but until then, he could not ask her to waste her waking hours in bed with him.

Besides, he had arrangements to make. Things to buy. Safeguards to put in place.

Pulling onto the street, Harlan gritted his teeth and forced himself to drive back to the manor. His tension came through loud and clear when he put a call through to Atticus, who had gone back to the manor after following them from the restaurant.

Atticus's voice was smug when he said, "I assume things went well?"

"Shut up," Harlan growled.

A deep laugh rumbled over the line. Slyly, he asked, "Did you have a good dinner, boss? I noticed you looked a little... *disheveled* when you left."

"I should have left you on the street."

"Oh, sure, but then who would give you shit?"

Shaking his head, Harlan commanded, "I want round the clock guards on Zia and a full security set-up on her house. No fucking gaps. If Julius comes sniffing around, I want to know about it before he even gets a look at her."

Switching to a serious tone with ease, Atticus replied, "That's going to be tough to keep from her, boss."

"Not a problem. She agreed to it."

"Really?" Atticus sounded perplexed. "How the fuck d'you pull that one off?"

"I told her the truth. She didn't have a problem with it." Dryly, he added, "Believe me, you can't be more surprised than I am."

"Damn. Good for you, boss." A burst of air came through the car's speakers: a reluctant sigh. "Gotta say, though, it'd make things a lot safer if she was on the property. I'm bringing Adriana up here just in case the sonuvabitch starts looking for her again. Couldn't you convince Miss North to move in?"

Harlan swallowed as the roof of his mouth pulsed with a renewed ache. Gods, he felt like he could still taste her on his tongue — cunt and blood both. He felt full for the first time in a year, but paradoxically, his first taste of her only made his hunger *worse.*

She tasted like fucking ambrosia. Sweet and rich and thick, like deep, dark molasses on his palate. Her blood was the best he'd ever sampled, and her cunt...

Fuck me. There's no way I'm going to be able to sleep today.

If he had his way, she would be getting a daily dose of venom. Maybe even twice daily, so long as he didn't take too much at a time. It wouldn't take long at all for her sleep cycle to switch.

And once that happened, there would be nothing stopping him from weaving her into every part of his life.

Voice rough, he answered, "I'm working on it. But you're right to move Adriana back for a while. I was going to suggest the same thing. If he comes looking for me, he'll definitely go after her, too."

Julius's budding obsession with Adriana was one of the catalysts for their move out of the New Zone. Harlan had always wanted out, but the moment they discovered Atticus's little sister was venom neutral — the rarest of the rare, a vampire that could have children with another vampire — they knew they had to get out.

The old bastard was fanatical about vampirism and family legacy. If he could get his hands on someone like Adriana, all his fantasies of creating a *pure* vampiric dynasty would take a dangerous turn toward reality.

Neither Harlan nor Atticus would *ever* let him lay a hand on her, though. They had practically moved the heavens to get her out once. They'd do it again if they had to.

"No vulnerabilities," Atticus said, each word hard and sharp. "That's what we're supposed to live by. No exposed weaknesses. I knew I shouldn't have let her go off into the city by herself. It's too fucking dangerous."

"You can't keep her prisoner, Atticus," Harlan warned. It wasn't the first time, and it wouldn't be the last. It didn't matter that they hadn't breathed a word of her secret since they found out. There was always the possibility of discovery, and that drove Atticus wild with worry.

Harlan understood it, even though he knew it could inadvertently hurt Adriana. Clenching his fingers around the steering wheel, he grated, "We can't lock up the people we care about, but we can keep our family safe when a threat rears its ugly fucking head. So bring Adriana home and get some damn guards on my anchor, will you?"

"Not a question, boss." There was a rustling sound. A few seconds later, Atticus's voice came from slightly farther away. "Hey, Damien, Vince! Put down your fucking bottles. I have a new job for you."

CHAPTER THIRTEEN

ZIA WOKE UP THE NEXT MORNING FEELING... different.

Not massively, of course, but there were definitely a few things she noticed. Firstly, she slept past sunrise. That was unusual for her, but not altogether surprising considering she spent the better part of the night trying to stay awake with her vampire. It didn't *necessarily* mean that she was already shifting her sleep schedule to match his, but her stomach still did a giddy little flip at the thought.

The second thing she noticed was the ache in her thigh.

It wasn't terrible — like a charlie horse, maybe, or the strain of a muscle slightly over-used — but when she skimmed her fingers over the two small wounds, Zia was surprised to feel feverish heat radiating from her skin.

If she held very still, she thought she could feel her pulse beating there.

She lay in bed for a long time, her palm cupped around the bite mark, as she went over the events of the night again and again. It wasn't the same as if she woke up curled up next to him, but the heat against her palm made her *feel* like he was there. It captured just a tiny bit of that intimacy she craved.

Zia rubbed her thumb over the puncture wounds as she pressed her free hand against her chest. Her heart beat a quick rhythm. Magic popped and fizzled under her skin at the memory of Harlan's touch, his raw voice, the way he tucked her possessively against his chest as she finally succumbed to sleep.

Is it normal to want to bond with someone so soon?

Of course, she was getting to the age when most witches bonded with a partner — romantic or otherwise. Human bodies weren't adapted to process magic without significant degradation over time. For witches with a lot of power, a bond was an essential thing. It passed their magic through another being before cycling it back to the original host, nullifying the effects of magical overload.

Her parents had begun to worry about her finding a bondmate, but Zia hadn't been in a hurry. She was only a hundred years old and not so powerful as to be at risk of burnout, the overload of magic that fried witches from the inside out, anytime soon. She could wait for the right person to trust with her magic.

None of her boyfriends so far had so much as aroused even the thought of a bond, and Zia had always assumed that whoever she chose would be someone deeply steady, even *boring*. Who else would she trust with her magic? Her life?

Her breath hitched as she smoothed her palm over the soft skin of her thigh. Was it crazy that when she thought of her bondmate *now*, all she pictured was Harlan?

He was a criminal. An *assassin*. He was also twice her age and a vampire.

Absolutely none of those things were on her list for traits a good bondmate should have.

And yet she felt so acutely alone without him there beside her — her magic reaching and reaching with desperate hands for a being who was not there — that she could not lie to herself. This was not simply about the chemicals of attraction making her moon over her boss. It was about a fundamental, singular connection.

Whuff! Lot to process, she thought, forcing herself to sit up and reach for her phone. Plucking it off of the charging pad, she was pleased to see a message from Harlan waiting for her.

Mr. Bounds - 6:01 AM: I am picking you up at seven tonight. Dress warm.

Mr. Bounds - 6:02 AM: On second thought, don't get dressed until I get there.

Mr. Bounds - 6:03 AM: Also, there are guards stationed around your property now. Let me know if they bother you.

Zia gnawed on her lower lip. The socially awkward part of her hollered at her to keep her cool, to play some sort of normal, casually sophisticated woman he might be used to. But who was she kidding? He knew she was a dork already.

Decided, she released her bruised lip with a determined grunt. *Screw cool.* Hoping that he might still be awake, she shot him a reply.

Zia - 6:35 AM: Thank you for the heads up about the guards. I'll tell you if I can't deal with them.

Zia - 6:36 AM: I can't wait to see you tonight.

Drawing on that heady sense of power she so briefly savored, Zia dared to send one more message.

Zia - 6:38 AM: P.S. Do panties count as getting dressed?

Cheeks flushing at her own audacity, she hastily tossed her phone onto the bed and swung her legs out from under the covers. Her toes curled against the thin carpet as she trotted down the hall to her small bathroom.

Running through her morning routine on autopilot, she tried very hard not to think of her phone, or her vampire, or her date tonight, or the pretty little wound that decorated her inner thigh. She tried.

By the time she made it back into her bedroom and managed to pull on some comfortable weekend lounge clothes, she was all but vibrating with the need to check her phone. Her heart jammed itself into her throat as she reached for it.

He's probably asleep, she tried to warn herself. *Don't get your hopes up. You probably won't hear from him until—*

Zia squeaked and nearly threw the damn thing when it began to vibrate in her hand. Fumbling with it, she managed to flip it over to see *Mr. Bounds - INCOMING CALL* flashing across the screen.

Before she could over-analyze or freak out, she hit the button. Too late, she realized it was a video call.

Zia stared at the image on the screen with her lips parted. Harlan was clearly laying in bed, the screen barely enough to illuminate the hard angles of his face, the lines of his upper body and long, black hair spilled across a jewel green pillow. His eyes were half-lidded, their night-glow translated strangely through the lens of the camera.

"Good morning, my Zia," he rasped, lips curling into a devastating smile.

He knocked the wind right out of her. Zia's knees turned to water, forcing her to sit down on the edge of her bed with a small *oof!* "Good morning," she wheezed.

Harlan, the bastard, stretched one arm back and under his head, showing off slopes of thick muscle covered in reddish-brown skin. "How are you feeling today?"

"I..." Zia had to swallow before she could get more than that one syllable out. "I feel a little tired. But mostly good."

He wasn't an easy man to read by any stretch of the imagination, but she liked to think that she was quickly getting better at it. There was a definite light of satisfaction in his gaze when said, "That's normal. The first bite can be intense, and some anchors react more strongly than others." His tone turned wry when he added, "You got a large dose of venom last night, too. I'm sure that's a part of it."

A small, uncomfortable feeling wormed its way through the warmth in her chest. Before she could think to censor herself, she asked, "Have you had a lot of anchors?"

She watched him blink slowly. His lashes, dense and curly like a cow's, fanned over his cheekbones before they lifted again. "I've bitten a few others," he admitted, expression unreadable.

Zia held her breath. Below the sight of the camera, she curled her fingers into her duvet cover. *Right, of course.*

How could she expect him not to have bitten anyone else? The man was a vampire. It was in his very nature. She could understand that even when she felt some of her confidence shrivel up at the thought.

In the space between heartbeats, a new thought dug its claws into her: *If he's had anchors before, how long will it be before he finds another one?*

She felt the blood drain from her face, though she did her best to keep her expression blank. It was fine if he wanted multiple partners, of course, but she needed to know before she got in too deep. Certainly she needed to know before she went and bonded with the man. She had no moral scruples against having multiple partners, but it wasn't for her.

She wanted to be more than just one of many. She wanted to be someone's *only.*

And, she now recalled, he said he wanted something *permanent.* Not *monogamous.*

"Zia?"

She blinked. Her eyes focused back on the screen to find Harlan sitting up, his brow deeply furrowed and his jaw tense.

"Sorry!" She tried to laugh the uneasy moment off. "I got lost in thought for a second."

"You are upset."

"I'm not upset," she protested.

There was something strangely comforting about watching him lift his lip to bare his fangs. He made that clicking noise again — that distinctly vampiric sound of annoyance that shouldn't have warmed her heart and yet did so anyway. He looked fierce and more than a little scary, but she *liked* that about him.

Harlan's camera moved as he sat up completely. For a moment, all she saw was long hair, a darkened room, and the slope of a bare shoulder. "I'm coming over there."

Zia made a small gurgling sound of panic. "No! Harlan, the sun is up! You'll get hurt!"

"It's not the first time I've had a sunburn, Miss North," he rumbled mulishly. "You are upset. I'm coming to you. *Now.*"

"No, you're not." She ran her fingers through her tangled, frizzy curls and let out a hard sigh. "If I tell you what bothered me, will you *please* lay back down? I'll start crying if you get hurt, Harlan. It'll make me so mad I might not even let you in!"

His face came back into view with dizzying speed. His expression was brutal, just on the edge of panicked, when he commanded, "You will *not.*"

"I will!"

He gnashed his fangs. "This would not be a problem if you were here," he muttered, vexed in the way that men who usually get everything they want tend to be when told *no.* "Tell me what upset you, Zia."

Queasiness settled in her stomach. She looked down at her lap and tried not to feel the low pulsing in her thigh, nor his gaze as it pierced her through the lens of his camera. "I... was just surprised that you had other anchors. I shouldn't have assumed, obviously, but I— Well, I did, and it made me wonder about what kind of relationship you're looking for. It's okay if you're looking for something casual, or..." She swallowed. "Multiple partners. But I need to know that before we go any further."

There. The big, grown-up, mature words were out. Now she just had to endure the consequences they came with.

"Pet, look at me."

Zia forced her eyes up. Her stomach rolled with nerves. When she looked at the screen, every muscle tensed, her fight or flight instincts immediately prickling to life. Harlan stared back at her with a look so fierce, it transformed his face into something savage.

His words came out clearly, concisely. It was as if he worried she would misunderstand him if the gaps between them were too short, or if the syllables rolled too quickly off of the tongue. "I said I had bitten others before, *not* that I had other anchors. They are not one and the same. Anchors are... special. They take time, effort. They are a gift. Most vampires only have the one — though there are always exceptions, or those who choose multiple partners."

He shook his head with a small grimace. "I have never had an anchor before you, Zia. I've never wanted one. Not until you. And I'm not the kind of man who shares well. I won't take another."

Relief was a wash of warmth through her, whisking away all that sour doubt. Still, she had to ask, "So you're serious about this being a... forever kind of thing?"

Harlan's expression darkened. "Yes, pet. This is a *forever kind of thing.*"

Zia let out a shaky laugh. "Oh, good. That's good. Okay. Yes. Good."

A question about how he felt about being witchbonded danced on the tip of her tongue, but she chickened out at the last second. There was only so much mature conversation she could handle in a day. Besides, she wanted to bask in the glow of this news before she broached another fraught topic.

Before Harlan could say anything, she plowed ahead. "You should probably get to sleep, right? You must be tired."

The look on his face wasn't exactly encouraging, but he did eventually sigh and lay back down. "Lay with me for a moment, pet."

She didn't have to think about it. Zia leaned back until she was flat on her bed, her legs dangling off of the edge. With the strategic use of a pillow, she managed to prop up her phone so he could see her when she turned on her side.

"Better?" she asked, drinking in the sight of her vampire lounging in his pillows.

"Better would have you here in my bed with me," he answered. "But this will do for now."

Zia tucked her hands under her cheek and bit her lip. That didn't stop her grin from spreading, though.

Harlan's expression softened, though a hungry light flared hotter in his gaze. "Tell me you can still feel me, pet. I can't rest without knowing you'll think of me today."

Reflexively, she lifted her right leg, drawing it up so her foot was planted on the mattress. Her wound gave a particularly sharp ache at the movement. Shyly, she answered, "I feel you. The bite's a little sore and... kind of hot. Like I've got a fever right there."

She watched the muscles of his throat move as he swallowed. A different kind of ache, hot and needy, began to pulse between her thighs when his tongue snaked out to trace his lips and the tips of his fangs.

"Show me, pet."

Goodness gracious gods in the sky. Zia felt a self-conscious fluttering in her stomach as she shifted onto her back to wiggle out of her yoga pants. She forcefully pushed it aside. It wasn't like he hadn't already seen the most intimate parts of her. There was nothing to be ashamed of. Besides, at least this time she had panties on.

It did feel strangely intimate, though, when she turned back onto her side and lifted her leg again. She nudged her phone a little bit, changing the angle to give him a better view of her thigh.

His sharply in-drawn breath came through the speakers of her phone like a bolt gun shot.

"Now that's a fucking sight," he murmured. "Look at how lovely your thigh looks with my bite, my bruises."

Zia bit back a whimper.

Harlan's gaze was locked on his bite, utterly focused and unblinking, even as his hand slid down and out of sight. Her breathing sped up. Gods, was he really— Yes. Yes, he was. She could see the way the scarred planes of his chest and shoulders flexed and relaxed with each slow stroke of his hand.

"Tell me where you want my bite next, pet," he demanded.

She wasn't quite brave enough to touch herself in front of him yet, but the power she felt *watching* him was... gods, there was nothing quite like it. Once more, Zia felt like she held the reins to a being of unimaginable strength — silly little Zia, who held this deadly man's desire in the palm of her hands.

The need to see how far she could push him asserted itself. It wasn't her nature to be bold, but for *this*...

Zia drifted her hand up her thigh to gently stroke the bloom of bruises around the puncture wounds. The slice of his fangs didn't cause them, she knew, but rather the suction of his tongue as he drew from her burst those tiny blood vessels just under the skin. It was something like a very large hickey.

"I'm not sure," she answered him, fingers stroking back and forth over the heated flesh. "I liked this one so much, I almost can't imagine it anywhere else." She paused, attention fixed on the way his shoulders moved, how his expression tightened with each rough stroke. In the silence, she could hear the soft sounds of flesh on flesh. Her mind whirred with the possibility of what he looked like. She was somehow more tantalized by *not* seeing his cock than she would be if it was smack in the middle of the screen.

Moving her gaze back to his face, she murmured, "Maybe it doesn't matter. Maybe I just want to see your bite *everywhere.*"

"Fuck." Harlan bared his fangs in a ferocious display. A shot of adrenaline coursed through her veins, giving her arousal a tang of something thrilling, *dangerous.*

"I'm going to mark up every inch of you," he promised, breathing hard. "I'm going to fucking fill you with every drop of venom I have, pet. You're fucking *mine.*"

Because Zia was feeling dangerous and powerful and in control, she bit her lip and pressed the edge of her thumbnail into one of the puncture wounds. It hurt far, far more than it did when he punctured her skin, but the pain was worth it when she saw Harlan's lips part and his eyes widen.

A single drop of blood made a hair-thin trail down the slope of her thigh, drawn down toward her cunt by gravity and the contours of her flesh. When it hit the edge of her white cotton panties, a vivid red stain bloomed.

In an instant, Harlan went from astonished to feral. His strokes became too fast for her to follow as he lifted his lip in a snarl that would have sent most beings running. His eyes, normally hard to read, were wide and white around the edges. They were wild with hunger.

Zia gasped. Her hand dropped to her cunt as her need became an unbearable ache. The wound pulsed hard, almost as fast as Harlan's furious pumping fist, as she roughly touched herself through the soaked, bloody material of her panties.

Her orgasm came on fast and hard, mingling with the pain of her wound and the hot exhilaration that came with power. Distantly, she thought she heard Harlan panting her name again and again, his voice so guttural it was almost impossible to understand, until he grunted sharply.

When she cracked her eyes open, she found him sprawled against his pillows, his head thrown back and his chest and throat gleaming with a thin sheen of sweat she wanted to lick and lick and *lick*.

"Harlan," she whispered, husky and out of breath. Gods, she wanted him more now than when they started. It was like she couldn't get enough of him, and every little taste only made the craving worse. Was that the venom talking, or was it just... them?

He kept his eyes closed when he said, "Those panties belong to me, pet."

Somehow, *that* was what made her blush to the roots of her hair. "Oh, I don't know—"

"They're *mine.*" He opened his eyes to fix her with a look so purely possessive, it made everything in her go soft. "I'll take them tonight after I get my fill of you."

She shuddered. Somehow, she managed to reply, "So I guess that answers the question of what I should wear when you pick me up, huh?"

"Pet, the only panties you should have on you are the ones you hand me when I get there."

CHAPTER FOURTEEN

HARLAN HADN'T FELT SO TIGHTLY COILED SINCE HIS first kill.

The act itself held no pleasure, but the *hunt,* that first thrilling dance between life and death, had marked him. Even as he began to loathe the business of coldblooded murder, his nature would always crave the chase.

He usually satisfied the craving with money. It seemed to activate the same part of his brain, however briefly, when he acquired something rare and precious. The hoarding of beautiful things was its own sort of thrill, after all. The manor was one such acquisition. His cars were another. Even the odds and ends in his kitchen cabinets satisfied a small part of that hungry beast who lived in his breast.

But that feeling paled in comparison to the roaring urges propelling him toward Zia's home.

The engine had barely turned off when he threw himself out of the car. His long legs ate up the thin gravel of her driveway. The sun, tinged orange and still far, far too bright for him, seared his skin with warning.

Sunset had only just begun, but he couldn't wait any longer.

He barely slept. All day he checked his phone, obsessively

scanning his notifications for signs of trouble, updates on the Amauri situation, or that she'd left her home. He hoped to see a message or two from her, too, but his sweet little witch left him in agonized silence. She probably thought she would disturb him if she messaged him during the day, but the opposite was true.

Going without the sound of her voice, even just seeing words on a screen written by her hand, made him feel increasingly uneasy.

Harlan had lost track of the number of times he checked in with the guards stationed around her home. He'd also stopped counting how many times he replayed the memory of that single drop of blood sliding down her supple thigh.

He was sleep deprived. He was hard as fucking granite. He was *hungry*.

It didn't matter that he was over an hour early for their date. He pounded on the door anyway.

The sun's weakened rays still hurt him, but he barely noticed the sting as he waited, breath held, for Zia to open the door. Though it hurt something fierce, he was too old to be at risk of dying in the weak light of sunset. Only babies and the sickly could be killed by exposure to the sun.

Not that it would stop him even if that wasn't the case, of course. Not even death could keep him away from his anchor.

Either she needs to move in or I need to pack a fucking bag, he thought, claws biting into the door jamb. *I can't live like this.*

And she thought he might want someone else in the future? The fact that the thought had even crossed her mind made him balk. He could barely *function* for wanting her. He had thought of her every day for a year. He was so consumed by her, he couldn't tell up from down anymore.

He wasn't sure if it took longer for her to answer the door than he anticipated or if it was time stretching like toffee in his mind, his perception made elastic by the bite of pain and relentless desire.

The door swung open.

It took him a breathless moment to understand what he was seeing: Zia, standing in nothing but a fluffy pink towel, her wet curls coiled over her olive toned shoulders, her cheeks flushed and expression slack with surprise.

"Harlan!" she squeaked, one hand curled around the top edge of her towel. "What are you doing here? You weren't supposed to pick me up for another..." Her eyes darted over his shoulder, taking in the angle of the sun, before she let out a horrified screech. The hand that had been loosely wrapped around the door knob fisted in his lapel.

He let her yank him over the threshold. The door slammed shut behind him.

Warm hands cupped his cheeks. Zia's eyes were huge as she arched onto her tiptoes to peer into his face. "Your skin is all pink! What are you doing here so ea— *Ah!*"

He clasped his hands around the sides of her neck, tilted her head back, and brought his mouth down to deliver a bruising kiss.

His anchor — so sweet, so giving — melted into him without so much as a flicker of resistance. Her fingers dug into his chest, clinging to his crisp dress shirt, as he slid his tongue against hers, tasting her with a desperation that might have humiliated him a year ago.

She made a needy sound that drove him even wilder. Hunger cramped his stomach even as his cock strained against his slacks. Venom gathered in the roots of his fangs, in the gland that gave him so much damn trouble, to press hard against the nerves around his teeth. It wanted *out*.

He should have forced some synthblood down his gullet before he came. Maybe if he had, he wouldn't want to devour his anchor quite so much. Maybe he wouldn't tear off her damp towel and palm her lush, full breast with a grip that bordered on bruising. Maybe he would be gentler when he walked her backwards, down the hall, and into her bedroom.

But probably not.

Fragrant steam billowed out from the open bathroom door to

perfume the air of the hallway and the bedroom. He inhaled deeply as he pressed her back onto the bed. *Sweet and earthy.* It lingered on his tongue; the taste of everything he wanted and more than he deserved.

Zia clutched at him when he stood up, a soft mew of protest escaping her throat as her hands skated down his chest. Harlan gave her thighs a soothing stroke before he curled his fingers around her knees and pushed her legs up and out.

His breath left him on a long, pained groan when he caught sight of the mark he'd left. The twin puncture wounds were framed by a swirl of soft purple bruises — like a blooming rose hovering just beneath her skin.

"My pretty anchor," he grated, tearing at his shirt, his belt, his slacks. His eyes bounced from Zia's flushed face to the soft swells of her breasts to her glistening cunt and back to his bite in a dizzying circle. Gods, he wanted to see all of her at once, to worship every inch of her for as long as he could.

He was gratified to see Zia watched him just as greedily. Her eyes slid over his naked skin, taking in his patchwork of scars, many of which he earned before he was even a man, until they landed on his cock. She tensed, fingers flexing in the duvet until her knuckles turned white, and then melted again. Her legs fell open a fraction wider as her breathing sped up.

"Harlan," she whispered, trepidation and awe giving her voice a husky quality, "are you going to put that monster inside of me?"

Gods willing. He dropped a hand to give himself a hard squeeze. The night before, just the taste of her blood had been enough to make him come. That would not be happening tonight. He had to be in control. He had to be *patient.*

His voice came out like cut glass when he answered, "Yes. You're going to take it, and everything else I give you, pet."

Zia's lower lip trembled when she sucked in a breath. "Are you going to bite me when you do?"

Fuck.

Harlan squeezed again. His cock didn't give a shit about the

almost painful pressure of his fingers, though. Pleasure streaked
down his spine as sweat broke out over his chest and back. "Yes,"
he answered again. "I'm going to fuck you. I'm going to bite you.
I'm going to fucking *gorge* myself on you. And then you'll get
dressed and you'll let me spoil you."

Her heart raced. The beat pounded in his ears, loud enough
to drown out good sense and raise the monster that lurked in his
soul. Harlan's lip lifted in a snarl, showing her the twin blades
he'd use to feast on her until he couldn't take another drop.

A flicker of naked fear passed through her expression. It was
stark, animalistic — the kind he'd seen in the eyes of so many
people just before he pulled the trigger, or sliced through flesh.

That fear might have stopped him then and there, if only Zia's
hand hadn't crept down to slowly slide her fingers through her
reddened skin, slick and plump with her arousal. Her confession
from the previous night rang in his ears.

It's like I want you to scare me.

His soft little anchor got off on being afraid. If the gods were
kind, she would love a touch of pain, too.

Harlan firmly brushed aside her glistening fingers. Keeping his
eyes locked on her expression, paying attention to even the
slightest shift there, he used one hand to gently spread her.
"This," he explained, "is mine now. All of you belongs to me. Do
you understand?"

Zia bit her lip and nodded, her hips tipping upward, seeking
more.

He clicked his tongue against his fangs. "I'll hear it, pet."

It was riveting, watching his witch flush from chest to hair-
line. Zia squirmed under his unyielding stare. "I... I..."

Her voice trailed off with a small moan when he trailed the tip
of his thumb's claw down to her entrance. He pressed the pad of
his thumb there, savoring the heat and slickness that greeted him.

"Do you understand that you're *mine?*"

Again, she hesitated, giving him the perfect excuse to test
another boundary. Rumbling low in his chest, Harlan gave her no

warning before he brought the tips of his fingers down onto her sensitive flesh. One quick, stinging slap.

Zia nearly bolted upright. A cry tore out of her throat. Her flush darkened as her hips moved under his hand, rolling hard. "I understand!"

A little fear and a little pain, he thought, astonished at his luck. *My perfect anchor. I'm never letting you go.*

"Good, pet," he murmured, soothing away the sting with delicate, teasing touches. She whimpered, thighs trembling, when he bent down to lick a path down her neck to her breasts. "Rule number one, sweet little anchor, is *always* do as I say."

Zia's thighs spasmed. "There... there are *rules?*"

"Yes, pet." He breathed against the taut skin of her nipple. "Do you like rules?"

There was not even a moment of hesitation before she answered, "I *love* rules."

Of course his witch loved rules. It was practically plastered over her forehead and across every record he found. No one who never even missed a *day* of college hated rules.

It was a good thing he loved to make them.

Harlan gently swept his tongue around her nipple, tasting freshwater and a hint of salt from her skin, before he murmured, "Rule number two, then, is to always tell me when you don't like something. I can't spoil you if you're uncomfortable. Understood?"

Zia arched her back, thrusting her breasts closer to his mouth. "Yes. Understood. Definitely."

He gave her a swift, appreciative nip with his fangs. "That's my pretty anchor. So good for me, aren't you?"

She made a needy noise. *"Gods,* I hope so."

He whispered things against her skin: confessions, hopes for their future, how godsdamned lucky he was to have an anchor such as her, and how he'd dreamed of fucking her every time he closed his eyes. All the while, he situated himself against her and slowly rocked his hips, the underside of his cock sliding against her with teasing pressure.

His breath exploded out of him when he felt how wet she was, how smoothly he glided. She was soft and wet and hot and *perfect.* The scent of her desire coated the inside of his mouth, his throat, and made frenzied need pop and crackle in his veins.

Harlan jerked his hips, skin slapping against skin, and felt the pressure build in the base of his spine. His own scent, sharp and barely present under the velvety weight of hers, warned him that soon it would not just be pre-come and her arousal slicking his way.

Zia canted her hips up, desperate to meet him, as he ran his tongue around a dark pink nipple. His palms kneaded her thighs, her sides, the soft skin of her tanned arms. There was not a single part of her lush body he disliked. Every bow of muscle, every elegantly shaped bone and taut sinew was erotic, precious in the extreme.

There was only one Zia in this world, and he loved every fucking bit of her.

Harlan released one well-loved nipple with an obscene *pop!* Looking up at her from under his lashes, he grated, "Do you want my venom, pet?"

She was breathing hard and her eyes were glazed, but her answer was strong. *"Yes."*

"Do you want my cock?"

Warm hands smoothed over his shoulders and upward to tangle themselves in his long hair. He let her draw him up until their lips hovered over one another, barely a breath apart. Speaking against his mouth, Zia answered, "Baby, I want everything you have to give me."

Harlan traced her bottom lip with the tip of his tongue, dipping in just enough to taste, before he pulled back. His hair fell around them like a waterfall of gray-streaked silk. Rising up on one hand, he used the other to position himself as he stared down at the center of his world.

Neither blinked or even breathed when he entered her.

Fuck.

She was tight as a fucking glove. A part of him winced, wishing he'd filed his claws so he could have prepared her better, but a larger part of him was savagely pleased by the idea that he was her singular focus, the source of both pain and pleasure.

Besides, he couldn't feel too bad when she looked at him like *that.*

Harlan took in the expression of exhilaration on her face, the way her lips parted and her eyes widened, and asked, "Does it hurt, pet?"

"Yes," she answered. Her chest moved with each deep inhale. Sweat gleamed in the golden light that snuck under her curtains. Her fingernails bit into his ass, trying to force him forward.

She licked her lips. "It hurts and I *love* it."

"Made..." He sank in another inch. "For..." Another. *"Me."* With one sharp thrust, he was seated firmly inside her.

Zia made a high pitched sound and threw her head back. Her spine locked as tension rippled through her. Knowing instinctively what she wanted, what she *needed* from him, Harlan didn't wait for her to adjust. Bracing himself on his elbows, he lowered his mouth to her throat and scraped his fangs against the sweat-slicked skin there.

The moment blood started to well from the tiny scratches, he began to thrust. Hard.

She bucked under him, a wild moan echoing off of the walls of her tiny bedroom, as he sucked at the little droplets. Her flavor burst across his tongue — sweet and earthy like the scent of dried grass, with the richness of fine wine. *Perfect.*

Her fingernails dragged up his back and dug in. *"Harlan!"*

He set a bruising pace. There was no softness in this, no delicacy or uncertainty. His anchor wanted all of him, so he gave her *all* of him. When he reached down to slide one hand under her back, angling her hips up, he gave her even more. He plunged deeper, faster, until he knew that each thrust edged closer to pain than pleasure.

Each brutal stroke made a luscious sound: wet skin meeting wet skin, the explosion of breaths over swollen lips, the stutter of a heart doing its best to keep up, the soft cries of his anchor as he hit just the right spot again and again and again.

When her back began to arch, Zia shoved a hand between their sweaty bodies and began to stroke herself. The scent of magic was thick in the air — like blood and green things, like Zia and something *more*. It bubbled between them until he felt like it was trying to press itself into his very pores.

It sought him out, coiled around him, *held* him. It felt... proprietary.

Desperate for her, Harlan reached back instinctively. But the magic was elusive, slipping out of his grasp like smoke the moment he touched it with his own. It danced around him, egging him on.

Zia's moan was ragged. Her hips rocked out of sync with his, moving as fast as they could as she chased her orgasm.

It took everything in his power to not let his own release overtake him as she began to tense, her muscles rippling around his cock. Only when she jolted, her body locked under his, did Harlan finally let himself go.

His hips moved on their own with a jagged, animalistic rhythm as he gathered a fistful of her wet curls, jerked her head to one side, and plunged his fangs into the fragrant skin of her throat.

His orgasm was *shattering*.

Lights danced in front of his eyes as his venom ejected from his fangs and into her bloodstream. In the same instant, he drove himself as deep as he could and came, painting the hot walls of her cunt with his release.

Euphoria wiped out everything but her.

He was not aware of his own body, of the sounds of the birds outside or the warmth of the room. All he knew was the ecstasy of emptying his venom into her bloodstream, sweetening it for him, and the thundering beat of her heart. He knew her breath, her scent, the soft, drugged sounds she made as she went limp. He knew only *her.*

When there was no more ache in the roof of his mouth, Harlan gently extracted his fangs. Slowly, he ground his semi-hard cock into her as he began to suck at the wound, pulling and pulling.

By design, a vampire's stomach could not hold enough blood to threaten the life of a grown adult anchor. He could gorge himself as much as he was able to and Zia would not feel more than a momentary wooziness when she stood.

But he didn't plan on letting her stand any time soon. He indulged himself, relishing the rich taste of her and the feeling of being *full* for the first time in a year.

His muscles relaxed and a content rumble made its way out of his chest as he sipped from her. Zia's hands drifted down his back, petting him, as she murmured sweet things into his hair. His hips flexed. One of his hands moved between them to circle her clitoris, matching the pace of his deep, blissful pulls.

Eventually, he was able to coax another short, intense orgasm out of her. When Zia went slack under him, he felt the telltale tingle behind his jaw that told him he was full. Instinct took over, shifting gears from the drive to drink to the need to look after his anchor.

The taste in his mouth changed as his saliva did — no longer the sharp, cloying flavor of his venom as it mixed with her blood, but the mellower notes that came with the compounds in his salivary glands.

Those compounds stopped bleeding, working to do the opposite of what the venom accomplished, and helped the wounds heal faster.

Harlan licked the twin puncture marks even after the bleeding stopped. Instinct was a low, satisfied purr in the back of his mind, urging him to stroke her, to kiss her, to make sure she was comfortable and sweetly sated. Aftercare for an anchor was biologically hardwired into all vampires. He couldn't have gotten up and left Zia even if he *wanted* to.

Slowly, he worked his way up her throat and over her jaw. When their lips met, their kiss was slow, deep, and luscious. Zia's arms curled around his neck as he hugged her close. For a while, they just breathed each other's air and basked in the closeness.

"Are you all right?" he whispered into her damp hair.

"I'm *great,*" she answered. She sounded almost drunk, but in such a smug, satisfied way, he found it deeply charming. "Better than great. I just had the best sex of my damn life."

Harlan grinned. He was full, warm, and holding his anchor. The hungry, violent little boy he'd been would have marveled at the man he had become.

He used to envy the wealthy. He used to make promises to himself that one day he would not feel like he was below them, and that he too would have beautiful things to wear, to collect. He would never be hungry, or forced to sleep outside, or beaten by the older boys in training again.

But no envy came close to what he felt when he saw people in love. Families. The boy he once was could not have cried for his losses, but he felt the pain anyway.

Now, though, Harlan did not feel pain. He was, perhaps for the first time in his life, entirely content. How lucky he was, that boy would have thought, to have someone as soft and gentle as their Zia.

After several long, blissful minutes, she dragged her lips over his cheek to whisper playfully in his ear, "So, do you still want those panties, or..."

Chapter Fifteen

In what felt like the blink of an eye, Zia's life bloomed with rich color.

As the weather grew colder and the ground harder, she and her vampire became nearly inseparable. It was not casual. It wasn't even really *dating*. It was the meshing of two lives that, though previously entirely unrelated to one another, were nevertheless made to be one.

Nights blended into days and weeks into months. He was a rock in her life; dropped into her lazy, drifting stream, Harlan provided her a stability she didn't even know she was missing. In turn, she began to wash away decades of quietly internalized self-reproach and doubt. Warmth blazed between them, and a bond that was one part friendship and one part roaring desire tied their souls together with ever-tightening knots.

It wasn't all lazy nights in bed, whispering soft secrets under the sheets, nor drugging kisses by the koi pond, though. True to his promise to give her anything she wanted, Harlan went above and beyond simply *dating*.

They went to incredible private concerts in Sacramento. He took her to five star restaurants and long shopping trips to plant shops. They spent a very memorable weekend in a spa and inn on the rugged coast by the city of Monterey, where he treated her to an after-hours, private viewing of one of the world's most incredible aquariums. Incredibly, the fact that they had sex by the moon jelly fish tank wasn't even the most memorable part of *that* particular trip.

Much to her delight, he showered her with thoughtful gifts constantly — a new workbench in the greenhouse, a set of silk pajamas, custom work boots with roses embroidered on the sides, an orchid imported from Indonesia, and even handmade pruning shears from Japan. This was all after she discovered a set of outrageously expensive diamond earrings, bracelet, and necklace waiting for her on the passenger's seat of his car the night they made love for the first time.

That particular gift flustered her so much that she only wore them at home. He was fine with that, saying, "I prefer to see you wear diamonds when you're naked, anyway."

Zia discovered that Harlan had a dry humor, and although he was not the most smiley man, he loved to trade barbs with Caldwell and gently tease her at every opportunity. He was also surprisingly chatty in his own somber, intense way. They spent hours talking on the phone when one or the other should be sleeping. Harlan peppered her with questions about her comparatively boring life, while Zia delicately probed at his bloody past.

He didn't like to go into details, but she got enough to realize that her vampire had lived a very, very hard life. It was no wonder he coveted beautiful things, when he'd spent half his life hungry, beaten, or sleeping the day away on filthy floors.

And that was when he was lucky. Apparently the man responsible for raising him, Julius Amauri, usually just told him to sleep outside.

He didn't want her pity, so Zia did not give it to him. What she *could* give was patience when he overstepped a boundary, or when he went full throttle on the protectiveness. She didn't give in to everything, but she tried to be understanding when conflict arose.

Overall, there was precious little to complain about. Her days shortened. Her nights grew longer, fuller. Her hunger for Harlan deepened with every bite he took, and her affection sweetened into something rich and nuanced with every word they exchanged.

With the way they couldn't get enough of one another, it didn't take long for his venom to take. Within two weeks, she was sleeping during the day and waking up just as the sun began to set. It was an adjustment, certainly. There was even a flare of panic as she walked out into the rose garden at night for the first time since that fateful night in October.

Questions swirled as she stood at the top of the brick stairs and stared down at the dark garden below. *Is this worth giving up the sunshine? The way I've lived my life for one hundred years? No more feeling the sun on my back when I dig in the dirt? No more light shining through rose petals as I prune?*

Harlan assured her that there was still time to turn back. The change took a while to become permanent. Theoretically, she could go back to the way her life was before. She'd since learned that venom withdrawal was an awful thing, but she would survive it.

The heartbreak was another story.

Zia knew she had already made her choice. The moment she felt her magic reach for him, there was no turning back.

And, she quickly realized, working at night wasn't so bad. Her fear of the dark lessened as her eyes adjusted to the venom, giving her better night vision, though she did still require *some* light. She could see perfectly fine with the lights Harlan installed. Most importantly, her plants reacted to her the same as they did before, reaching up through the soil to meet her magic with the same ready affection.

Besides, if she ever really *needed* to, she could stay up late and walk in the sun again. She wasn't harmed by the light like he was. A pair of good sunglasses and an energy drink would get her through a day in the sun.

Not so bad when I get Harlan in exchange, I think.

There was, of course, the added benefit that now her vampire could visit her during her hours in the garden.

It wasn't an easy change, nor a thoughtless one, but it was one she was willing to make. What was the sun compared to the way he looked at her?

Nothing.

Harlan made her feel special. To him, she was not silly Zia, little sister to five talented older brothers, underachiever and consummate crybaby. She was sensual and interesting and important.

He said she would be the center of his world, and Zia was slowly coming to understand exactly what that meant.

Her vampiric shadow rarely left her side. The only time he went off on his own was when he needed to have meetings with some of his business partners — people who rented out the buildings he owned, or those who were looking for investments. She learned he had sprawling interests, and he liked to dabble in all sorts of businesses mostly for the fun of it. She was delighted to learn that it wasn't all real estate and shares and other nonsense.

The man owned a *bakery!*

The news tickled her so much, Harlan was forced to bundle her into one of his cars and drive her all the way to Auburn, a town about an hour away from the estate, to give her a tour. And a taste of the goods, of course.

That night, as with every date and errand they did together, they were accompanied by a small fleet of Harlan's guards.

It was jarring at first, but as October passed into November, Zia simply got used to it. This was helped along by the fact that Caldwell — *Atticus,* he insisted — had also become a fixture in her life. Like Harlan, he wasn't nearly as stern as she initially thought he was.

Atticus had a mischievous sense of humor, and he delighted in poking at Harlan until he growled something scary. It was clear from the moment she first spent time with them together that they had an enormous amount of love between them. It was also clear that for all that Atticus was less impassive than Harlan, there was no missing the fact that he was raised by him.

They stood the same way. They spoke with a similar cadence. They even gave her the same eyebrow arch when she said something they found particularly outrageous.

They were father and son. Seeing that bond helped ease some of the cold ache she felt when she thought of Harlan's life before their paths crossed. For all the horrible things he went through, at least he had family.

When Atticus brought his sister, Adriana, up to stay with him for a while, Zia was pleased to discover that she, too, was lovely. Even though Adriana was unhappy about her temporary relocation from San Francisco, they got along instantly.

Gone were the lonely days in Zia's little cottage. With her shift to nocturnal life, her world overflowed with connections, laughter, kisses, and bonds that drew her into a brand new family.

There was a part of her that boggled at the sudden change in her life, too. Sometimes she lay awake, her back tucked against Harlan's naked chest, and wondered if she would wake up from the blissful dream she had been snared in.

Surely this couldn't be *real*. This kind of happiness, this connection, *Harlan,* couldn't want her as much as she wanted him. Doubt was a shadow in the back of her mind. It was thin and weightless, but still held the power to tie her tongue into knots whenever she tried to work up the courage to bring up bonding.

But every day that shadow lessened. Doubt crept back. Her confidence grew.

Really, the only problem was that while *she* got more comfortable, her vampire seemed to get more and more tense.

He lavished her with attention, of course, and he insisted on spoiling her every chance he got, but as the weeks passed, she could tell something was wrong.

When she wasn't on the estate, he insisted on an escort of

guards. A couple turned into a few, then more and more. Her home got an upgrade in wards, at his insistence, as well as a new security system and a full-time rotation of guards. It didn't matter that she rarely slept there anymore. On the subject of her security, Harlan was utterly immovable.

Several times she caught him muttering angrily into a phone, or speaking quietly with Atticus, who wore a hard, grim expression.

Considering his past, she was surprised that when she asked him about it, he told her the truth: the Amauri family was in upheaval, and he worried that the chaos would reach them, too. Zia was skeptical that anyone would be foolish enough to bring Syndicate drama into the EVP, but she didn't want to dismiss his feelings. He would know better than her, certainly, so she did her best to adjust. Temporarily, at least.

It helped that Adriana, a beautiful vampire with wavy auburn hair and an infectious, dimpled smile, was there to commiserate with her.

"It sucks," she agreed one night. They were sitting on the manor's living room floor, both clad in festive sweaters and matching fuzzy socks. A board game lay between them, and two steaming mugs of apple cider sat beside one another in front of the crackling fireplace. Adriana couldn't drink more than a sip of hers, but she said she liked the smell of food, so Zia gamely made her a cup.

"They aren't always like this, are they?" Zia pressed, eyeing her tiny plastic figure's place on the colorful board. She had never been very good at games and couldn't rightly tell if she was winning or not. "I feel like things have escalated since I've been with him."

"Yeah, you're not imagining it." Adriana tucked her fangs against her lower lip as she plucked a card from the deck at the edge of the board. Her nose wrinkled as she read it, scrunching her freckles. "They're bad on a normal day, but when they're *worried?* It's a whole new level." She glanced up to meet Zia's eyes and shrugged. "And you're Harlan's anchor. It's different."

"Why?"

"You're *literally* his lifeblood, Zia," she answered, moving her figurine back three squares. "He loves me like a daughter, but instinct tells him that his very life, his whole existence, depends upon your safety and happiness. So yeah, he's gonna be pretty feral about danger. Particularly Julius."

Zia took a nervous gulp of her cider. Licking her lips, she whispered, "Do you think there's really a threat?"

Adriana shrugged again. She was pretty, with long limbs and an hourglass figure, but there was something almost withdrawn about her. It was not quite shy and not quite stand-offish. Instead, it was as if she hoped to fade into the background whenever an eye landed on her.

But perhaps Zia had it wrong. Maybe Adriana was just an introvert. She was, after all, someone who spent most of her life sitting quietly in front of a canvas, restoring damaged paintings with tremendous skill and technical know-how. It was entirely possible that she was just *quiet*.

She didn't think so, though.

Adriana's answer came slowly as she toyed with her figurine. She looked up through her lashes when she said, "I... think that Julius would do anything to get Harlan back into the fold, and without Dora there to keep him in check, he really *could*." She swallowed. "But I also think that he's fickle. He was interested in me for about half a second before he apparently forgot all about me, so... With everything going on, he might not even spare a thought for Harlan."

Another shrug. This one came with the distinct impression of a woman intentionally shucking off worries she could do little to fix. "If we get lucky, someone else will deal with him before Atty and Harlan have to."

Zia shook her head and set her mug aside. Her stomach was

too knotted with anxiety to accept anymore cider. "I guess I just can't imagine it. That whole world seems totally unreal to me."

She watched Adriana's expression tighten as she lifted her nearly untouched cider in a half-hearted toast. "Here's hoping it stays that way."

CHAPTER SIXTEEN

NOVEMBER GAVE WAY TO DECEMBER. THE GROUND became too frozen for Zia to work in the garden, so she gave her roses her warmest wishes as they quietly settled into their winter dormancy. Instead of going outside, she started spending her nights in the manor, writing her paper.

Gradually, her things migrated into Harlan's home, too. Her plants came first, since she had begun to spend weeks at a time in the manor. Her wardrobe moved over in fits and starts. This was helped greatly by the fact that Harlan enjoyed hiding gifts for her in the closet — mainly fine wool sweaters, satin nightgowns, and an assortment of expensive coats. What she didn't have tended to just *appear* one day, sneakily eliminating any need to run back to her cottage for even a simple errand.

It was a foregone conclusion that she would move in permanently, though Harlan restrained himself from demanding it more than once a week. It had become something of a game between them — the push and pull versus the inevitably of her choice.

Mostly, though, she knew that having her under his roof eased some of the stress she saw mounting every day. It was no hardship to spend most of her time in the manor, anyway. While she still

danced with the topic of moving in completely — and silently
wrestled with how to broach *bonding,* of all things, when she still
felt like she was in a dream she might wake up from at any
moment — it was easy for her to make the adjustment.

Harlan was worried enough. She didn't need to add to his
load by pretending like she *wanted* to stay in her cottage. At the
very least, his water pressure was *way* better than hers.

By the time the first snow stuck to the ground, she was living
with her vampire in every way that mattered. It was also around
that time that Zia reluctantly broke the news of her relationship
to her mother.

"...a *vampire,* Zia?"

"Yes, *Anne,*" she replied, watching her mother's expression on
her phone's screen warily. Harlan sat just out of sight on the
couch beside her, his thigh pressed against hers while he leaned
over the coffee table and worked on cleaning every part of a
wicked looking bolt gun. It was a wordless gesture of support that
made her chest swell with warmth.

"But—" For once in her life, Zia's mother apparently didn't
know what to say. She looked entirely flummoxed until, with a
small furrowing of her brow, she asked, "Your *boss?*"

She tried not to squirm. Tucking a curl behind her ear, she
stuttered, "Uh, yeah. Mr. Bounds. Harlan, actually. I've
mentioned—"

"Zia Alexandria Serafina North, you are not telling me, your
mother, that you started an intimate relationship with your
vampire boss." Her mother's voice rose in pitch and volume as her
temper flared. "You are *not.*"

If she could have melted into the couch, she would have. Since
that wasn't possible, Zia's body decided the second best option
was to simply start crying. It didn't matter that she felt exactly
zero guilt or shame about her relationship. All that mattered was
that her mother was upset.

"*Anne,* it's not like that. Harlan and I are so happy together.
Please don't make it out to be something predatory when it's

not." Zia blinked hard, trying to force the reflexive tears back. *No waterworks! If you start crying, she'll really think there's something to be upset about!*

"He's a p*redator*, Zia! Of course it's predatory!"

"That's not fair. You haven't even heard everything I have to say!" She sniffed hard and firmed her jaw. "This isn't some fling. We've been together for two months already. Harlan's *it* for me."

"How can you know that? Didn't you say he was almost the same age as your father and me? Zia, he's so much *older* than you. That kind of unevenness in a relationship is unhealthy." Her mother's face pinched. "Your father is going to be upset."

"Dad doesn't care about who I date," she shot back, unwilling to take that particular guilt-trip. "You know that as well as I do. The last time I talked about a boyfriend, he zoned out so hard he missed dessert. Dad would rather chew glass than talk about my relationships!"

"That was when you weren't dating a vampire twice your age, who happens to be your *boss.*" Her mother's face flushed. Worry made her tone harsh when she demanded, "Zia, what are you *thinking?* He will use you up and leave you heartbroken! Men like that don't just *date* women like you."

Harlan set the parts of his gun down on the polished coffee table with a dull thud. Zia made the mistake of glancing at him when he straightened.

His expression had hardened into something ice cold.

She tried to subtly shake her head, conveying that she was fine and that he didn't need to interfere, but it was no use.

In one swift movement, he plucked the phone out of her hand and angled himself into the frame.

"Good evening, Mrs. North," he murmured, voice pitched to what Zia had come to think of as his *I'm warning you not to fuck with me* cadence. His eyes glittered with a deep, dark anger that made the animal part of her brain want to run and hide.

Zia shrank into the couch cushions as her mother's mouth opened with an astonished gasp. Before her mother could get a word in, Harlan continued, "I understand that you have some concerns about my relationship with your daughter. I will handle those now."

Recovering a little, she managed to reply, "Oh? And how are you going to do that?"

"By telling you that I made it *very* clear to Zia when we started our relationship that it would never affect her position as the estate's rosarian." A corner of Harlan's lips quirked — such a subtle smile that it took Zia's trained eye to catch it. "That will change, of course, when Zia officially becomes my wife under the eyes of the law. Then she will *own* the garden. *That* is what *men like me* do with *women like her*, Mrs. North. We *marry* them."

It was Zia's turn to gasp. Flushing to the roots of her hair, she hissed, "Harlan, you can't just say things like that to my mother!"

He didn't look the least bit chagrined. "It's the truth. You are mine. The paperwork and the vows are just a formality."

Well, *she* might know that, but her mother didn't. Going by the astonished look on her face, it appeared she was having some trouble processing this news. Her voice was faint when she asked, "You want to marry my daughter?"

"I *will* marry your daughter." Harlan clicked his tongue against his fangs. "It is as good as done. Zia is my anchor, Mrs. North. She is my *mate*. If your concern is that she will not be taken care of, then rest assured that I have the means to keep her comfortable for the rest of her life."

His expression sharpened with a raw sort of aggressiveness when he added, "If it's that you think I do not love her, then you are simply fucking wrong."

Her mother's eyes flicked to Zia. The blood began to drain from her face as she absorbed the seriousness of the situation, as well as the sheer intensity of Harlan's expression. "Zia, what about…"

Dread was a lead weight in her stomach. This was *not* how she wanted to broach the subject of bonding with her vampire. Zia held up her hands in a stalling gesture and hoarsely begged, *"Anne, please don't worry about that."*

Harlan aimed a frown at her. His eyes narrowed dangerously when he asked, "Worry about what?"

"Noth—"

"If she'll bond with you," her mother helpfully supplied. "Zia, can you really trust this man with your magic? What if this is a mistake?"

She felt Harlan stiffen. *Shit.*

Zia rubbed her eyes to avoid looking at both him and her mother. *"Anne,"* she said, firm despite the annoying prickle of tears behind her eyelids. "I am a grown woman. Who I do or do not bond with is my business. Who I *marry* is my business. I love you, but you are overreacting to this news. Harlan is my partner now. You will accept it."

Great, she thought, wincing, *now I'm giving orders, too.*

"At least let the family meet him before you do anything hasty," her mother begged. "We just need to know you're in a good place, *gülüm.* "

Sighing, Zia opened her eyes to gauge Harlan's expression. It was, of course, perfectly inscrutable. He'd thrown up the mask as soon as her mother brought up bonding, making it impossible for her to tell how he felt about going to visit her family.

Well, since he's being unhelpful... She squared her shoulders and announced, "We'll come down and visit for Moonrise, *Anne.* "

"But Zia, that's only a ni—"

"Talk to you later! Love you!" She swiped her finger over the screen and then plucked her phone out of Harlan's hand.

Gods, that really couldn't have gone any worse.

Feeling self-conscious for the first time in weeks, Zia stood up from the couch and swept her dishes from the coffee table. "I'll be in the kitchen," she muttered, beating a hasty retreat.

She was loading up the super advanced, ten minute dishwasher Harlan had installed just for her when she felt his heat radiate along her spine. The bites decorating her body, all in various stages of healing, gave a deep throb of welcome.

Harlan's heavy hands settled on her waist. His voice was a dark rumble through her back when he asked, "What is this about bonding, Zia?"

She braced her palms against the cool marble of the kitchen counter and lowered her head. A deep sigh filled the silence.

Eventually, she said, "I'm sure you've heard of witchbonds."

His hands tightened on her waist. "Of course. I just didn't realize you needed one."

The unspoken accusation hung in the air between them. *Why didn't you tell me?*

It hurt her to think that she hurt *him*. That was never her intention. Harlan had been hurt enough by life. He didn't need his anchor doing the same.

Forcing herself to turn around and meet his dark, wounded gaze squarely, she explained, "It's not because I don't trust you, or that I don't *want* to bond with you. I just... didn't know how to bring it up. It's such a personal, permanent thing, and it wasn't pressing, so I just thought I could put it off until I absolutely had to."

Harlan's jaw ticked. Slowly, he moved his hands up to cup the sides of her neck. His thumbs stroked down over fading bites. "Witch, you *sustain* me. Do you not think I would kill for the honor of doing the same for you?"

Zia's lip wobbled. "Harlan... I know you would. I'm just— I think a part of me is still a little bit in shock that you want me. I keep kind of waiting for a punchline, or to wake up and realize I drank a bunch of cold medicine before bed." She swallowed thickly. "I keep waiting for it to end."

"That will pass." It was an order from a man utterly unwilling to compromise. His grip tightened infinitesimally on the sides of her neck. "You will bond with me, Zia. You will tie yourself to me like I've tied myself to you. I *will* feel your magic in my veins. I swear I feel it reaching for me every time I'm with you, but I didn't know—" He cut himself off.

Harlan sucked in a deep breath through his nose before he rasped, "Don't deny us what we both clearly want."

Gods, how could she still, after months of dating, still find this man's commands *charming?*

Zia leaned forward to rest her forehead on his shoulder. "Right *now?*"

His arms curled around her. The heat of his body was soothing, his scent familiar and luscious. He crushed her to his chest and rumbled, "When you're ready, I will be open to the bond. Any time, any day. But if I had a choice, I'd like it to be sooner rather than later."

"I love you," she whispered, anxiety slowly melting into nothing but mist.

Harlan sighed, long and low. "My Zia, all my love is yours. You *own* me."

She peeked up at him through her lashes. "Even after I said we'd go visit my family for the holiday?"

The smile came back. It was wry and small and just barely crinkled the crow's feet around his eyes, but it was still heartstopping. "Yes, *gülüm,*" he teased, using her mother's nickname for her. *My rose.* "I love you only a tiny fraction less than I did yesterday."

Giggling, she wrapped her arms around his back and playfully nipped at his throat. "Watch it, Mr. Bounds."

He palmed the back of her head. "Always, Miss North."

CHAPTER SEVENTEEN

"I REALLY DON'T THINK THE GUN IS NECESSARY."

Harlan slanted a look at his anchor, who stood in a puffy coat, a knit beanie, and tall leather boots beside him. Under the coat was a garish sweater covered in stars, a twin to the one she had somehow coerced him into wearing. In her hands was a deep glass dish full of fluffy pastries she'd spent all of the previous night working on.

The air was cool in San Jose, but lacked the bite of snow that came with each breath back home. It was the first night of Burden's month-long holiday and the street that stretched out before them was ablaze with lights. Every home was decorated with bulbs and string lights and artificial candles — each one a reminder that even in the darkest, coldest time of the year, there was warmth to be found.

Harlan was not, as a rule, particularly conscious of holidays.

He was not religious. The gods held no interest for him, and he never found comfort in the stories other vampires whispered about the gift Grim had given them, how their goddess was the truest, most powerful one of all.

He didn't listen when they spoke about how one day all the

Earth would be her domain, and how the vampires would rule a land of the dead.

What was religion to a man who delivered death in exchange for money? Where were the gods when he pulled the trigger, or when his mother left him in the sun to die as a defenseless newborn?

If Harlan had to guess, the gods probably didn't exist. If they did, they were cruel, capricious bastards, and he'd sooner swallow his own tongue than worship at their feet.

...But he liked the lights.

He liked that they made Zia's golden skin glow, and that, though she fairly shook with nerves, the excitement in her expression was undeniable. She was happy to be home with her family, and *she* wanted to celebrate Burden's Moon. He would make sure she got both of those things, no matter the personal cost to him.

That being said, he absolutely was not leaving their home without a gun.

Harlan hoisted their bags out of the trunk of his car. In his, there were two guns — companions to the one he strapped to his back. "We talked about this," he replied, watching the trunk's lid come down automatically. "I will keep you safe, no matter the cost, Zia. That includes your pouting when I bring guns to your family's home."

"I just don't think it's *necessary*," she argued. "You haven't heard a peep from Julius, right? Do you really think he'd do something now, when we're with a houseful of people?"

Harlan gestured for her to walk ahead of him, toward the two story house bursting with color directly across the street. A dark SUV was already parked in front. Another was down the block. Both were full of his men, who were almost as tense as he was.

He tried to be as honest as he could be with Zia about the possible dangers ahead of them, but no matter what he said, he never could convey what two hundred years of instinct told him was true: silence meant danger.

Something bad was headed their way.

His witch couldn't feel it, but he could. The smart thing would have been to outright refuse her request to visit her family, but he just didn't have the heart to do it. He rarely had the will to say no to her, but he was especially weak when it came to her love for her family.

Her devotion to her loved ones was one of the things he *loved* about his anchor. How could he punish her for it?

Besides, she had a point. Julius was arrogant, but he wasn't an idiot. He wouldn't risk having a squadron of Patrol officers descend on him by making a mess in a quiet suburb of the EVP.

He was grateful that Zia was being as accommodating as she was. She didn't complain about the extra guards, nor that they would spend the day in a high security hotel in San Francisco before they returned to the manor. Most people wouldn't have tolerated his paranoia, but she took it in stride.

Still, he wasn't going to give up his guns.

"Keeping you safe is my number one priority," he told her. Somewhere, muffled by walls and laughter, a jaunty holiday song began to play. "Don't think about the guns. There's only a slim chance I'll have to use them."

Zia paused. Standing a pace behind him on the cleanly swept sidewalk, she demanded, "What do you mean *slim chance?*"

Harlan shot her a small smile over his shoulder. "If your brothers don't like me, I might need them."

"You will *not!*"

She hurried to catch up to him, her cheeks pink with cold and exasperation. Harlan nudged her to take the low steps up to her parent's house first. He watched her back. Always.

When she gave him a playful glare, he leaned down to press a kiss to her rosy cheek. "Pretty pet," he whispered against her skin, "it's cute when you order me around."

"I'll show you *cute,*" she huffed.

He smiled. "I'm certain you will."

Of course, she gave him the stink eye when she turned to continue up the stairs, but he wasn't fazed. He rather liked it when she got huffy with him. It had been a very, very long time since anyone dared to do so, and he thought it showed just how comfortable Zia had become since that night in the greenhouse. *That* woman wouldn't have dared to give him an order.

This woman wiggled her hips as she walked, teasing him, and fearlessly crowded into his personal space as they stood in the doorway.

She was completely, unreservedly comfortable with him. By some miracle, she even loved him.

The only thing he was missing was the bond.

Forcing that thorny thought aside, as he so often did, Harlan fell back into habit and schooled his expression into something neutral as Zia activated the doorbell with a touch of her elbow. Her fingers went white around the edges of the casserole dish in her hands.

"Feels weird," she whispered, breath clouding in the air.

"What does?"

"Ringing the doorbell."

Harlan cocked an eyebrow. "Why? Isn't that what everyone does?" When they weren't breaking in, of course. Historically, he rarely had use for doorbells.

Zia licked her lips. "Well, yeah, but I lived here for a hundred years. I don't think I've ever done it before."

"Then why do it now? Couldn't we just... go in?" He didn't exactly know the protocol for holiday visits, let alone big family gatherings, but he suspected it wouldn't be an issue if she walked through the door unannounced.

She shrugged. Her expression was pensive when she answered, "Dunno. Just didn't feel right. This isn't my home anymore, I guess."

Harlan's chest tightened. "Where is your home now?"

Her eyes met his. The lights strung around the doorframe reflected in them, making them sparkle with little flecks of blue, pink, gold, and green. Her expression was soft when she answered, "With you, of course."

For a moment, it felt like he couldn't breathe at all. Harlan stared and stared, trying to sear the image of her into his mind forever, before he finally rumbled, "You'll officially move in with me when we go home."

A grin stretched across her face. The little dimple on her chin looked even cuter when it was framed by a smile so big, it crinkled her eyes. "Is that an order, Mr. Bounds?"

"Yes, Miss North," he answered, fighting the temptation to kiss her senseless.

Gods, he loved her more than life itself.

Somehow, her smile widened. "Good."

Footsteps approached the door. There was the sound of the lock disengaging, then the door knob turning. Just as the door began to open, Zia leaned over to whisper, "You ready to face the mob, big bad criminal?"

Harlan firmed his spine. There was no way he would be intimidated by her family, no matter how fiercely they might disapprove of him. "For you, my Zia, *anything.*"

She winked. "Keep that attitude. You're gonna need it."

Things were, to put it mildly, *chaos* in the North household. Harlan had never seen anything like it.

On the whole, vampires tended to have small families, and they were deeply possessive of their kin. They didn't throw big parties, or invite the whole extended family over for dinner on Saturday nights. Vampires could rarely stand each other's company for too long. Packing a dozen of them into a room for hours at a stretch was a good way to end the night with fewer family members to keep track of, if nothing else.

But Zia's family was so far removed from that world, they might as well have come from a different planet.

It was a gauntlet of light and sound, scent and contact. Not only were all of Zia's brothers present, but so were their partners, children, and pets. Cousins were there. Aunts and uncles were there. He even thought he spied some people who could only be friends. Turkish flew through the air, mingling with good-natured American drawl as upbeat holiday music played through it all.

Every table was strewn with a mind boggling array of foods — from what he recognized as traditional holiday fare, to international delights, to things that he could only assume appealed to little hands. Plates of olives and dates and cookies and sliced fruit and cheese were everywhere. Someone had even thoughtfully provided a few bottles of synthblood for him, though he never would have asked them to.

For a man who preferred a more or less solitary life, it was entirely overwhelming.

But it was worth it. The cry of delight that tore from Zia's throat as she embraced her frazzled mother, almost an exact, matured copy of her daughter; the wet gleam in her eye when she swooped up babies and kissed their faces; the enthusiasm with which she tackled her eldest brother onto the floor when his back was turned — all of it was worth the pain in his eyes and the sensory overload.

Besides, it wasn't like he was worried about the outcome of the evening. No amount of suspicious looks from her mother or probing questions from her lean, keen-eyed father could shake his confidence. Not even the combined, thinly veiled suspicion from her brothers made a dent in his mood.

Zia was his. End of story.

It helped that he'd been through worse obstacle courses, anyway. He wasn't sociable by any stretch of the imagination, but he stuck by Zia's side as she moved from person to person. He answered questions and remembered everyone's names, which seemed to impress several people. He even held a baby or two, though he was unsettled by how easily they melted into him, their little heads nestled under his chin and their breathing slow.

"Must be a vampire trick," Zia's second eldest brother speculated as he watched his daughter's eyes droop. "I've been trying to get her to sleep that easy for six months. Care to tell me what kind of magic you're using?"

Harlan could only shake his head. His guess was as good as Ahmet's, though he suspected it might have something to do with an instinctive predator response. After all, if a baby lay still and quiet, they were less likely to be noticed by a big bad monster who wanted to eat them. It was the same reason people used mobiles.

He didn't say that, though, and he didn't hand baby Elif back for some time. It felt... nice to be trusted with something so precious. It was a taste of how he felt when Adriana used to ask him to read to her when she couldn't sleep at daybreak, and, if he was lucky, how he might feel again in the future.

Slowly, in fits and starts, Zia's family seemed to forget that he was a vampire, and that he was twice her age. The wariness faded from their eyes the more he put up with childlike manhandling and being asked to fetch this, pass that, find so-and-so.

By the time all of the children were bleary-eyed and the gifts had been distributed, even Zia's mother, the elder Elif to the *baby* Elif he'd spent much of the evening with, had unthawed somewhat.

"You be good to my daughter," she warned, pressing two quick kisses to his cheeks. They stood in the doorway, their coats on, and their bags considerably lighter after all the gift-giving. The one full of weapons remained mostly the same, of course. "And you bring her back to visit all the time. No more of this months and months without seeing my daughter, do you hear me?"

While he didn't enjoy taking orders from anyone but his anchor, Harlan respected her mother's directness — and her protectiveness over someone they both treasured.

"We will visit," he offered. It wasn't quite the answer she wanted, but it was all he would dare commit to with the shadow of Julius looming over their heads.

"*Anne,* don't harass him." Zia hugged her mother from

behind, then turned to give her father an equally tight embrace. "We'll come back for Moonset, okay?"

"You'll relax during the holiday, won't you?" her father asked. He spoke to Zia, but his eyes met Harlan's over her head.

Francis North was lean and pale, with thinning dirty blond hair and an easy smile. But there was a hard sort of intelligence that gleamed behind his blue eyes. Despite his cushy little life, Harlan would bet any amount of money that Francis knew his way around a bolt gun.

That sense of tightly controlled danger slid smoothly beneath his words when he commanded, "Don't work yourself into the ground on that paper, Ziabean. You know how you get."

"More like you know how *you* get," she quipped.

Her mother let out a greatly put-upon sigh. "You do get it from your father."

Harlan inclined his head toward them both. "I will make sure she relaxes."

"Good." Mrs. North gave him a look that wasn't quite approving, but it wasn't hostile, either. *Small improvements.*

"Goodnight *Anne*, Dad." Zia stepped back to slide her hand into the crook of Harlan's elbow. She looked sad to go, but her smile lingered, soft and full of warmth for the people who loved her so much, they could hardly stand to watch her go. Her voice was soft when she whispered the traditional blessing, "May your nights be warm."

Harlan watched her parents' expressions melt into a painful mix of tenderness and sadness. "You as well, *gülüm,*" her mother breathed, misty-eyed. "We'll see you at Moonset."

CHAPTER EIGHTEEN

THEY DID NOT HEAD BACK TO THEIR HOME FOR THE night, though the drive wasn't too strenuous. The m-grid automatically set their speed for far higher than normal on the long road through farmland and the delta, so it only took about forty minutes. Still, Zia was told that it was too dangerous for them to travel the long, almost desolate stretch between the Bay Area and Sacramento in the dead of night, when any number of vampires could have plenty of time to set up an ambush. So they drove the smooth, traffic-free highway to San Francisco, where they would stay at The Palace Hotel.

Despite the dour reason for their visit, Zia was thrilled.

The Palace was famous all over the world. It was one of San Francisco's oldest and most luxurious hotels, and it hosted everyone from Taevas Aždaja, leader of the Draakonriik, to mega pop stars. Situated in the throbbing heart of downtown San Francisco, it was surrounded by people every second of every day — exactly what Harlan wanted.

It wasn't a vampire's style to attack in a crowd. They were stealth hunters and ambush predators. She was told it was highly unlikely he would try anything bold when they were surrounded by hotel staff and other guests. Privately, she thought that it was unlikely he'd try anything at all in the Solbourne's city.

Zia thought the choice had a lot to do with Harlan's unabashed love of luxury, too. She was an earthy type, but even she could appreciate the magnificent crystal archways of the entrance, the soaring ceiling of the lobby, and the Italian marble floors. Fresh bouquets the size of shopping carts perfumed the air, and a nocturnal crew of dapper employees welcomed them and their guards without batting a single eyelash at their entourage.

She tried not too *ooh* and *ahh* too much as Harlan escorted her up to their suite, but it wasn't easy. Even though she was tired from spending the evening with her intense, chatty family, she still bounced on the tips of her toes when they passed a particularly gorgeous painting, or when the concierge explained that they had a lush indoor pool and spa.

Stressed as she could tell Harlan was, he was patient with her. He didn't rush her, or make her feel silly for being so excited about staying in a hotel that he had likely visited a hundred times.

"I'll bring you back for a longer stay," he promised her as they stepped into their suite.

Zia flicked the heavy, sunlight-proof curtains back from one huge window and peered out at the blazing streets just below them. Neon lights spilled color across the glittering sidewalk, and m-enhanced cars zoomed confidently through intersections. Somewhere not too far away, just across a stretch of dangerous water, Solbourne Tower loomed over it all.

"When things are safer?" she finished for him.

There was a small, frustrated sigh behind her. "Yes."

Zia cut a look over her shoulder and felt her chest constrict. Her poor vampire looked wrung out as he stood by a velvet couch, his eyes on his phone. "Still nothing?"

The skin around his eyes tightened. "Still nothing. War has officially broken out between Felix and Yvanna, but there's no sign of Julius. He's gone completely dark."

Concern for him was a heavy weight in her stomach. Harlan

was constantly checking his phone, getting updates from his guards, and fretting about her safety. She also suspected that he was anxious about how she was taking his increasingly strict rules, and that only added to the stress bunching the muscles in his shoulders.

"We'll be home soon," she reminded him. Drifting back over to where he stood, she shucked her outer layers and tossed them onto the couch.

Zia gently pressed on his wrist until he lowered the phone. Harlan's eyes snapped up to meet hers. They were dark with worry, and the lines on his handsome face were deeper, etched with the weight he carried.

Heart swelling with tenderness for this man who had known so much cruelty, she slipped her arms around his back and held him tight. Her voice was muffled by his chest when she said, "Thank you for doing this tonight, baby. I know it was hard for you."

A warm hand cupped the back of her head. His other arm banded around her waist, holding her so tightly, she thought she felt him tremble. "My Zia, there is nothing I wouldn't do for you."

She knew it. Gods, did she know it.

The poor man barely even slept anymore, but still he did everything in his power to please her, to shower her with affection. Not a day went by when she felt like an afterthought, or that he wished he didn't have to worry about her. She felt *loved*.

Zia tilted her head back and propped her chin on his chest. "Just because I *know* you would do anything for me doesn't mean I should ever stop thanking you, Harlan. That's not how this relationship works."

His lips quirked up in a small, very *Harlan* smile. "I know." His thumb swept over her cheek. "I love you, my Zia."

"I love you, too," she answered, smoothing her hands up and down his back. "You did great with my family tonight, by the way."

Immediately, his expression went from warm to faintly disbelieving. "Did I?"

"Baby steps were made," she insisted. "My mother didn't yell at you, and my brothers thought you were mysterious and cool. They'll warm up more with every visit. This was just a test run. Besides, all the kids liked you. As far as the rest of the family is concerned, that makes it a done deal."

Harlan tilted his head slightly. Something in his expression changed, though she couldn't put her finger on exactly what. "I liked the kids," he said, slow and measured. With no warning at all, he bluntly asked, "Do you want children?"

Her heartbeat stuttered. For a moment, Zia's mind blanked. "I..."

Did she want children? Did she want a crowded home full of screaming babies with fangs? Did she want to sing silly songs and put too many bubbles in the bathtub and plant a special garden with her children? Did she want to feel the visceral terror of holding a newborn for the first time, knowing they were *hers?*

Did she want to touch baby soft skin and look into dark brown eyes just like Harlan's?

"Of *course* I want babies," she breathed. "I've always wanted kids, and if they were yours, I'd— Yes. Yes, I want to have babies someday."

Harlan blinked slowly once before his expression softened. "Then you'll have babies," he promised her in that imperious way she loved so much. "As soon as you want them."

"Is now too soon?"

She was only half joking, considering she would at least need to get her IUD removed before they really started that journey, but he seemed to miss the humor in her tone when he answered seriously, "It usually takes about six months for the venom to change your body enough to allow for impregnation, and I don't want you pregnant while Julius is still a threat."

Zia moved her hands to his waist. Gripping his narrow hip bones, she asked, "So... what? Three more months?"

He arched a brow, but he couldn't quite hide the excitement shining in his dark eyes. His tone was dry when he replied, "So eager to have my children when you won't even bond with me?"

She stretched up onto her toes to kiss the scar on his chin. "I've been waiting for the right time."

"When is that, exactly?"

"Hm…" Zia slowly began to untuck his dress shirt from his slacks. His holiday sweater had been stuffed in his bag after baby Elif spat up on it, so she was free to undress him easily as she walked him back toward the couch.

"You know, you were *so* wonderful tonight that I think you've earned a reward," she murmured. Her lips skimmed his throat, following cords of muscle she knew so well. A little nip made him gasp almost imperceptibly.

"What kind of reward?" His voice was husky; that baritone she loved so much dropping even deeper.

"The sexy kind." She worked on his belt as she began to lick and suck at his throat. Harlan's fingers plunged into her hair. His claws pricked at her scalp when she popped the button from the hole and pulled down his zipper. She hooked her fingers into the waistband of his briefs and tugged everything down around his thighs, freeing his rapidly hardening cock.

"Sit," she murmured, nudging him down onto the couch. Harlan didn't argue about how *he* was the one who usually gave the orders. Like the smart man he was, he simply sat his ass down on the couch and stared up at her like he wanted to eat her.

Harlan gripped her hips as she pulled her sweater over her head and tossed her bra on the floor. His hungry gaze roved over the swells of her breasts and the soft flesh of her stomach. He told her that he loved to look at her — simply *look* — because he loved beautiful things, and she was the most beautiful creature he'd ever seen.

This also meant that he had a certain fondness for both mirrors and watching her touch herself, but those were delights to be savored on another night.

Tonight, she wanted to spoil him a little. Recalling how Arif had taken him outside to inspect his car for nearly an hour, she thought, *Gods know he's earned it.*

Sinking down to her knees between his spread thighs, she smoothed her hands down his chest and stomach to tease the silky skin of his cock with the tips of her fingers. That drugging sense of power — of having a predator at her mercy — still hadn't faded. In fact, it had only *increased.*

Harlan's presence still raised the hair on the back of her neck. Her stomach still did a fearful swoop whenever she caught him moving out of the corner of her eye. When he sank his fangs into her skin, she still felt that deep, animal terror.

But she was a master of this dangerous being. Like a tiger trainer, she knew exactly what he was capable of, and from that knowledge came the rush. No one else would get this close to him. No one else would feel the gentle touch of those claws. For no one else was he *tame.*

When Zia licked a hot stripe from base to tip and heard him choke, the rush she felt was unparalleled.

This was *her* predator. *Her* killer. *Her* vampire.

Magic was hot in her blood, bubbling and fizzing with the desperate need to claim, as she sucked him into her mouth and began to move. Knowing how much he liked it, she kept her eyes on his as she hollowed out her cheeks with one long, hard pull.

That was one of the first rules he taught her: *Never look away.* He wanted to see everything in her eyes and know that he was the center of her world, just as she was the center of his.

Harlan's hips lifted off of the couch with a bitten off curse. His claws dug into the tops of the cushions as she stroked what she couldn't take in her mouth. His moan was low and throaty when she took him deep, then pulled back to lick and kiss every inch of him.

Finally, when he couldn't take the torture anymore, Harlan's hand found its way into her hair with a grated, "Fuck, Zia, take it."

Rule two: *Do as he said. Mostly.*

Feeling powerful and just a little wicked, she gave him one last lingering kiss before she did as he needed her to. Harlan slid over her tongue like a dream — salty and smooth and *delicious.* His hips pumped shallowly as she took him deeper and deeper, faster and faster, until he tugged gently but urgently on her curls.

"Zia," he gasped, panting hard. "Zia, I want—"

Rule three she learned on her own. *Give him a show.*

She pulled back with one hard suck. The flushed tip left her mouth with an *pop!* Her lips were swollen and her throat ached just enough to make her voice slightly scratchy when she said, "I know, baby."

Using one hand, she gathered up the rest of her curls that weren't in Harlan's grip. The other stroked him hard and fast, her palm sliding over wet skin with ease. Leaning down, she opened her mouth and stuck out her tongue just in time to catch his release.

Harlan's eyes didn't leave hers even when his orgasm wracked him, tightening his spine and making the muscles of his neck stand taut. His flavor burst across her tongue, but she couldn't catch all of it. That wasn't the goal, anyway.

His come slid down her chin and splattered onto her chest, painting her breasts and chin in the way that sent her vampire into a frenzy.

When he was finished, Zia had barely swallowed before he was hauling her up into his lap to bury his fangs in her throat. She let out a short, ecstatic shout as his venom pumped through her veins. Her hips ground down, seeking friction, until his claws tore at the fastening of her pants.

Harlan thrust his hand in and ruthlessly circled her clitoris, giving her everything she needed as he released his fangs and began to suck. Her orgasm meshed with the high of his bite. The world took on a gauzy, dreamy shine even as her magic pushed and pushed and *pushed.*

Normally she became sleepy after a bite, but not this time. *This* time, she had something to do.

As soon as she felt him lick her wound, sealing it, Zia threaded her fingers into his hair and yanked.

Harlan's head snapped back. His eyes were heavy-lidded and dazed, his lips swollen, and his cheeks pink. Utterly irresistible.

"I *love* you," she whispered against his mouth.

His voice was thick when he answered, "I love you, my Zia."

She crushed her lips against his, tasting her blood, his release, *him,* as she framed his cheeks with her hands and *pushed.*

Magic exploded. Color and light popped behind her closed eyes as she rode the wave toward him. She felt herself sinking into him, seeping into every crack and scar and hollow place. Her magic arrowed into every cell he possessed with a singularly proprietary swiftness.

He is mine, it crowed, filling him until his body could take no more. *We are his!*

She felt her magic glide back to her, calmer than before, and with a distinct tang of *Harlan.* It was the start of a loop that would sustain her life for centuries to come.

A tremor rolled down her back as she gradually pulled away. Giddiness threatened to send her flying in a hundred different directions, but exhaustion was rapidly closing in. Zia exhaled a shaky breath as she leaned her forehead against his.

"Happy now?" she rasped.

There was no response.

Zia forced her eyes open. Peering through her lashes, she found Harlan's eyes closed, his lips slightly parted, and his head resting against the back of the couch. He was entirely limp underneath her.

Oh, she thought, fighting an exhausted giggle. *I knocked my poor vampire out.*

It was just as well. He hadn't been sleeping enough anyway.

CHAPTER NINETEEN

Zia woke up early, as she usually did, and found Harlan in exactly the same position she had arranged him in the night before. He'd woken up on the couch a few hours after their bonding and blearily allowed her to guide him to their bed, where she stripped him and lovingly tucked him under the covers. They slept the day away, tangled up in one another under the sheets.

But her poor vampire was still tuckered, it seemed. He usually began to stir not long after she did — some deep instinct alerting him that his anchor was up and about, or perhaps it was his years of criminal life that made him a chronically light sleeper.

Either way, the bonding seemed to have knocked Harlan sideways.

He didn't so much as twitch as she climbed out of bed to take a long, hot shower in the palatial bathroom. She expected him to be awake by the time she finished, but when she checked on him again, his expression was blank and his breathing deep. His long black hair was fanned out over the pillow — a silky river she ran her fingers through with an appreciative sigh.

All in all, their bonding didn't seem to have affected her nearly as much. While she had a sharp headache behind her eyes and a strange, overall sort of internal soreness she couldn't put her finger on, Zia felt otherwise great.

Quietly closing the bedroom door, she stepped into the suite's living room and gave Damien, Harlan's second most trusted guard, a call. Normally she would have called Atticus, but since he stayed home to be with his sister, she had to break the news that they would be leaving a bit later than planned to the dark-skinned, hazel-eyed vampire who had been assigned as her personal nocturnal bodyguard.

The plan was for them to leave as soon as the sun set, so Damien wasn't too happy to hear things had changed.

"Why isn't he up?" he pressed, confusion clear. Harlan was *never* late.

Zia nervously tucked a curl behind her ear as she peered into the mini fridge by the feed screen. She was pleased to note that the hotel had thoughtfully accommodated their vampire guests by providing several bottles of synthblood.

Knowing there really wasn't a way around explaining the situation, she said, "We bonded last night, and it took a lot out of him, I think. We might have to stay another day."

She could practically hear Damien's scowl through her phone's speaker. "You really couldn't have waited until you were home?"

One nice part of her burgeoning confidence? She didn't feel an ounce of anxiety when she answered, "Nope!"

Zia frowned at the bottles lined up in the fridge. While Harlan mostly subsisted on her blood, he still needed to supplement his diet with synthblood while she finished adjusting to being his anchor. Unfortunately, the brand stocked in the refrigerator was one she knew he didn't like and upset his stomach.

A deep sigh puffed over the line. "Fine. Guess there's no helping it. He'll call as soon as he's up."

"Mm-hm. In the meantime, maybe you and the boys should try out the pool or something. I'm gonna get some room service."

Incomprehensibly, Damien didn't seem particularly enthused

by that idea. *She* longed to jump in the pool and spend some time in the sauna. Unfortunately, she knew that Harlan didn't want her spending extended periods of time out by herself. Instead of indulging in those luxuries, she contented herself with ordering a large breakfast and asking the front desk if they had any other brands of synthblood available.

Unfortunately, the answer was no, but they did direct her to a boutique grocery store a couple blocks away that sold a variety of specialty foods, including synthblood.

Normally, she wouldn't have bothered. Harlan fed the previous night, which typically meant he wouldn't need anything more for another twenty-four hours. However, the longer he slept, the more she worried that he would need the extra energy when he woke. Who knew what becoming a walking, talking magical filter did to a person's appetite?

After she finished her breakfast of eggs Benedict with smoked salmon and a side of fresh fruit, all served on a funny little cloth-covered cart, Zia checked on Harlan one more time.

Peering into the dark bedroom, she found that he had moved into her vacated spot to bury his face in her pillow. He was on his stomach, the sheets twisted around his hips, and appeared more or less dead to the world.

Okay, he'll definitely be hungry when he wakes up, she decided, closing the door once more.

After making another quick call to the front desk to extend their stay, Zia put on her jacket and boots to venture outside. Worried that he would wake up and fly into a frenzy when she was gone, she left him a quickly scribbled note on the hotel stationery explaining that she stepped out to get him something to eat.

She knew that he wouldn't be happy to hear she had gone out for a bit by herself, but she wasn't about to ask one of the guards to run a five minute errand for her. Not only was it a holiday — one they were *already* working — but it was a task she was happy to do for him. Besides, it wasn't like she was venturing into a desolate part of the city by herself. It was a five minute trip in the most populated part of San Francisco.

According to the concierge, the little grocery store was only two blocks away. She would be fine.

Tugging her hat over her ears, she shoved her phone in her pocket and slipped out of the suite. A quick scan of the ID chip in her palm would unlock the door on her return. In the meantime, Harlan would be safe and snug as a bug in their suite.

Despite that knowledge, a brittle sense of unease edged into her giddy mood, its presence increasing with every step she took toward the bank of elevators down the hall, but she refused to let it bother her too much.

Of *course* she felt uneasy. They had a fresh bond so tightly woven, it made every instinct balk at the idea of leaving his side for even a moment. It felt unnatural to walk away.

But, she sternly reminded herself, it was only five minutes. Ten minutes at the maximum. Soon enough she could change back into her pajamas and tuck herself underneath the covers with him until he finally woke.

The air outside of the hotel was crisp and wet. Around her, people walked by in thick coats and high heels — some nocturnal folk on their way to work, and others perhaps headed to holiday parties. The street was lined with shops and high end bars, every single one of which was decorated in some holiday paraphernalia. Lights were everywhere, and window displays were opulent.

She had been to San Francisco on school trips before, but never as an adult, and not during Burden's Moon. It seemed like every square inch of the city was decked out for the holiday, and all the people who passed her had somewhere important to be.

The sidewalk was faintly bouncy under boots as she followed the concierge's directions. Though she wanted to stop and look at everything, Zia tried to hurry. They would come back for a longer, less tense visit. *Then* she could explore.

She found the grocery store easily enough. Lanzo's Fine Foods was just across the street from a piano shop and a stationery store, and it was one of those places that clearly tried to capture some European magic in its aesthetic. It was small and seemed to specialize in luxury and imported specialty foods, which suited her just fine. They had Harlan's preferred synthblood in stock, so she bought a six pack and quickly headed back out, the handles of the paper bag dangling from the tips of her chilled fingers.

On her way back, she stopped for a moment to look in the window of a high end baby supply store. They had gone all out for their window display. Fancy strollers burst out of synthetic snowbanks, and a great silver moon hung behind a cascade of baby booties suspended from the ceiling.

Soon, she thought, biting back a smile. *Soon.*

Prying herself from the window and the temptation to peek inside the store, just to get a feel for all the itty-bitty baby things, Zia crossed in front of a narrow alley. She didn't notice the parked SUV there, nor the man who leaned against the wall by the passenger's side, just out of sight until it was too late.

CHAPTER TWENTY

HARLAN WOKE UP WITH A SPLITTING MIGRAINE.

He groaned as he turned over onto his back. Every muscle ached. Even his *internal organs* hurt. It was like he'd been kicked from the inside out. Repeatedly.

Disoriented, he struggled to recall how he'd gotten this way, or even where he was.

The last time he felt this bad, he'd nearly gotten himself killed doing one last favor for Dora. Killing her eldest son was a damn near herculean task. That sociopath had nearly broken every bone in Harlan's body before he managed to get a bolt through his skull.

The discomfort he felt as he reluctantly swam back to consciousness wasn't quite as acute as the injuries he sustained four years ago, but it was just as pervasive. Every inch of him hurt..

He was also fucking *starving*.

Hunger cramped his stomach in a rolling wave as instinct took over. He was nothing but raw urges when his claws dug into the silky sheets, pawing the space beside him, searching for a warm body he knew so well.

He needed Zia *now*. He needed to plunge his fangs into her tender throat and gorge himself as she welcomed him into the tight heat of her cunt. Instinct knew that feeding from his anchor would take the pain away, that it would soothe this awful, pounding ache in head. It knew that she would be soft and pliant under him, and that the more venom he pumped through her precious veins, the sooner she would be fertile.

That deep, animal need to see her sated and flush and bred was a dull roar in his mind, growing louder and louder with every desperate swipe at the tangled sheets.

They were bonded now. They were one in all ways. He could—

His memories of the previous night came back in the same instant he realized her side of the bed was empty.

Harlan jolted upright. Spots exploded in front of his eyes as he swung his gaze around the darkened hotel bedroom. Joy bubbled under his skin, fizzy and hot and—

No, that wasn't just joy. It was *magic.*

He pressed a clammy palm against his naked chest, astonished. *Gods, I belong to her now.*

Harlan had never had much by way of magic. Like most vampires, his m-paths were narrow and few, making the channeling of magic incredibly difficult. His skills lay mainly in dismantling wards without detection, which was something that required very little magic but extreme technical skill. It was the main reason Julius took an interest in him at all.

But *now,* it was like something inside of him had tripled in size. He felt internally expanded, his senses stretched. When he held his breath, he thought he could *feel* a hum of magic in the air, connected to something deep, earthy, and welcoming.

It was luscious and heady and foreign and—

Harlan's heart began to pound. He lurched out of bed, but found his legs hopelessly tangled in the sheets. All of his hard-won predator's grace deserted him as he tumbled off of the high bed and onto the floor. Cursing, hissing, and laughing all at once, he tore at the sheets until he freed himself.

"Zia!" he called out, hoarse and overjoyed, as he scrambled

onto his feet. He swayed, braced his hands on the bed, and called again, "Zia!"

He wanted to kiss her until he couldn't breathe. He wanted to crush her against his chest. He wanted to know everything about this new connection they shared, the gift she had given him. He wanted to sink his fangs into her and give her the babies she wanted and watch her write her paper and just *love* her until the day Grim swept him off to her riverbank.

But there was no reply.

Harlan stumbled toward the door, expecting to hear her padding around the suite in her fuzzy socks at any moment. The shower wasn't running, so she wasn't in there. Perhaps she had ordered some breakfast for herself and simply couldn't hear him through the heavy door separating the bedroom from the living area of their sprawling suite.

Except, when Harlan threw that door open, the living area was empty.

It took him several seconds for his sluggish mind to catch up to what he was seeing. There was a room service cart by the couch, and their bags were exactly where he left them the previous night. The curtains were still drawn tightly over the windows, though he could sense that it was well past dusk. There was nothing amiss.

Nothing, of course, except for the notable absence of his anchor and her purse, which she had set on the table by the door when they came in.

His stomach dropped.

He spun around and charged across the bedroom to slam his fist against the bathroom door. Panic made his voice sharp when he called again, "Zia, answer me!"

Nothing.

His hand shook when he turned the knob and found the room dark and empty, just as he knew it would be.

Fear, as cold and painful as a sudden drop into frigid water, stole the breath from his lungs.

Harlan was across the room again in a flash. Dropping to his knees, he pawed at the discarded clothing on the floor until he found his cell phone. The only messages he found were a handful from Atticus and one from Adriana that read, *"he slipped"* with an attached photo of her brother facedown in a snowbank.

When he frantically called Zia's phone, it went straight to her voicemail. Her cheerful voice told him to leave her a funny message.

No, he thought, vision blurring. His chest sawed up and down as he fought to get air into his compressed lungs. *No. No, this can't be happening.*

His next call was to Damien. Hope threatened to choke him as he ran through every single possibility in the seconds between hitting the button and raising the phone to his ear.

She could be at the pool. She could be exploring the hotel. Maybe she decided to do a spa treatment while I slept in. Surely one of my men is with her. She's probably forcing them to get a mud mask with her right now. Everything is fine.

"Hey, boss. Are we headed ou—"

"Where the fuck is Zia?" he snarled.

There was a dreadful pause. Then, slowly, "Isn't she with you?"

The world spun out from under him.

"She said that she was calling the desk to request another night, since you were... ah, indisposed."

Harlan fell back onto his ass. His bones felt like they had been turned to jelly. In an instant, every ache and pain and joy and hope vanished. There was nothing but a cold hollowness left.

"She's not with me," he heard himself say, from some great distance. "She's not in the suite."

Damien was smart and well trained. Barely a second passed before his confusion disappeared, replaced by the cold calculation of a soldier on a mission. He didn't ask where she might have gone, or suggest that she might come back soon and all his worry could be in vain.

Damien was a vampire. He knew the instinct an anchor

inspired as well as anyone. An anchor was *life*. They were not simply lovers, or meals, or partners. They were a singular obsession and the source of all hope.

To lose one was utterly unimaginable.

"I'm going to call the desk. Michael will get access to their security footage. If she's in the hotel right now, we'll know in ten minutes."

Unspoken was the certain knowledge that if she wasn't, Zia had been taken.

Harlan hung up the phone without saying goodbye. His aches and pains, even his empty stomach, were distant memories as adrenaline took their place. It rushed through his veins as he forced himself to throw on clothing. His gland ached with a fierce, aggressive pulse when he did a circuit through the suite, trying to determine how stale her scent was, how recently she might have left — or been kidnapped.

Instinct howled with pain and rage. He could barely see straight. His anchor was missing. His lifeblood, the greatest treasure in his possession, the woman he loved and didn't deserve, was *gone.*

It went against everything that made him a man and a vampire to realize he'd simply slept through her disappearance. Her protection was his top priority, and he'd simply— what? Drooled into a pillow as she was snatched from their suite?

Did she scream for him? Did she cry? Did she suffer?

It was the smallest relief that the more he looked, the less he thought she had been taken directly from under his nose. If it was a ploy with a fake hotel employee, there would not have been a room service cart *in* the room. She wouldn't have had time to finish the coffee he saw on the corner of the cart, certainly.

This was confirmed when he circled around to the entrance of the suite, determined to try and pick up on any foreign scents that might linger there, and instead found a note.

The sight of Zia's familiar, looping handwriting made his

heart skip a beat. He felt his throat tighten when he read the words scrawled on the hotel stationery.

Baby—
    I'm running to the store to get you some food. They only have junk in the fridge. >:(Be back in 5. Love you!!!
    —Zia

~

In the end, it took ten minutes to determine where Zia had gone, and half as long as that to discover an abandoned bag of Sipiron in a damp, shadowy alley by a children's store a block from the hotel.

The Palace's security footage, backed up by the nervous concierge who gave her directions, told Harlan and his men that she had been missing for approximately an hour.

Their faces were grave as they watched the footage again. Amidst several other guests, Zia's lush form stood out as she sauntered through the lobby and toward the glass doors, a tiny skip in her step. She looked content but determined, like she really was trying to make the errand a quick one.

When she turned her head slightly, a giddy little smile curled the corner of her mouth up. The sight of it gutted him.

Harlan was too numb with fear to be angry at her or his men, though the rage he felt lashed at his insides. Mostly, he was disgusted with himself.

Why hadn't he done *more?*

He didn't think to station men outside their door. They weren't fucking foreign dignitaries. They didn't need guards standing on alert at all times. He thought they would be safe enough with his men a door away, relaxing in their own suites but on call if there was trouble.

It was his fault he wasn't paranoid *enough.* If he had been, she would have been stopped at the door, or at the entrance to the hotel, and turned right back around. She would have huffed but returned to bed anyway. He would have woken up with her in his arms, safe and maybe a smidge annoyed, like he was fucking supposed to.

It was also his fault that he didn't explain to her *exactly* what could happen if they slipped up, if Julius took any tiny opening they provided. He didn't want to frighten her with the realities of his old life, so he had been honest but vague. Even knowing that Zia remained skeptical about the truth of the threat, he didn't try to correct her.

He never wanted to expose her to the world he left behind.

And because of that, his sweet anchor saw nothing amiss with running a quick errand as he slept. She wanted to do something nice for him. She was just trying to be a good partner and look after his needs. It was *his* fuck-up that got them here.

For once in his life, Harlan felt like he was frozen.

There was no outlet for his rage, no course of action in which to channel his fury. Instead, it coiled into a dark ball in his gut, leaving the rest of him to simply shut down.

The greatest assassin in the New Zone had been rendered completely powerless with one act, and now he was adrift. No matter how he tried to gather the frayed ends of his composure, his centuries of experience, he could not come up with a plan to find her that would not immediately get her killed and her body dumped somewhere for him to find.

As if reading his mind, Atticus's hard voice came through the speaker on his phone like the crack of a whip, "We know she's not dead. We're going to find her."

Harlan's tone was flat when he replied, "Do we know that?"

"Yes, we do." The sound of a car door slamming briefly interrupted him. Atticus had spent thirty minutes assembling a guard to keep his sister on complete lockdown before he hopped in his car to assist in Zia's rescue — or recovery.

There was a low rumble of an engine in the background when he bit out, "Julius isn't a fucking idiot. He might not know that she's your anchor, but we know he's probably been watching you, which means he's seen you with her. He'll know she's important to you. There is not a chance on Burden's Earth he's gonna kill her when he can use her as leverage instead."

There were, of course, worse things than murder, but no one in the room pointed this out.

The air was thick with anger and anticipation. Harlan got the distinct impression that every single person took Zia's kidnapping almost as personally as he did.

Most of his men were themselves vampires. The others were an assortment of demons and predatory shifters. All of them knew that a mate was a sacred, precious thing, and all of them would kill to get Harlan's anchor back because they understood he would do the same thing for them.

More than that, though, Zia was *theirs*.

All of his men were hardened soldiers pulled from bad situations, and all of them were possessive, greedy bastards who knew when to latch on to a good thing. They adored Zia in their own quiet ways because she was kind to them without reservation.

When they went out, she often insisted that they join in the conversation. She invited them into the manor to play boardgames, and roped several baffled soldiers into assisting her in the garden. Michael helped her hang garlands of pine around their fireplace, and even Tarrence, a particularly antisocial lynx shifter in charge of cyber security for the estate, surprised her with an elaborate light display around the fountains.

Her loss wasn't just devastating for Harlan. It was a fatal blow to the ugly, patchwork family they had scraped out of the gutters of the New Zone.

Harlan dropped his head and squeezed the back of his neck with both hands. He fought to throw off the hopelessness and the fear that clouded his judgment. Zia needed him to be the assassin, the ruthless criminal he was trained to be. She needed him to be her *protector*, not this weak creature crippled by terror and inaction.

"She's not dead," he rasped, mostly to himself. "I'd know if she was dead. I would *know.*"

But would he know if she was in pain? If she was being tortured? Harlan felt the bond, the magic that flowed in an invisible current even across whatever distance lay between them, but he couldn't get a handle on much else. It was too new and he was an amateur when it came to nuanced magic. When the idea came up to track her using their new bond, he was immediately crushed to realize that he simply didn't know *how.*

But he was certain he would feel it if she died. Even without the bond, he would feel it.

"Think about what you would do in his position," Atticus said, drawing Harlan's eyes away from the tops of his shoes and back to the phone on the coffee table. "Julius is going to let you stew for a while, really make you sweat, and then he's gonna call you. He's going to taunt you because he's a sick sonuvabitch, but ultimately he's going to demand you meet him somewhere to negotiate Zia's return. He wants something from you, boss. He's not gonna risk damaging his best bet of getting whatever that is."

Harlan squeezed his neck harder, to the point of pain, and used the feeling to ground himself. His voice was raw when he replied, "Yes, that sounds like him."

Like what I would do if I had no heart, no fucking honor, no godsdamned soul.

"Right. So what the fuck do you want to do when he calls?"

He felt every eye on him as his men waited, silent and still, for his answer. One sharply drawn breath cracked the ice that had encased him since he found Zia's note — it splintered, the pieces falling away to reveal that molten core of pure, unbridled rage.

His anchor had been *taken.* There was no greater sin. There was no retribution cruel enough.

Zia was the blood in his veins, the heart outside of his body, the mother of children yet to come, and the soul he did not know he possessed.

Julius thought he had the key to controlling Harlan in the palm of his hand.

What he really had was a gun pointed at his own fucking head.

"We get her back," he answered, lifting his head to look each of his grim-faced men in the eye. "And then we make him answer for his crime."

Chapter Twenty-One

THE CALL CAME AT NINE, EXACTLY TWO HOURS AFTER Zia's kidnapping.

Everyone froze as his phone rattled against the coffee table, their eyes swinging to the device like it more closely resembled a bomb.

Atticus had arrived only a few minutes before and hadn't even taken his jacket off yet. When he stalked across the room, away from the temporary crisis station of half a dozen monitors and men attempting to comb through the city's extensive security network for a glimpse of Zia, his long black coat billowed around his legs.

The tattoos on his neck and hands stood out ghoulishly as the muscles there tensed with barely concealed aggression.

He sank onto the couch beside Harlan. They both stared at the screen for the span of a ring. The caller was unidentified, the number scrambled, and the video feature disabled. It couldn't be anyone else.

Harlan was calm when he raised the phone to his ear and answered, "Julius."

"Little Harlan. It's so good to talk to you after... what has it been? Four years?" Julius's voice was almost *bubbly*. There had always been a saccharine outer shell to the man that only made his rotten core more stomach-churning.

He used to think that Julius played a character to disguise his terrifying lack of empathy, but as he got older, Harlan came to the chilling realization that he did it simply because it made people uncomfortable. He never tried to fit in, nor pretend to be anything other than what he was.

If he laughed, it was because he knew it raised the hair on the back of a person's neck. If he cooed, it was because he knew it made sweat break out across their skin. If he soothed, it was only because he was about to cause unimaginable agony.

The sick bastard only loved two things: making people afraid and himself.

Harlan's stomach did a familiar turn. For many years he was both afraid of and desperate for Julius's attention. When he was hand-picked out of the group of Amauri-claimed orphans at six years old by the son of Dora Amauri herself, he'd been so briefly full of hope. Finally, he would be special to someone. He would no longer live in the cramped room full of other forgotten children, fed once a night and told to make themselves neither seen nor heard. He would have somewhere to belong, and someone to care for him.

Julius shattered those dreams in less than twenty-four hours. The hope, though...

That took years to die.

Once that was gone, what was left was little more than hatred tinged with disgust. Julius was pathetic and broken in ways that Harlan couldn't comprehend. Regret for not eliminating him when he had the chance four years ago burned a path through him. Dora had freed him from the Amauri family's control, but she had also made him swear to never raise a hand to a member of the family again.

He didn't give a shit about promises made to someone like Dora Amauri, a woman who had her own son murdered and oversaw the misery of countless others for the sake of profit, but the desire to get Adriana out of there as quickly and quietly as possible outweighed his need for justice. He didn't kill the bastard when he should have.

He wouldn't make that mistake twice.

"If you don't want to suffer, return her," he commanded, voice low. His rage was vast and hot, but it was also still. It held itself tightly coiled, waiting for the right time to strike.

Julius's laugh — hollow, practiced, and a sound that haunted his childhood nightmares — rang over the line. "Are you talking about the sweet little bite I found walking all by herself? Really, Harlan, you should know better than to let your leftovers out of your sight. Someone else might just gobble them up. This all could have been avoided if you just finished your food like I always told you to."

Old memories assailed him with that one simple phrase. *Finish your food.*

Vampires weren't designed to kill the beings they drank from, but that didn't stop people like Julius from doing it anyway. Some purists believed that was the *right* way. To truly take in the power of the blood they consumed, a life had to go with it.

And Julius, for all that everything else about him was artifice, truly, wholly believed in the purest ideal of vampirism.

For many of his boyhood years, Harlan's job had simply been to *take out the trash* his master left after a meal.

That coil of rage drew tighter, hotter in his gut. The threat to Zia's life was clear, but Harlan didn't act on the instinct that demanded violence in response. Not yet. Instead, he clicked his tongue against the roof of his mouth and drawled, "So desperate for my attention, Julius? You could have just written an email."

"And miss sampling such a sweet little creature?" There was the faint sound of fabric rustling, then a soft, urgent noise of distress.

The hair on the back of Harlan's neck stood up. Every muscle tensed as he fought the urge to spring up from the couch and rip the room apart.

A ripple of tension went around the room. Every man leaned toward him unconsciously. The aggression had been high before, but now it radiated out from every one of his soldiers like blistering heat.

That was *Zia*. He knew it. He knew that breathy sound of panic — the very same one she made when he found her in the greenhouse that fateful night in October.

His mind spun as he imagined what Julius was doing to her. Was he using his claws on her? Was he drawing a knife over her throat just for fun? Was he pressing on a bruise, or pulling her curls?

Surely he wouldn't kill her. Not yet. Not if he guessed that she was his anchor and so much more valuable to him alive. *Surely.*

"So pretty," Julius cooed. "Such soft skin. I can see why you like her. Even if she didn't belong to you, I might have plucked her off the street anyway. You know how I have a sweet tooth."

It was an effective taunt, though Harlan didn't think Julius would be stupid enough to try it. An anchor's blood was poison for another vampire unless their venom was identical to that which already flowed through the host. That was a one in a million bet. No vampire in his right mind would risk taking even a sip from a host with clearly visible bite marks.

And Julius, for all his arrogance, wasn't stupid. That was the only way he managed to stay in Dora's good graces for so long, after all.

Or perhaps it was willful ignorance on Dora's part. She had to know that her son had a love for torture and murder. Was it a mother's love that turned her head away, or was it the millions of dollars he brought into the family's coffers through drug smuggling that did it?

Reining in the desire to snarl at even the suggestion of another vampire sinking their fangs into his anchor, let alone *hurting* her, Harlan asked, "Did you really call to talk about a woman, or did you have something important to say?"

There was a soft, almost disappointed sigh. "We need to talk about your return to the family."

"Then we'll talk." Harlan clenched his left fist on his thigh until his knuckles bleached. "Tell me when and where."

He could *hear* the empty, almost vapid smile Julius wore when he answered, "Let's meet up for a drink."

～

There weren't a lot of vampire bars in San Francisco, but the few that existed fell into two categories: extreme luxury and back alley filth.

Harlan had spent much of his life in the latter type, taking out vampires that pissed off the family in one way or another as they drunkenly swayed their way to the restroom, or stepped out back for a smoke.

Only in his later years of service did he begin to warrant enough respect — and no small amount of fear — to be allowed into the places people like Julius frequented, and more often than not, *owned.*

The Lush was one of those places.

Situated on the corner of Haight and Cole, The Lush was easy to miss amongst the flamboyant storefronts and art installments that surrounded it on all sides. Its exterior was painted a minimalist dark gray, and the letters that spelled out its name were a brilliantly shined silver bolted to both street-facing walls. The windows were replaced with shimmering black glass, opaque from the outside, and soft white lights glowed around the inside of the doorway from floor to ceiling.

The only way an outsider might possibly guess it was a vampire establishment at all was by the extremely subtle symbol of Grim etched into the black glass set in the stainless steel door — two circles, one filled in, with the second forming a thin halo around the other.

Depending on who you asked, it was a symbol of eternity or

the Earth itself. Many vampires subscribed to the Earth interpretation, if only so they had some flimsy excuse for their belief that they would one day rule the world.

All will return to Grim's hands when the time is right, her acolytes preached, *and we will inherit the Earth when blood flows.*

It was all bullshit, and he doubted the Merciful One would appreciate her symbol being used as decoration at a bar. Especially not a bar like Lush.

Harlan had only been there once before, back when he first moved to the EVP. He had lived in the city for a handful of weeks as the sale of the estate went through and thought to check out the vampiric community that eked out a living under the noses of the elvish government.

One visit had been more than enough for him.

He opened the door to find interior dimly lit and crowded. Behind the black glass and darkly painted walls, there was no holiday cheer, no sweetness or twinkling lights that lit up the street. A sprawling room lay before him, dotted with circular leather booths with high backs. A sleek black glass bar spanned most of the left side of the room. Glass shelves full of expensive alcohol and rare, alcohol-infused synthblood lined the wall behind it. Music, soft and sensual, drifted through the air.

The scent of blood did, too.

It was the scent of all kinds of blood — human and non-human — and every drop fresh. Though the booths were designed for privacy, making it nearly impossible to see who was in each one unless you were sliding into them, he knew exactly what was happening in them.

The Lush didn't just serve expensive synth. They paid the beautiful, the sweet-smelling, the foolish, and the exotic to drink and to sit in those booths to *be* drunk.

Servers moved around in dark clothing, their hands covered in thin black gloves for hygienic reasons, delivering cocktails and warmed bottles of synthblood to the tiny tables inside each booth.

They walked quickly, darting between vampires who lingered outside of the booths and in front of the bar.

They moved like people who knew that at any moment they, too, could become a meal.

Harlan's stomach turned. Despite the hollow pang in his gut, he was suddenly glad that he couldn't force anything down his throat before they left the hotel. Just the thought of his Zia being in a place like this made him want to retch.

It didn't matter that establishments like The Lush needed to have strict codes of consent and compensation to operate. Harlan knew what happened to so many of the hosts who stepped into those booths, and what the vampires who indulged themselves thought of them.

They were little more than fuckable food.

Harlan tried not to breathe through his nose as he made his way through the milling crowd. The lowest hum of static in his right ear told him that his audio implant was live, though Atticus remained silent on his end of the line.

His men were spread out around the outside of the club. Within a few minutes, some would begin to trickle in, melding with the normal clientèle, while the rest would be quietly slipping through the service entrance.

Julius wasn't an idiot. He demanded that Harlan come alone and unarmed. At any sign of trouble, he said he would take great pleasure in "twisting your treat's pretty little neck."

Harlan wasn't about to test his threat, but he also wasn't stupid. His men were well-trained, and most of them would be unrecognizable to Julius's guards. They wouldn't be able to pick them out from the crowd if they acted like they belonged there.

Though...

Harlan tilted his head, his gaze sweeping over the bar again. He picked out three men immediately, but the rest were obviously not part of Julius's retinue.

Counting the guards he saw across the room, he was unsettled to realize there were only five men.

Harlan touched the corner of his jaw, activating the implant there. Speaking quietly, he said, "Atticus, do we have eyes on Julius's men outside?"

Deep in his ear, he answered, "We've got the building surrounded. Only four men are on guard, as far as we can tell."

"What the fuck is going on here?"

"What? What's wrong?"

Harlan stepped lightly around a drunk fey, whose wings were buzzing loudly as he leaned against a dark-eyed vampire.

"Nothing," he grunted. "There's five men inside."

"...Only five?"

"Five."

"What the fuck?"

"I don't know," he replied, jaw clenched. "But I want you to move in as soon as I clear the doorway."

"Got it, boss."

Harlan did another quick sweep as he touched his jaw again, deactivating the mic. Unless there were more men hidden in the booths and in the back of the bar, then Julius had come woefully under-guarded.

Back when he was still living under his thumb, Julius used to travel with no less than twenty-five men. And that was when he was *comfortable.*

So either he had an ambush planned, or something had gone seriously wrong for his old master in the four years since his defection. People in the New Zone flocked to those with power and money. The unsettling suggestion that Julius might no longer have the following that he once did spoke of a dire loss of both.

He thought Julius had been laying low to bide his time, but if he had almost no soldiers to fight for him, it would explain why he was so very desperate for Harlan's skills.

What the fuck is going on here? Is this Felix's doing?

If he was right, then he had the upper hand, but that didn't mean he relished the unease he felt. It didn't sit well with him that he didn't know exactly what was going on. Neither his years of being an assassin, nor his dizzying whirl of instincts cared to step into a situation full of unknowns, let alone allow his anchor to sit in the middle of it all.

Harlan tasted iron on the back of his tongue as he pushed his way to the back of the bar, where a stainless steel door emblazoned with a much more obvious Grim's Circle gleamed. It was the entrance to the VIP floor, and it was guarded by two hulking vampires in cheap suits.

Stopping a few feet away from them, he nodded at the door and then lifted his arms.

The guards shared a wary look before the one on the right slowly approached him. They knew exactly who he was and what he was capable of, apparently.

Heavy hands patted down his sides, his back, and his legs in quick, nervous bursts. That done, he pulled a small, portable scanner from his pocket and did a quick pass from head to foot. Of course, it revealed nothing. His implants were extremely advanced biotech, stolen from the EVP's very own research division. The scanner wasn't built to pick up anything organic, so it would simply pass over it like any lump of flesh or lock of hair.

As for weapons he might have hidden: Harlan didn't have any. For all that he had risked Zia's displeasure over bringing so many weapons for their visit with her family, he didn't bother taking anything with him now.

His guns had gone to his already armed men. Bringing them wasn't worth risking Zia's safety. *Especially* when he had every intention of ripping off Julius's head with his bare hands.

"You're clear." The guard stepped back, nearly plastering himself against the wall. Beads of sweat broke out across his lined forehead. His voice cracked when he said, "You can go up, sir."

Harlan dropped his arms. Taking a calculated risk, he stepped toward the door but stood there for a moment longer than necessary. He could feel the tension of the two men ratchet up with every second that ticked by.

Who the fuck are you recruiting, Julius?

These boys looked like they were about to wet their pants and he hadn't even said a word. He didn't recognize them, either, which meant that they were new and probably, knowing his former master, not being paid enough to truly risk their lives for him.

Certainly they weren't paid enough to face *Harlan*. No one was.

Harlan turned his head one way and then the other, deliberately resting his gaze on the side of each man's pale, sweaty face.

Quietly, he asked, "Do you know what he did?"

They didn't answer, but their throats bobbed. More sweat beaded, then slid down to soak into the collars of their dress shirts.

"That man kidnapped and threatened my anchor," he explained, calm and low. "He has probably hurt her in some way. At the very least, he's scaring her as we speak." He paused, watching as horror tightened the skin around their eyes. Their shock and repulsion was written in every line of their faces, no matter how hard they tried to hide it.

Of course they didn't know. Why would they be told the truth about the job they were given? To Julius, they were expendable thugs. They were nobodies, like he was once a nobody, and they would probably end up face down in a gutter sooner rather than later even without Harlan's help.

Julius would use them up and toss them out like trash without a thought. All for control of a family he couldn't win without his pet assassin there to pick up the slack.

Both guards were ashen when he continued, as bland as if he was explaining what errands he planned to run after this was all over, "I'm going to kill him in the worst way I can conceive of, and then I'm going to kill every single person who helped him. I'm going to make it *hurt.*"

He let that hang in the air for several terrible seconds before he tilted his head toward the exit. "Go."

He didn't wait to see what they would do. As soon as he stepped past the swinging door, he knew that they would bolt.

No amount of money was worth crossing a vampire whose anchor had been stolen.

When the door swung shut behind him, Harlan stared down the dark hallway and tapped the corner of his jaw, reactivating the implant.

Too quiet for anyone but the mic to hear, he said, "Just cleared the VIP door. No guards yet. There are two men headed your way. Make sure you stop them and offer them a job."

Atticus's voice buzzed deep in his inner ear. "Picking up strays again, boss?"

"No," he answered, walking toward the single black glass door at the end of the shadowed corridor. He wasn't shocked to discover it was empty. Not a single vampire stood between him and Julius's long overdue justice.

The darkness of the hallway was a familiar shroud. Only his feet were illuminated by tiny lights in the floor, scattered to look like stars. Instinct took over as his shoulders rolled forward and his heartbeat slowed.

Bloodlust was a high, keening note in the back of his mind when he finished, "I'm here to take out the fucking trash."

CHAPTER TWENTY-TWO

WHEN ZIA WOKE UP WITH A DRY MOUTH AND THE TANG of chemicals in her nose, she felt like she was swimming up to the surface of a deep, deep pool.

Her senses were dull; her thoughts were sluggish. Something in the back of her mind *screamed,* but she couldn't hold onto any thoughts long enough to understand what her instincts were trying to tell her. All she knew was that she was late for something, or...

Had she been in a hurry? Yes, that sounded right. She had been rushing to get back to Harlan so she could cuddle up beside him in bed.

Zia's muscles twitched. Gradually, she became aware of stiffness in her limbs, and the ache of being in a strange position for too long in her neck and shoulders. Had she fallen asleep in a weird position? Maybe Harlan had rolled on top of her again. Being an extremely clingy sleeper, he tended to do that sometimes.

Except, when she shifted to get out from under him, Zia was baffled to feel the familiar slide of leather under her thighs and against her back. She was in a chair.

The screaming in the back of her mind got louder, more

focused, as she tried to force her eyes open and rise at the same time.

She wasn't successful in either endeavor. Her eyelids felt like they weighed a thousand pounds each. Her arms wouldn't move from the armrests, and when she flexed her knees, she was chilled to realize that she couldn't move her legs.

I'm... Am I cuffed to this chair?

Fear, sickly and cold, seeped through the haze of confusion. How in the world did she end up locked to a leather chair in a dimly lit room?

She couldn't puzzle it out for several long, fuzzy seconds, and then—

Memories came back in a flood of broken pieces.

The bond. An awareness that her magic no longer simply belonged to her, and the soft comfort of feeling not quite alone in her own mind anymore.

The hotel. Something about the pool, and synth, and then babies.

She remembered the heaviness of the bag's handles cutting into her fingers as she walked back to the hotel. She remembered busy thoughts of making an appointment with a healer in a few months to get her IUD removed, and to look up how vampire pregnancy worked. She remembered her heart soaring at the joy the future held. She remembered speeding up her steps when she thought of how ecstatic Harlan would be when he finally woke.

And then she remembered, with terrifying clarity, a hand closing over her mouth from behind. The sensation of being dragged, kicking and screaming, into a damp alleyway came next. A bloom of foul smelling chemicals had seared her nose and throat for just a moment before her vision swam, faded, and eventually blacked out.

Cold sweat slicked her palms as a mixture of terror and guilt assailed her.

She wasn't a rulebreaker, but it had seemed like such a small thing at the time that she waved away the consequences of doing something she knew her vampire would disapprove of. What was a five minute errand? It wasn't like when she stayed after dark on the estate, or stealing, or putting one of her brother's m-grid hackers in her car so she could break the speed limit. It was just a run to the grocery store to get Harlan something he liked.

And yet it landed her... *Where?*

Zia forced her heavy eyelids to open. She squinted and tried to peer through her curls without showing any obvious signs that she was awake, though all her squirming would have already given her away to anyone looking.

She vaguely remembered waking up once before and being afraid — very afraid of *someone,* though her memory was patchy. Whatever they used on her had left her groggy, weak, and nauseous.

Bile crawled up her throat as her eyes bounced around the room. Was she alone? Instinct said no, but even with her improved night vision, she struggled to make out shapes in the shadows.

From what she could make out, she was being held in a small room scattered with black leather furniture. Huge abstract paintings hung on the walls, and low music filtered in from hidden speakers. She was sitting in a chair, and in front of her was a low, glass table covered in an elaborate planter full of lush ferns, moss, and the tiniest of blood red miniature roses.

Across from the table was a half-moon shaped leather booth. It was strangely made. The back was tall and curled over, creating something like a shell that hid the occupants from sight if you stood at any other angle than the one she found herself at.

It took her several passes to see him there, watching her. The drugs made her sight swim, but the moment her eyes snagged on the twin night-glow eyes hidden in the darkness, her blood turned to ice.

Animal instinct took over. That wasn't *her* vampire.

"You have a lovely heartbeat."

Zia flinched. Fight or flight instincts threw all thoughts of pretending to be asleep out of her mind in an instant. She jerked backward until her head hit the high, padded back of the chair. Her arms and legs, she quickly discovered, were locked in place against the chair with silver cuffs. Magic hummed against her skin, hot and foreign. No matter how hard she pulled, she couldn't move an inch.

Recognition hit her. She knew what these restraints were, though she had never seen the real things in person. Patrol used them to subdue criminals, and she'd glimpsed schematics for similar sigilwork on her brothers' work tablets once or twice.

Her father and brothers worked in m-tech research and development for the EVP. They were part of teams responsible for fusing magic and tech to make things *just* like these cuffs — specially crafted metal restraints that could stand up to the strength of beings more powerful than her and inlaid with wards that could only be deactivated by the one who set them.

While Zia yanked fruitlessly, she prodded at the magic netting that she could feel pressing against the skin of her wrists. She was not an expert like her father, but she was well-versed in sigilwork. It was her most powerful skill, though she rare used it. If she could unwind the wards—

Except there *was* no unwinding them. In a painfully simple failsafe, the designers of the cuffs had made it so the wards could only be accessed through skin contact with the outside of the metal.

Another genius failsafe? The more she prodded at the magic, the heavier the metal became. Zia was forced to stop her meddling when the cuffs began to cut into her skin, making her struggling even less effective.

"Oh hush. Don't go thrashing around like that." The voice was oily in its sweetness. Almost a *coo.*

Zia's chest rose and fell fast as a man emerged from the booth. He stood up slowly and stepped out of the shadows with one hand tucked into his pocket and his other dangling casually by his thigh. His thumb moved restlessly over a heavy gold ring on his middle finger.

Julius had never been described to her, but she knew with absolute certainty that it was the second son of Dora Amauri that stared out at her with those glowing green eyes. The only father figure Harlan could claim — and a monster.

He was pale, with a lined face and hair that had clearly been black once, but was mostly white now. Despite his advanced age, there was still a handsomeness to him, a vitality in the breadth of his shoulders and the set of his mouth, that was utterly destroyed by the terrible vacancy of his eyes.

There was nothing there. No heat. No hatred. No glee or worry or even lust. Nothing. Meeting his gaze, Zia got the dizzying sense that she was standing at the edge of a cliff over a black abyss, and that the abyss wanted nothing more than to swallow her whole.

"Ah, that's my favorite sound," he purred. A grin broke out across his face — an awful, empty smile that did little more than show off the points of his fangs.

Julius prowled forward until he was barely a foot away from her chair. Instinct demanded she hold perfectly still, as if doing so would stop the predator from noticing her. Her heartbeat was like a fist banging against the inside of her ribs.

"I'm very sorry about all this." He casually took a seat on the edge of the low table and rested his wrists on his knees. Still, his thumb twirled that chunky gold ring. "I really do hate to make such a fuss, but Harlan has always been a stubborn boy. Never would do what he was told unless he had good enough incentive."

She had no idea what to say to that. Anger made her skin flush, but terror tied her tongue into knots. She knew exactly what kind of *incentive* he spoke of. Harlan told her about how he would withhold synth from him as a boy, how he would use basic things like blankets, sleeping inside, *showers* as both punishments and rewards for *good behavior*.

She flinched back when Julius reached out to brush hair out

of her eyes, his fingers skimming over a bruise she didn't notice until he pressed on it deliberately. When a hiss of pain escaped her, his smile stretched into a thousand-watt grin. "Do you know who I am, little bite?"

Her voice was barely a breath when she answered, "You're Julius Amauri."

His grin widened, deepening the lines around his mouth and eyes, as he pressed his thumb a little more forcefully into her brow bone. Pain bloomed, forcing a yelp out of her throat.

"Smart little bite," he praised, drawing his hand away. She watched with horror as he lifted his thumb, smeared with blood from a cut she couldn't see, up to his nose.

Julius's nostrils flared. His upper lip lifted in a snarl before he dropped his hand to wipe his bloody thumb on his slacks. "I suspected as much, but I really didn't want to be right. You're his anchor, aren't you? Such a waste. I would have paid top dollar for a taste of you, but now I'll have to wait until you flush his venom. I *hate* waiting."

Horror was a wave of needles washing over her skin, each one a new and hideous possibility.

Harlan won't let that happen.

The thought was clear and cold, slicing through her terror like a sharp knife. Her vampire would never, *ever* let anyone hurt her. He wouldn't let another vampire bite her, and he wouldn't let her kidnapping stand.

And, she realized, Julius had to know that, too.

I'm a bargaining chip, not a meal.

It was an awful thought, but one that managed to calm her nonetheless.

He wouldn't hurt her while he still needed Harlan for... whatever it was he needed him for. Getting control of the Amauri family? Simply having Harlan back under his thumb because he was a possessive little monster? Zia couldn't fathom what reasons he used to justify this, but she *did* know that he was a dead man walking.

"You won't have to wait," she replied, words tumbling out before she could stop them. She hated this vampire with everything in her. She *wanted* him to know that his death was coming, because he had earned every second of dread and pain that was coming to him. "He'll kill you before you get the chance."

She jolted when Julius slapped his thigh, a roar of laughter bouncing off of the dark walls. "Oh, I *like* you! You're going to be so much fun for me, little bite!"

He leaned forward, hands reaching for her cuffs. Zia shrank back as far as she could go. Her skin crawled when his fingers brushed her wrists and then moved down her legs. There was a burst of magic against her skin, almost too hot for comfort but gone in an instant.

The restraints popped off and fell to the floor, and the grating hum of magic ceased.

Before she could process her release, he yanked her up and out of her seat. She stumbled, her balance shot, as he maneuvered her around the table and into the booth. Her head swam as she attempted to right herself.

"Make yourself comfortable," he said, nudging her deeper into the booth. "I'll order you something to drink so you can relax as I talk business with my wayward protégé. What would you like, hm? Maybe something sweet?"

Zia shook her head, both to clear the spots from her vision and to reject his offer. There was no fucking way she would accept any sort of drink from this man.

Julius *tsked*. A twinkle of malicious interest lit his night-glow eyes. "Now, little bite, you're not allowed to say no to me. I'll ask once more. If you give me an answer I don't like, you won't enjoy the consequences. What do you want to drink?"

Her heart jammed its way into her throat. The sugar-coated tone only made the very real threat in his words scarier, more real. This man *wanted* her to do something wrong. Whatever those consequences were, he actually looked excited by them.

That, she decided, was far, far worse than the emptiness from before.

"I—" She dug her fingernails into the leather of the seat. "I want a—"

Julius pulled a sleek phone out of his pocket. He held out a hand, telling her wordlessly to shut up. That wide grin returned. "Oh good," he said, tucking his phone away, "he's here!"

An uneasy mixture of relief and terror locked her muscles until she was frozen in her seat. Zia was overjoyed to know Harlan had come to her rescue, but the thought of what could happen to him now because of that made her want to throw up her fancy breakfast.

She knew that he was dangerous, but this man was clearly deranged — and had a grudge she couldn't begin to guess the complexities of.

He also had the upper hand. Harlan would never risk her life, which meant that Julius could probably get him to do whatever he liked, so long as he kept her under his thumb.

Her breath stalled. Dark spots floated in front of her eyes. *Gods, what if he hurts Harlan because of me?*

Her darling vampire who had been through so much, who only wanted to keep her safe and happy, would endure any pain for her. She knew this instinctively, just as she knew her magic connected them on a level even an exchange of blood couldn't match.

The idea of her bondmate suffering because of her was utterly unbearable.

A fluttering hand skimmed the back of her head, pressing her tangled curls down. "Breathe for me, little bite," Julius commanded, all mocking concern. "I can't have you passing out before he gets here, can I? What kind of impression would that make?"

Zia wanted to snap at him, to break his hand or burn his flesh, but she was powerless. While magic buzzed in her veins, she had no real offensive abilities. Her telekinesis was negligible, her psychic abilities non-existent. She couldn't channel heat or sound or electricity to wound. All she could do was tinker with wards and talk to plants.

"I said *breathe.*" Sharp pain in the side of her neck forced her to suck in a lungful of air. Her eyes snapped toward Julius, who was making himself comfortable next to her in the booth. He was frowning at his claws and, as she watched, he flicked her blood off of them. Splatters flew across the glass table in the center of the booth. They caught the low light like a galaxy of tiny rubies.

There was nothing dangerous about her — except her blood.

Zia clutched at her neck. Blood oozed between her fingers from a long, shallow slice. A little pool began to accumulate in her cupped palm, hot and sticky and awful. She gasped out a panicked sound.

Julius made a shushing gesture with his bloody claws and rolled his eyes. "Hush now. It's only a scratch. Just a reminder to be on your best behavior for me, little bite, or you'll get far worse."

She didn't have time to tell him that Harlan wouldn't think it was *just* anything. If he thought he could escape her vampire's wrath before, there was absolutely no possibility now.

Just as the thought flitted through her mind, the silver door on the opposite side of the room slowly eased open.

The hallway beyond was so dark, she struggled to make out the familiar form in the doorway — broad shoulders, lean waist, long hair. The familiar silhouette, the one she had fantasized about for a year, made her heart stutter. She didn't need to see his features to know exactly who he was.

Harlan.

Something deep behind her breastbone pulled her to him. Magic sang in her veins, bubbling and fizzing with recognition. *Safe,* it said, reaching for him. *We're safe now.*

Julius's hand closing over the nape of her neck shattered that fleeting moment of relief.

"Harlan," he greeted, grinning from ear to ear. "So good to see you! Take a seat. Have you enjoyed your vacation?"

She bit back a whimper as her vampire closed the door behind him. His eyes lingered on her face for only a moment before they moved slowly over the oozing wound she covered, to Julius's extended arm, and up to the man himself.

"Julius."

It was one word. Just a name spoken softly. And yet it felt like a boom of thunder in the quiet room.

Harlan walked slowly until he stood beside the chair she had woken up in. He glanced down — barely a flicker of his eyes — and she knew the moment he spotted the fallen restraints. His expression was shuttered, but there was a subtle tightening of his jaw and the slightest flex of his claws by his thigh.

Slowly, he rested one hand on the back of the chair. "I haven't been on vacation. Dora released me from service and I retired."

Julius's fingers tightened around the nape of her neck. She could feel the tension building in him, though his tone never once changed from the sweet, gentle one he had used from the start. "Oh, I know my mother promised you all sorts of things after you helped her kill my brother, but you must know that dear old mom died recently, don't you?"

He killed Dora Amauri's son? Zia's mind spun. Was that why Julius wanted him so badly? Was it some element of revenge? If so, then she thought they had a lot more to worry about than just a shitty job offer.

Harlan's eyes didn't stray to her face again, but she felt his focus on her through the bond. It pressed against the back of her mind, insistent and dark and safe, like a shadow reaching out to embrace her.

"I do know about Dora's passing," he answered, easing himself into the leather seat. "That doesn't explain why you've gone so far to get my attention, though."

"You're stubborn." Julius shrugged. Releasing her neck, he moved to pet her hair again — as if she wasn't actively trying to stop the bleeding from her throat while he did so. "After you left and Dora said no one was allowed to contact you, I knew you'd be a pain to get back. I thought that sending all those pesky flies your way would annoy you enough to give you a little push, but I got distracted when my mother started deteriorating."

Julius spoke of his mother's health in the same way she might have talked about her car needing new brakes. "Things have been messy back home. My mother really fucked things up for me as a final maternal gift." An edge of real anger entered his otherwise cheerful voice. "Can you *believe* she made that boy her heir? That fucking welp has been undercutting me for twenty years."

Harlan tilted his head, considering something. "You want me to kill Felix, I presume."

"Of course I do." Julius looked at him like he'd just asked if the sky was blue. "And whoever else I want dead, of course. I knew you'd just need a little convincing, so..."

He twirled one of her curls around his bloody finger. His smile turned sly when he finished, "Why not just snatch something you care about? I know how much you covet pretty things. You get that from me, you know."

CHAPTER TWENTY-THREE

HARLAN BENT SLIGHTLY TO PICK UP TWO OF THE CUFFS. Julius watched him move with an indulgent expression, saying, "Nice, aren't they? I caught a shipment of military gear smuggled out of the 'Riik last year. Those cuffs are state of the art sigilwork. Look how well designed they are! They could even restrain a rogue dragon."

Her vampire held them in his palms and examined them for a moment, his expression bland. It was like he was looking at two lumps of granite rather than magically reinforced restraints.

He rubbed his thumbs over the edges of each cuff, circling slowly, and looked up through his lashes at his old master. "I suppose I get my love of beautiful things from you, though I tend to keep my treasures in better condition than you do."

Julius made a derisive noise in the back of his throat. Flicking her curl aside, he leaned forward to brace his elbows on his knees. Threading his fingers together, he rested his chin on them as he replied, "See, that is your problem. I always told you that you should never get attached to things — or people. It just gives me more to play with."

He tilted his head and with a disapproving little frown, admonished, "Really, Harlan. An *anchor?* You should know better than that. Now I'm going to have to flush her, and that won't be very nice for her at all."

Zia held her breath, her eyes glued to her vampire's stoic expression. Harlan's voice was unnaturally calm when he asked, "And why do you have to do that?"

"Because I'm going to keep her for a while," Julius answered, like it was the most obvious thing in the world. "Once we're back home and you're doing what I trained you to do, maybe I'll consider giving her back. We'll see."

"You don't want an anchor."

"Grim, *no.*" Julius looked disgusted by the very idea. She was too relieved to be offended. "You wouldn't catch me *breeding* with a witch even if my life depended on it. Once I've got control of the family, I'm going to find myself a lovely little bloodbond to give me an heir."

The sly look returned, but this time it had a hungry edge that made her stomach bunch up into a series of painful knots. "Tell me, Harlan, how is little Adriana doing these days? I hear she's living it up here in the city. I thought I might stop by her apartment to say hello."

The threat hung above them all, thickening the air to the point where it felt like it was hard for Zia to breathe. She was scared for her vampire, but she was *terrified* for Adriana. What kind of misery would this monster force on her friend? She didn't pretend to know everything about vampire culture, but she knew enough. It would not be simple pain. Not just suffering.

It would be a lifetime of torture, just because Adriana happened to have a coveted genetic quirk.

Her eyes darted between Harlan and Julius as they stared at one another, communicating silently.

Eventually, her vampire tilted his head to the right. His eyes flicked to hers for barely a second before they went back to watching the predator at her side. "She's well," he answered, like the question was sincere, "and untouchable."

Julius *tsked* once more. He was so focused on Harlan, that he didn't notice when Zia began to inch ever-so-slowly to the right, toward the empty side of the booth.

"Oh, we'll see about that. She really was such a pretty, sweet little thing. I wonder — why did you never have her tested? Was it because you wanted her for yourself? Or maybe you planned to sell her to the highest bidder." Julius's saccharine tone vanished. His voice rose in pitch and volume as he speculated, "Maybe you promised her to Felix. Maybe you always planned on betraying me. You know how far a bloodbond would go to solidify his claim over the family."

Zia watched Harlan's thumbs circle the cuffs again, this time counter-clockwise. She bit back a surprised little squeak when she felt another deliberate brush of his consciousness in the back of her mind. This time, it was accompanied with the distinct sense of *drawing* — magic moving out of her gently, in a steady current, as he did something she couldn't see.

Blood trickled down her wrist as the pool in her palm over-flowed. She didn't think she was at risk of bleeding out, but fear made her breath choppy anyway. She couldn't black out. That would make her even more of a burden for him than she already was.

She had no idea what he was planning, or what this monster sitting next to her would do. She just hoped she could keep herself together until the escalating tension broke.

"So you don't just want your pet assassin back to help you take back the power you've obviously lost," Harlan surmised, bland and entirely unmoved by the horrifying implications of Julius's accusation. He said it like he was simply confirming something he already knew. "You want Adriana, too."

"You could get rid of Felix and Yvanna in an afternoon." Julius waved his hand. That gaudy ring winked in the low light. "That would solve fifty percent of my problems with only a little bit of mess. Adriana would solve the other fifty percent with none."

"Why are you so certain that Adriana is neutral?" His thumbs disappeared behind the cuffs, tracing shapes she couldn't see against the metal. Zia felt the pinpricks of magic moving under her skin as she inched across the padded bench. There was a whole two feet between her and Julius now.

"Please," Julius scoffed, straightening his spine. He slapped his hands on his knees. "Why would you go so far to hide the girl if she wasn't?"

Harlan narrowed his eyes. There was a swift popping sensation deep in the churning magical core that bound her to him. It was familiar, and when she recognized what it was, Zia had to fight to keep her eyes from widening to the size of saucers.

He broke the ward.

He was going to use the cuffs. But what would they do? She doubted he planned to just restrain the man. There was no way her vampire was going to let Julius walk out of this room alive. But if he didn't have a weapon...

Zia felt the trickle of blood over the pounding pulse at the base of her throat. *But he does, doesn't he?*

"Because I care about her," Harlan answered simply. "She's my daughter in every way that matters."

"And *that's* why it's always been easy to control you."

The world turned upside down in an instant. Like someone had waved a flag, both men acted in the same second: Julius snatched her arm and drew her roughly into his lap as Harlan lunged over the glass table, cuffs in hand.

She felt the hot barrel of a primed bolt gun pressing against her temple, but had hardly processed the revelation before Harlan snapped a cuff onto Julius's wrist and attempted to wrestle his arm back against the booth.

They were snapping and snarling, all pretense of civility vanished like a puff of smoke, and Zia was caught in the middle. Outside the room, the faint sounds of screaming and dull whine of discharged bolts filtered in — just before the much louder sound of a bolt gun going off next to her ear made her jerk. It took her a frantic second to realize the bolt missed both men and instead went over Harlan's shoulder to hit the ceiling. Plaster rained down onto the glass table and its pretty miniature roses, and the acrid scent of hot plasma stung her nose.

There was a stunned second where they all held perfectly still.

Zia didn't think. She didn't wait to see if Harlan had been shot, or if *she* had. Taking advantage of that tiny opening, she pulled her hand away from her wound, wrenched herself around in Julius's lap, and shoved her cupped palm against his mouth.

He made an incoherent, outraged sound just as Harlan forced his hand back against the cushioned booth. Magic hummed in the air. The cuff locked in place. There was a wet crack as Harlan tore the gun from Julius's hand — breaking bones in the process.

The older vampire's head thrashed, fighting to tear his mouth away from her hand. Julius gasped and then gurgled as her blood was forced into his mouth. When he tried to spit it out, Harlan's big, scarred hand covered hers. A rough command filled the suddenly too-quiet room. "Pinch his nose."

There was a brief, hysterical moment where she wanted to ask why *he* didn't just do it. She wasn't built for this sort of thing, after all. But he was busy holding onto Julius's other hand, she realized, and it was not the time to take umbrage with his commands.

Adrenaline bubbled in her veins as she followed his instructions. Using her forefinger and thumb, she cut off Julius's air. Within a handful of seconds he was struggling in earnest, attempting to dislodge them so he wouldn't be forced to swallow her poisoned blood.

Zia had never even thought of what it might be like to watch a man die, but when the air loss became too much, she couldn't say she was sorry to see Julius choke on her blood.

Once it was clear it wouldn't be coming up again, Harlan snapped the other cuff on his wrist and fixed it to the table, forcing his former master into an awkward spread-armed pose. That done, he hooked his arm around Zia's waist and hauled her away. They were halfway across the room before Julius began to convulse.

Oh, gods. Zia felt her gorge rise as she watched him jerk his splayed arms, desperately trying to free himself as pink-tinged foam began to leak from his lips. His eyes were wild as they rolled backward, almost animalistic in their desperation. Gone was the sophisticated man with the sugary charm and vacant gaze.

This creature was nothing but flailing, gurgling meat.

When the blood vessels began to pop in the whites of his eyes, Zia felt Harlan's hand on the side of her head. She let him turn her face into his chest as he backed them up. His spine hit the wall by the door with a dull thud.

Across the room, the sounds of agony got louder, more disgusting.

Zia tried to block them out. Instead, she retreated to the soft shadows in her mind, where warmth and safety waited. She buried her nose in the collar of his shirt and breathed in his scent, felt his heartbeat against her chest, and thanked every god in the pantheon that her vampire was *hers.*

She didn't know how long it took Julius to die. It felt like hours, but it could have been less than ten minutes. Whatever the case, Harlan held her tightly until his last breath. She could feel the warm muzzle of the bolt gun against her hip, gripped in his tense hand, and the way his heartbeat thundered until, at last, it calmed.

"He's dead."

Zia was shaking too badly to do more than nod.

Soft fingers slid under her chin, gently coaxing her to tilt her face up. Her vampire stared down at her with an agonized expression. "My love," he whispered, voice breaking, "I am so sorry."

Tears spilled over. "I shouldn't have l-left the room," she blubbered, clutching at his bloody shirt with all her strength. "I'm the one who— it was my fault!"

"It's *not* your fault." His voice was whip-sharp. "He was waiting for any opening, Zia. If we didn't give him one, he would

have made his own. I should have done more, but even then..."
He shook his head. His expression was slack with disbelief. "I
didn't realize how desperate he was. We were his only shot at
getting his power back. Even if I'd done everything right, he still
would have found a way to get to us."

She sniffed hard. A hard knot of dread and guilt made a lump
in her throat. "You're not angry with me?"

"Gods." It was as soft as a breath. "Gods, Zia... I was out of
my mind when I found you gone. When I walked in and saw your
blood and his hands on you, I thought—" The sentence ended
with a single, cracked syllable. "Zia, you are my beating heart. I'm
not angry with you. I could never *be* angry with you. Please
believe me."

The knot loosened, making it easier for her to breathe. "I love
you," she replied, hiccuping. It was about all she could manage to
articulate, and summed up everything she felt, everything she
needed, in three simple words. "I love you so much. I'll never
break another rule, I promise."

A soothing rumble built in his chest. Harlan leaned more of
his weight against the wall, like relief had stolen some of the
strength from his spine. "Ah, pet, you can break rules. I love it
when you surprise me. Just don't ever leave my sight again. At
least for a while. Maybe forever."

A raw laugh climbed out of her aching throat. "Deal, Mr.
Bounds."

Very, very gently, he tilted her head to one side and began to
lick at the cut on her neck, cleaning up every drop of blood and
sealing the wound with his saliva.

She went lax in his hold as her body responded to what was
his usual after-bite care. A flood of endorphins dulled the edge of
hysteria that threatened to cut her in two. *Safe,* instinct whispered. *Cared for. Loved.*

"So brave," he murmured against her throat. "So smart. I
never would have thought to use your blood against him. I was
just going to snap his fucking neck, but I like your way better.

Blood poisoning is the worst, most humiliating death a vampire can suffer." There was a dark pride in every word.

Zia didn't quite know how to feel about that, but she didn't argue. So long as she never had to do anything like this again, then she would accept the macabre praise. Her voice was slightly sluggish when she asked, "Is it done?"

"We will never have to worry about him again, my Zia. You're safe. You'll *always* be safe."

She sagged against his chest. Burying her face in the crook of his neck, she croaked, "But is it *over*-over?"

"Yes." Harlan kissed the crown of her head and squeezed her so tight, she felt the breath *whoosh* out of her lungs. "Atticus and the other guards have taken care of the few men who were loyal to him. It's done, pet."

Relief made her shudder. "What about— How are you gonna..."

She couldn't even get the words *"dispose of the body"* out of her mouth. While she wholeheartedly believed that monster got what he deserved, it was impossible for her to comprehend the realities of murder or its aftermath.

Harlan combed his claws through her hair. When they caught on a snag, he stopped to very carefully unwind the knot before he continued his strokes. "Don't think about that. Let's just get you back to the hotel and taken care of."

Her voice was very small and watery when she asked, "Can't we just go home?"

"We will go home tomorrow," he promised. "But I need to make a few calls first."

CHAPTER TWENTY-FOUR

FELIX AMAURI WAS A YOUNG MAN NOT TO BE FUCKED with.

That was the impression Harlan got when he met him the first time fifty years ago, and it was the same impression he got when he met the vampire in the deserted main floor of The Lush approximately six hours after he ended Julius once and for all.

It didn't take much to get Felix onto a private m-jet headed for San Francisco. All it took was a photo of Julius's right hand — and his bloody ring.

"Who owns this place?"

Harlan eyed the younger man as he stood in the center of the room, his hands on his hips and his eyes roving over the empty booths and overturned tables. His guards stood at the door, arms loose at their sides and expressions coolly focused.

Unlike Julius's hired help, *those* men would die for Felix in a heartbeat. They would kill for him even faster.

"Some local family," Harlan answered, his tone brusque. He didn't care about the bar, nor Felix. He just wanted to get back to his anchor, who he had left in the heavily guarded suite drowsy and full of venom. It kept her calm, and it soothed the bone-deep terror that she might be snatched from him again that he still felt hours later.

Itching to be near her, he cleared his throat and nodded toward the bar. "Small time shit. Mostly drugs and smuggling through the Underground. I think they call themselves the Vance family."

Felix hummed. His eyes, a cool blue that bordered on gray, fixed on Harlan with a familiar intensity. He was a man raised by Dora Amauri and it showed.

He was utterly self-possessed and ice-fucking-cold.

His expensive leather shoes barely made any noise as he made his way across the floor to join Harlan at the small table and chair he commandeered for their meeting. A black body bag lay by his feet.

Felix was taller than Harlan, but leaner, with a swimmer's build and long black hair that curled around his neck and ears. His most notable feature, besides his pretty face, was the lock of white hair that curled over his forehead. It was a signature feature of the Amauri family, and one he knew Felix wore proudly.

That, and a bad attitude.

Felix nudged the edge of the body bag with the toe of his shoe. His lip lifted with disgust. "That him?"

"Yes." Harlan fished the ring out of his pocket and set it on the table between them. It was a gaudy thing — thick gold, with the Amauri crest engraved in the center — and had delivered more wounds to Harlan's face than any real weapon ever had.

Felix glanced at the ring, then back to the bag, before he cracked a wide, pleased smile. Sinking down into a chair, he spread his arms and announced, "I need a fucking drink."

Harlan watched one of his guards peel away from the door to slip behind the bar. He disappeared through a discreet door for a handful of moments before he came out again, this time with a pale, scowling woman in toe. The guard pushed her toward the bar. "Get him a drink. Best alcoholic synth you have."

The waitress, dressed in a severe black cocktail dress and

gloves, firmed her angular jaw but didn't talk back. Instead, she used a keycard to unlock a compartment behind the bar and retrieved a bottle of extremely expensive alcoholic synthblood called Velvet.

She kept her eyes down and her movements efficient as she cracked the lid and activated the heat seal. Walking briskly, she didn't bat an eye at the body bag on the floor as she moved to deposit the bottle in front of Felix.

Harlan suspected it was not the worst thing she had seen in The Lush.

The blonde waitress was barely a wisp of a thing. Small, fine-boned, and pale, she looked like she was made to make people like Felix feel powerful when they served them. Harlan didn't get the appeal of any of it, but when he watched Felix's eyes trace her form, his fangs pressing into his bottom lip, Harlan suspected *he* did.

"Thank you," he said, breaking the tension. He didn't want to be the reason the poor waitress ended up as Felix's plaything, so it was best he shooed her away as soon as possible.

Putting a firm order in his tone, he commanded, "Go home now. If your boss gives you shit about leaving the bar, send him to me."

Her eyes flashed to his for just a moment before she nodded. She turned on her low heel to walk away, but not before Felix's arm shot out. His large, clawed hand circled her wrist like a manacle. The waitress stiffened, her delicate shoulders bunching.

Still, she kept her eyes down.

Smart girl. Men like Felix loved a challenge, and tended to look for it everywhere — in a tone, a gesture, and even a single glance. He suspected she'd dealt with her fair share of people like Felix in The Lush, though he doubted she had ever encountered someone with as much power as him.

"Tell me your name before you go."

Harlan was impressed by the way such a waif could manage to

look so coolly uninterested. Her expression was blank as she stared at a spot on his shoulder.

In a pretty, lilting voice, she answered, "Dahlia, sir."

Felix hummed again, except this time it sounded unsettlingly like a purr. His eyelids lowered as he gently released her wrist. "Pretty name."

When she was sure he wouldn't grab her again, Dahlia beat a hasty retreat. Felix's eyes followed her until the last strands of her golden hair disappeared through the doorway behind the bar.

Almost to himself, he said, "Really is a nice bar, though they're fucking stupid to have a woman like that serving drinks. Someone is going to snatch her." He flicked his tongue against a fang. "I'd run this place better than the *Vance* family."

"Take it, then," Harlan grunted, increasingly annoyed by how long this was taking. He had a traumatized anchor to get back to, and all the stress made his body work overtime. Already he could feel his gland aching, filling with more venom.

The desire to possess Zia was stronger than it had ever been. Now that he knew what it was like to have her ripped away from him, Harlan struggled to control the urge to keep his fangs buried in her throat indefinitely. Until the day her body was fully in tune with his and his seed firmly fucking planted, he might just do that.

It wasn't a reasonable urge. It was primitive and raw and a little bit ugly, but it was a desperate sort of need born from a fear that he would never be able to shake.

Felix shot him a smile as he lifted the bottle of Velvet to his lips. "Just might. Couldn't hurt to expand operations westward now that you've taken care of my little problem."

You'd be a fucking idiot to bring the Syndicate to the EVP, he thought, eyeing the young man coolly. *But if anyone can, it's probably this arrogant motherfucker.*

Because unlike Julius, who was arrogant to his rotten core but otherwise average, Felix was wickedly intelligent.

That cleverness glittered in his eyes when he lowered the

bottle onto the glass table top. "So," he drawled, nodding toward the ring that sat between them. "What do you want?"

"Peace."

The younger vampire eyeballed him with open disbelief. "Really? You know what I'd pay you to work for me, Bounds? The kind of rank I could give you?"

"I don't want your money and I don't want a high rank. I want to be left *the fuck* alone."

Felix rolled his eyes. "What if I offered you a position as my right hand man on the west coast? You could be the head of the entire operation on this side of the continent. All I'd ask is that you help me take out Yvanna."

Maybe before Zia, Harlan would have considered it. The poor, lonely boy in the gutter would have jumped at the chance to have that kind of power and respect he was being offered.

But that boy now had a family to think of — not just Zia, but Atticus and Adriana, Zia's brothers and her parents. Sooner rather than later, they would have their own children, too.

He didn't want any of them getting dragged into the Syndicate. Not after he worked so hard to keep them out of it in the first place.

Besides, he wasn't tempted. Not really. He had everything he needed — more than he ever thought he deserved, certainly.

"I don't want half the continent," he answered, utterly immovable. "I eliminated one of the biggest threats to your power today. All I ask for in exchange is that you leave me and my family alone. *Forever.*"

He could tell Felix wanted to argue. Like him, he was not a man who gave up something he wanted easily. But he could also see that the younger vampire knew it was not a fight he could win. He could give him this, or he could make himself Harlan's enemy.

And Felix had more than enough enemies to deal with already.

Snatching up the bottle, he took a long drink before he slowly inclined his head. His eyes cut briefly to the bar before they moved back to Harlan's forbidding expression. "Fine. I get the bastard's body and you get out for good."

They shook on it before Harlan stood. "Try not to die too young, Felix."

"Don't plan to, old man." The younger vampire laughed as he stood up from his chair as well. Instead of heading for the door like Harlan, he knelt by the body bag and began to unzip it.

Harlan was nearly at the door when Felix called out, "Grim's tits! What the fuck happened to him?"

His hand pressed against the cool metal door, opening it just enough to let in the dull light of pre-dawn. Without turning around, he answered, "Blood poisoning, I'm afraid. Awful way to go, isn't it?"

EPILOGUE

JUNE 2050 - EMPIRE ESTATE, THE ELVISH PROTECTORATE

"WHAT'S THIS ONE AGAIN, *ANNE?*"

Zia looked up from her task of attempting to gently weed out the overgrown mint plant in their kitchen garden to find her daughter holding a bristling twig of rosemary about an inch from her nose.

"Give it a smell," she gently encouraged as she rocked back on her heels. She was already getting tired, and that annoyed her to no end. It was the first time since the birth of her son that she'd felt anywhere near well enough to get some night air. She *needed* to get out of the house, but her enthusiasm didn't make her body recover any faster.

It wasn't easy keeping up with a four year old, either.

Serafina squinted her big brown eyes at the twig in her chubby fist for a long moment, mimicking her father's narrow-eyed expression of concentration, before she brought it up to her nose for a noisy sniff.

"Blegh!" Her little fangs flashed with her disgusted grimace.

She shoved the twig back at her mother, who took it with a grin. "So smelly!"

"That's rosemary, baby. It's used for food," Zia explained, pulling her daughter's soft little body into her lap. She reached around her to pluck a leaf off of the mint. The plant didn't mind losing a leaf or two, since it was beginning to overstretch its resources, but she gave it a small pulse of magic as a thank you anyway.

Handing it to her daughter, she said, "Smell this one. It's called mint."

Serafina's little black pigtails bobbed when she dipped her head to sniff the leaf in her mother's hand. "That's toothpaste!"

"It's what toothpaste is flavored with, yes."

Harlan's baritone came from the doorway to the kitchen. "Are we getting a botanical lesson tonight?"

Mother and daughter swiveled their heads to look at the vampire leaning against the door jamb. He wore running pants and no shirt, but a baby sling was strapped over his chest. Zia could just make out a tiny brown fist curled against his scarred pectoral muscle and a wisp of curly black hair from deep within the sling.

Like always, her heart swelled with warmth when she glimpsed the long-healed marriage sigil between his brows. Designed to look like a blooming rose, it held a spark of magic in it — a symbol of the unbreakable bond that stretched between them, forged in blood and magic both.

The night they married, Harlan told her that it was the only scar he wore proudly. She still felt a rush of warmth when she remembered those words, and the long, blissful night that followed them.

"Daddy, smell this!" Serafina hopped out of her mother's lap to scurry over to Harlan, who immediately squatted down to be at her level. Her little bare feet flew over the brick path until she halted with a clumsy half-step in front of her father.

When she held the nearly crushed leaf up to his nose, he

sniffed dutifully. "Hm," he hummed, putting on a thoughtful expression. "What does that smell like? I can't quite put my finger on it."

Serafina, who relished learning to an almost unhealthy degree and who had inherited her mother's tendency to ramble, sucked in a deep breath and clapped her hands on her father's cheeks. "It's *toothpaste*, Daddy!"

Harlan's eyes crinkled when he glanced over their daughter's shoulder to meet Zia's amused gaze. "Is that right? I had no idea."

Careful not to over-exert her abdominal muscles too much, Zia carefully levered herself up from her spot on the ground by the flower bed. Cupping the back of her daughter's head, she said, "It can also be used as a tea. You've seen me drink it lots of times."

Serafina wrinkled her nose. "That stuff from when you were sick with Leo?"

"Sometimes, yes."

She looked up at her mother like she was questioning her taste. "I didn't like that one very much."

"That's because you're a growing vampire, and vampires prefer synth." Harlan rose up from his crouch to gently usher their daughter inside the kitchen with one hand. "Speaking of which — it's lunchtime, princess. Go pick your bottle from the cupboard."

"But how come Leo doesn't hafta drink synth?" Serafina shuffled her dirty feet in the dust by the door, her lips pursed. "And *Anne* doesn't either."

"That's because I'm a witch, not a vampire," Zia answered, unfazed by the question. She'd already answered it close to a dozen times since Leo's birth. "And your brother drinks milk until his fangs come in, just like you did."

"Well, I don't *remember* drinking milk," she muttered, eyeing her brother's tiny form dubiously.

"You were too young to remember, but you did." Harlan nudged her again, edging her over the threshold and into the kitchen where he and Zia had their first quasi-date all those years ago. "Go pick your bottle, or I'll do it for you. You need to eat before your auntie gets here with her anchor, remember? If you don't, you'll be too cranky to play with—"

Serafina was off like a shot. Her feet pitter-pattered against the tile floor as she rushed around her father. "I'm goin', I'm goin'!"

Zia shook her head. "I swear, she'd do anything for her uncle. I just don't get it."

Personally, she found Adriana's anchor to be one of the prickliest, haughtiest men she'd ever met, but both she and Serafina thought he was the best thing since synthblood. It almost certainly had something to do with all the gifts he came with — mainly rare books and toys that made a truly egregious amount of noise.

Echoing her thoughts, Harlan dryly replied, "He spoils her."

"Like you don't?" she teased, dusting off her hands.

Harlan stepped out of the doorway to wrap his arms around her middle. Drawing her close, but not enough to wake the baby pressed between them, he dropped his face into the crook of her neck and pressed a warm, wet kiss there. Zia's toes curled in her custom boots.

"I spoil you, too, don't I?" The words were a deep rumble against her skin. Goosebumps broke out all over her body, and a familiar heat settled low in her stomach.

Smoothing her hands up his bare back, she felt the muscles there ripple in a sensual wave. "I don't have any complaints."

Harlan huffed a laugh.

It was true, though. Zia didn't have anything to complain about. Her life was so full of laughter and color and love that some days she felt overwhelmed by it all. It took her a year to truly believe that Felix would keep his word, but every day since had been treated like the gift it was.

There was never a single moment where she regretted her choice to break the estate's one cardinal rule, nor her participation in the death of Julius Amauri.

Both choices had led her to this moment. Three days after her kidnapping, they led her to asking Harlan to marry her, which he happily did at Moonset a few weeks later. A year after that, they led to the birth of their daughter, named after her grandmother. Four years after that, those choices led to the birth of their son Leo.

Their world wasn't perfect. Harlan was still extremely paranoid about their safety — and was somehow *worse* when she was pregnant — but instead of feeling hemmed in, Zia felt safe. Her family was protected on all sides by an elite force of guards who acted more like family, and the connections that spiderwebbed out from Atticus and Adriana and Zia's brothers.

They were a force to be reckoned with, though no one dared do so after Felix took bloody control of his family. The announcement that the Bounds family was officially off-limits, and that anyone who crossed that line would be dealing with the full force of his wrath, had gone a long way to soothing their minds.

Harlan kissed her neck lazily, lavishing old bite marks with attention. Zia sighed and stroked his back with her fingertips, taking in the comforting mixture of scents from her vampire and the newborn cradled between them.

"Do you think she's making a mess in there?" she asked, voice low so Serafina's keen ears wouldn't catch it.

He scraped his fangs over her pulse point and slowly lapped at the tiny beads of blood that welled there before eventually answering, "Absolutely."

Zia giggled. "Shouldn't we go check on her, then?"

"Not yet." Harlan lifted his head to skim his lips against hers. It wasn't quite a kiss, but it was close enough to make her close her eyes and sigh. "Have I told you how much I love you today, pet?"

"You tell me every night when we wake up, Mr. Bounds."

"I'll tell you again, then." He twined one hand into her curls, holding her head still as he gave one slow kiss after another. "I love you, my Zia. Somehow, I love you more every single night."

She melted into him. Hearing him say how much he loved her, how much he loved their *life*, never got old.

"I love you too, my scary vampire." She gave his bottom lip a tiny nip, earning herself a low, rumbly growl. A wide grin made her cheeks ache. "Thank you for hunting me down the night I trespassed."

His night-glow eyes glinted with a familiar heat. "My pet, I'd hunt you down across the entire fucking continent if I had to. You can't escape me."

Zia kissed the tip of his nose. "Wouldn't dream of it."

Harlan opened his mouth to reply, but this was stopped by a sudden crash and childlike *eep!* from the kitchen.

They both turned toward the doorway just as their daughter's round face popped out from around the kitchen island. She made a disgruntled face that showed off her fangs. "Daddy, which bottles are mine again?"

Harlan shook his head. He was way better at hiding his smile than Zia was. Cupping their son's back with one hand, he sighed and walked back into the kitchen. Tugging lightly on one of Serafina's pigtails, he said, "Come on, princess. Let's go clean up the mess you made."

Zia watched them walk away. Butterflies filled her stomach, and a golden satisfaction suffused every part of her being. She moved to follow them, but stopped just before the threshold to glance over her shoulder.

The sky was a deep, inky black speckled with a spray of stars. The air was heavy with the day's heat. Around the edge of the property, bugs sang in bushes and an owl called out from the shelter of the trees.

When she looked out over the brick patio that overlooked the koi pond and the gardens below, her heart lurched. She couldn't see beyond the balustrade, but the glow from the lamps Harlan installed for her was a gentle warmth in the distance.

The estate was quiet. The guards were patrolling the grounds.

Mr. Eisele had gone home hours before, his golf cart safely parked in the staff garage. All was hushed, and still, perfect.

Zia turned to step into the kitchen. Just as the latch clicked into place, she heard her son's high-pitched cry from within the pantry. It was shortly followed by Serafina's exasperated exclamation of, "But you said Leo was hungry! He can't even *try* some of my synth?"

Zia grinned. *Nothing to complain about, indeed.*

THE END

A SNEAK PEEK OF STRIKE...

DECEMBER 2044 - THE ELVISH PROTECTORATE

She was once boundless.

It was the only way she could describe her life before the storm, and the dragon, and *newness*.

She was immeasurable, a gossamer veil between the horizon and the dome of stars; formless, with neither body nor true mind, but *presence*, personhood, all the same. Consciousness did not come all at once. It grew over eons, in starts and stops, and not always in isolation. In quiet moments, she thought she could reach deep into her memory, to that wild primordial time, and touch other beginnings, other beings, who joined to become *her*.

Her first clear thought came as a surprise. She had no eyes, no ears, no body at all, and yet she sensed the world below her and felt the thought in every part of her being. It was fully-formed, a strike of electricity through a haze of dull awareness: *What is that?*

More thoughts came, each one quicker, more focused than the last. Existing as magic and thought, she could do little more than watch the world below her and *hunger*. For what, she didn't know — at least, not for many, many years. How could she, when she did not have words for the concept of curiosity? For loneliness? Despair?

And yet she felt, and wondered, and decided that if ever there was a chance to be reborn into something else, she would trade her vastness for even a moment of *life*. Drifting over the world, she watched those below and felt envy. It took many thousands of years for her to recognize that they, too, were beings with thoughts. Watching them closely revealed previously unimaginable differences between them.

Sound. Movement. Community. *Change.*

They did not make sense to her, but one day she began to wish she could know what it was like to be small and strange and together with others. There was no one to hear her silent pleas, but she wished anyway.

It came as something of a shock, however, when that wish came true...

ALSO BY ABIGAIL KELLY

Find all new releases, bonus chapters, and exclusive content on the
Works by Abigail Patreon!

FRAGILE BEINGS: A NEW PROTECTORATE NOVELLA COLLECTION

In the first volume of The New Protectorate Stories...

Fate can't be contained.

#376: A fey Changeling is rescued from captivity by a reluctant demon on a quest to find his fate. Of course Dom expects trouble, but he is shocked to discover his fate is tied to an imprisoned fey woman. Charlotte's a kicking, spitting, hissing little Changeling — and she's his.

A dragon's kiss burns cold.

Astray: When Paloma Contreras, arrant scientist, accidentally dooms a rogue dragon to death, she'll do anything to save his life. If that means giving up the mountaintop she's called home her entire life, so be it. Too bad Artem Aždaja has no plans to steal her roost. He only wants one thing: *her.*

Desire fogs the mind.

Weathering: Elise Sasini, an intrepid reporter and weather witch, sets out to uncover the story of San Francisco's legendary sentient fog and gets a lot more than she bargained for. The mysterious elemental agrees to tell his story in exchange for a taste of the life — and the woman — he craves.

Three novellas. Three couples. One fractured world. Step into a magical near-future where love builds, breaks, and defies boundaries.

Available in Kindle Unlimited, ebook, and paperback!

bonus chapters, and exclusive content on the Works by Abigail Patreon!

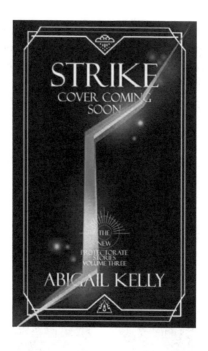

STRIKE: THE NEW PROTECTORATE STORIES VOLUME THREE

Passion is electric.

After a millennia of longing, Hele has finally gotten her chance to live. A lightning elemental with a voracious hunger for knowledge and experience, she takes to her new life with a gusto that surprises everyone she meets. After two years of learning how to navigate the world she's been thrust into, Hele is only missing one thing: love. She wants one particular dragon, but when he turns her away, she decides that life is too short to wait.

Vael has been a loyal soldier of the Draakonriik for nearly one hundred years. He's never wanted anything more than to serve his clan and his leader... until the day he snatches a beguiling elemental from the sky. For two torturous years, he's resisted the call of his Chosen, trying to give her a chance to fly before he claims her and hides her away in his nest.

But when Hele decides to set out on a quest to find a mate, that resolution goes up in smoke. His lovely elemental is about to learn a very valuable lesson: a dragon will do *anything* to win his Chosen.

Available in Kindle Unlimited, ebook, and paperback!

Consort's Glory: The New Protectorate Book One

Margot Goode, healer extraordinaire, knows that being noticed is the fastest way to getting herself murdered — or worse. But even with a secret like hers, she can't stay cloistered forever. On her own in San Francisco, she's on the hunt for the one person who can stop her magic from turning against her in a catastrophic meltdown.

Margot doesn't expect things will be easy, but even *she* is surprised when someone plants a bomb in her Healing House, nearly killing her and wiping out her anonymity in one fell swoop. Attacking a healer is an egregious breach of the laws that keep the races from war. Attacking

Margot Goode, granddaughter of the terrifying Goode Matriarch and leader of the most influential coven in the country, is not just blasphemous — it demands retribution.

Theodore Solbourne, newest sovereign ruler of the largest Elvish territory in the West, has waited his entire life for the woman he will one day claim as his consort. With the power to keep her finally in his grasp, he's planned their meeting down to every last detail... only to have all the carefully crafted steps in their courtship blown away when she's nearly killed before he can even say *hello*.

With her life and his kingdom on the line, there's no time for subtlety. Earning the trust of the woman he's been mad about his entire life just became much harder: the speculation of war is sweeping through the city, a goddess's acolytes call for justice, and a traitor's shadow looms over his household. But nothing, not even Margot's single-minded determination to keep him out, will stop him from winning her heart.

Available in Kindle Unlimited, ebook, and paperback!

Courtship's Conquest: The New Protectorate
Book Two

Their future hinges on a promise.

In the wake of her mother's death, Camille Solbourne is determined to follow through with her deathbed promise to arrange a union with a suitable partner and get out of the Solbourne family. A union is cold, more business than love, and negotiating them is a dangerous political dance. It's not what she wants, but sometimes happiness is found in compromise – and keeping one's promises.

Their choices haunt their past.

Nearly twenty years ago, Viktor Hamilton, alpha of San Francisco's lone coyote shifter pack, let his mate go. Becoming someone his pack could rely on for safety and guidance is the only thing that kept him sane in the long, lonely years that followed. When the opportunity to make a life-altering choice for the betterment of his people arises, he makes a promise to see it through.

What he doesn't expect is for the world to change around him in the blink of an eye. After a volatile run-in with Camille reignites the flame between them, he knows he can't leave the past alone. The only thing standing between them is their fraught past and Camille's furious determination to tie herself to another man. Pursuing Camille means gambling with the future of his pack, but Viktor won't let his mate go a second time – even if it means he has to put his life on the line to keep her.

Available in Kindle Unlimited, ebook, and paperback!

GLOSSARY

A full character directory and map can be found at Abigailkkelly.com

PLACES

United Territories and Allies: What we would consider the continental USA. A loose federation of sovereign states established after the Great War. The UTA capital is United Washington, in the Neutral Zone.

The Elvish Protectorate: Also known as the EVP. Stretches from Oregon to New Mexico. Capital city is San Francisco. Led by the elvish sovereign Theodore Thaddeus Solbourne.

The Coven Collective: Also known as the Collective. Encompasses Washington state. Capital city is Seattle. Led by a large coalition of witch covens, with Sophie Goode acting as their leader.

The Orclind: Encompasses much of the Midwest. Led by the Iron Chain, a close-knit government made up of orcish clans and family groups. Capital city is Boulder.

Shifter Alliance: Takes up a section of the midwest and all of the south. (Unfortunately includes Florida.) Run by a very, very loose alliance of shifter packs from three capital cities — Minneapolis, Oklahoma City, and Atlanta.

The Draakonriik: Also known as the 'Riik. The second smallest territory, it takes up all of the Great Lakes region and stretches to New York. Led by Taevas Aždaja, the *Isand* (ee-zand) of the dragon clans. Pronounced: *dra-kon-reek*

The Neutral Zone: Also known as the New Zone. Technically it is held by a coalition government consisting of representatives from the UTA, but in reality it is run by a syndicate of feuding vampire families. It is a small strip of land squeezed between the Draakon-riik and the Shifter Alliance.

GODS

Light & Darkness: The primordial gods who created all the others. Also known as The Lovers and First Union. Both are generally represented as female.

Loft: God of the sky and creator of flying beings. Twin sibling to Tempest. They know no gender. Also known as the Boundless One.

Tempest: God of the ocean and creator of all water beings. Also known as the Hungry God and the god of love.

Burden: God of the Earth, creator of all beings who live within it — most notably the orcs. Husband of Glory.

Glory: Goddess of sunlight, magic, and creator of elves. Worshipped by witches for giving the gift of magic to humanity.

Blight: God of forested places and disease. He works in partnership with his daughter Grim and shares her dominion over demons and all reviled creatures.

Grim: Goddess of death. Known as the Merciful One and the Brilliant Lady. She is widely beloved.

Craft: God of change, newness, and messengers. Creator of humanity and viewed warily by non-worshippers as the Chaos Maker. They change their gender frequently, but generally is referred to using he/him pronouns.

TERMS

Arrant: someone born without m-paths, or the ability to channel and use magic.

Dragon: a person with a dual form. In their bipedal form, they have claw-tipped wings, horns, and a tail. In their quadrupedal form, they are roughly the size of a standard SUV and can fly at extremely high altitudes for weeks at a time. They come in a variety of extremely saturated colors that shift with the time of day (light to dark). They breathe cold blue fire and can see the Earth's magnetic field. Identifying mating feature is marked change in behavior, including the overwhelming urge to nest.

Elemental: a being created by a spontaneous magical eruption. They often take on the attributes of whatever weather they happen to be born into, *i.e.* a lightning storm might produce a lightning elemental, or a blizzard might make a snow elemental.

Elf: someone born with jewel-toned skin, claws, pointed ears, and four fangs. Very secretive and considered apex predators who require a strict hierarchy to function. Average height of 6-7ft. Identifying mating feature is the retraction of claws.

Fey: a person with nearly vestigial, insect-like wings, small fangs, and claws. Usually live in large groups. Identifying mating feature is bioluminescence.

Foresight: the ability to see multiple possible futures. The average number is between 2-4, with the likelihood mental instability increasing with each subsequent possible future.

Healer: a person who possesses the ability to see into and heal bodies through touch.

M- : M- is frequently used as shorthand to denote when something is infused or otherwise combined with a magical element.

Met: acronym for *magically enhanced tech.* A branded home assistant that can do everything your Alexa can, as well as small, low-level magic to help around the house.

M-siphon: a containment device used to imprison a magical being and siphon off their magic. Highly illegal.

R-siphon: also known as *reverse siphon.* New technology that redistributes magic away from the siphon instead of into it.

M-lev: a play on *maglev,* meaning a high speed train that levitates using magnets. In this case, magnets *and* magic.

M-weather: magic weather. Very common, but can result in "clusters" or storms that wreak havoc if not properly contained. In rare circumstances, it can also produce a sapient being known as an *elemental.*

Orc: a person with green, gray, russet, or blue skin, two fangs, and claws. Widely renowned for their strength and beautiful voices.

Identifying mating feature is "the kohl", or altered, dark pigmentation of the hands and feet developed after meeting their mate.

Pixie: a small, winged creature with compound eyes with about the same level of intelligence as a rat. In the wild they live in trees and in burrows, but have adapted to living in walls, pipes, mailboxes, etc.

Shifter: a person who can shift into an animal form. They can partially shift (changing only parts of their bodies at will) and often take on characteristics of their other half. Famous for their strength and tenacity, as well as their dual-voiced "shifter purr" which many people find deeply attractive. Usually found in packs.

Sigil: a symbol used to channel magic. Western countries use the alchemical alphabet formally codified in the 1800's, though many, many variations are used all over the world.

Syndicate: a group of loosely affiliated vampiric crime families who control the Neutral Zone.

Vampire: a person who drinks blood to survive and cannot go out in sunlight without injury. Vampirism can only be "caught" with the exchange of fresh blood, and as of 2045 is much more widely spread through procreation. Vampires can only breed with their *anchors*. Identifying mating feature is marked change in behavior, including overwhelming sexual desire and need for total isolation.

Were: a person infected with the were virus, a much mutated strain of the vampirism virus, resulting in altered physiology and magical ability. They can be identified by their heterochromia, or different colored eyes. They are the newest magical race and viewed warily by the general public for a variety of earned and unearned reasons. Identifying mating feature is marked change in behavior, including highly increased territorial instinct and the urge to nest.

Witch: a human with the ability to use magic. It is a gender neutral term. It is often affixed to another word to denote exactly what a witch's speciality is. Ex: *greenwitch.*

PRONUNCIATION GUIDE FOR NAMES OF IMPORTANT CHARACTERS IN THIS BOOK

Zia North: Zee-ah Nohr-th
  Harlan Bounds: Hahr-lan Bown-z
  Atticus Caldwell: At-ih-kus Cawl-d-well
  Adriana: Ay-dree-ah-nah
  Julius Amauri: Jool-ee-uhs Aw-mar-ee
  Felix: Fee-licks

ABOUT THE AUTHOR

 Abigail Kelly is a writer of alternate histories, love stories, and women with drive. Her work is heavily influenced by both her modest family roots and her passion for history. A former illustrator, she is now a bookseller at an independent bookshop where she gets to badly influence impressionable young minds and put her favorite books in eager hands. She is also the host of the Kingdom of Thirst podcast, a show all about romance novels and why they matter.

Her favorite authors are Shirley Jackson, V. E. Schwab, Ursula K. Le Guin, Kresley Cole, Nalini Singh, and just about anyone who writes about the weird and wonderful. She lives in San Francisco with her dog, Babs, who remains stubbornly illiterate.

CONTENT WARNINGS

Content warnings: Violence, murder, kidnapping, organized crime, past child abandonment, blood play, discussions of fertility/pregnancy, past child neglect, and sexual situations.

Made in United States
Troutdale, OR
09/29/2023

13286989R00146